Ambition's pinnacle, for Anglo-Celtic authors, is uniquely tackling King Arthur's legend: Merlin, Morgan le Fay, Wort, and all. Such quests take decades to conceptualize, execute, and refine. Welcome to Elfindale.

to

Susan Backus

"She Takes care of everybody."

Sept 15/08   Kerstin White

1 of 4 a/c First editions

JH

ELFINDALE

ELFINDALE TOO

ELFINDALE FAREWELL

by

Ian Lauder

Trafford
PUBLISHING

Order this book online at www.trafford.com/07-0437
or email orders@trafford.com

Most Trafford titles are also available at major online book retailers.

Cover Photograph: Pamela Grier
Cover Design: Jon Willis

Mud Valley Productions
mudvalley.com

Note for Librarians: A cataloguing record for this book is available from Library
and Archives Canada at www.collectionscanada.ca/amicus/index-e.html

Printed in Victoria, BC, Canada.

ISBN: 978-1-4251-2033-7

www.trafford.com

North America & international
toll-free: 1 888 232 4444 (USA & Canada)
phone: 250 383 6864 ♦ fax: 250 383 6804
email: info@trafford.com

The United Kingdom & Europe
phone: +44 (0)1865 722 113 ♦ local rate: 0845 230 9601
facsimile: +44 (0)1865 722 868 ♦ email: info.uk@trafford.com

10 9 8 7 6 5 4 3 2

Contents

ELFINDALE

"Früher order später findet jeder topf seiner deckel."
Sooner or later, every pot will find his lid.

old German saying

to
extra-large harvest moons

BOOK ONE

THUNDER

Chapter One

FINALLY

$\mathcal{F}$or her fifth, sixth, and seventh birthdays, after asking for a puppy, Angelica Pearson politely enjoyed the Barbie stuff, Easy-Bake Oven, and croquet set her parents gave her instead, before placing them in a storage chest and returning to her primary love—reading books.

For her eighth birthday she asked for a puppy, and received a dozen volumes she hadn't read yet. Sensitive, as always, to her parents' feelings, Angelica didn't tell them she could get those, and thousands more, free, at any library, at any time she wanted; so she read them all, then sequestered them in the storage chest hosting her previous presents.

When her parents asked why she'd put them away, she said there were so many great books in the world nobody could read everything in one lifetime, so she wasn't planning on reading many twice; which made sense to them. In fact, it made so much sense they went into a huddle, profoundly worried, and talked about her well into the night.

Why were they worried? Well, like most parents who'd personally replaced literature with television, they were afraid their child might spend the rest of her life reading, and wouldn't fit in anywhere. This concern resulted in her father taking her ice fishing and bowling and to Monster-Truck rallies, which she enjoyed because it gave him so much pleasure. It also resulted in her mother taking her shopping and to afternoon matinées, which she enjoyed because it gave her mother so much pleasure.

It would be a mistake, however, to think her parents failed to notice she mostly enjoyed doing those things because they liked them so much; so by the time her ninth birthday rolled round they were understandably trepidatious as to her present, till she insisted all she wanted was a puppy, and they not only secretly agreed she was old enough, they jumped at the chance to finally give her something she clearly coveted.

Chapter Two

THE NOTE

$\mathscr{A}$t breakfast, on the morning of her ninth birthday, Angelica knew something was up because her parents kept exchanging sappy grins, so when they gave her a big, prettily-wrapped box after her usual cereal, she decided she was going to really like whatever was inside, no matter what.

Carefully opening the box, she found a smaller prettily-wrapped box inside, and inside that box was another prettily-wrapped box, and inside that box was another box, and inside that was another, and so on and so on, until she came to the very last one, which was so tiny it balanced easily on the end of her finger.

"A ring," Angelica thought, "They've given me a ring. Some valuable old family heirloom, I bet. Well, that isn't so bad. I'll wear it to please them, and give it to the daughter I hope to have one day."

Smiling lovingly at each, she then undid the tiny box and found a piece of paper inside, all folded up into a teeny square.

"A cheque," she guessed, "They've given me a cheque. Well, that isn't so bad; even a nine-year-old likes to have money. I'll open a bank account."

But it wasn't a cheque. Oh no, it was something more desirable. Something *way* more desirable. It was, in fact, her heart's desire. Something better than a puppy. Something *much* better than a puppy. It was a note. A note which said:

This certificate guarantees Angelica her choice of puppy.

J. Pierpont Huxtable

Proprietor

Pierpont Puppy Farm

"My choice," marveled Angelica, stunned and happy, "My choice. Not just *any* puppy, but the puppy of *my* choice."

The birth of Angelica had squeezed her parents' hearts, as had her first step, her earliest words, and any photos they'd taken of her as a toddler in bonnets; but nothing in the past ever squeezed their hearts like the silent tears of joy presently springing from her eyes while she stared up to nowhere, holding the precious little note in her hands.

"We did it this time," they thought, "This time we really did it."

They were so happy they didn't even think to tell her all the usual stuff that takes the edge off the pleasure of getting a puppy. Stuff like: "Don't forget, it's *your* puppy; *your* responsibility; *you* have to clean it and feed it and walk it and keep it from barking and chewing up the house", which was just as well, because in Angelica's case, there wasn't going to be a problem, as far as she was concerned.

Little did she know, and little did they know, that she would pick the puppy of all puppies, who would grow to be the dog of all dogs. Little did any of them know that 'Thunder' was on his way.

Chapter Three

THUNDER'S CHOICE

While all this was going on at Angelica's house, Thunder, in the spacious, fenced yard of the Pierpont Puppy Farm, was acting up once again. Only two months old: big, black, lean, and mischievous of soul, he'd just squirmed from the lap of a large woman who'd decided she wanted him for a guard dog, jumped out of her hands, gorped down three bowls of food meant for other puppies, and was busily running circles around J. Pierpont Huxtable himself, yapping his head off delightedly.

"Don't worry 'bout how he's acting," advised Mr. Huxtable to the large lady, "It's a sign he'll make a great guard dog. Lots of spirit. Chained and trained, he'll be just the ticket."

"W-e-e-e-ll," hesitated the large lady, "If you say so."

"He'll have to catch me first," vowed Thunder to himself, "And it won't be easy: I'm fast and he's fat and I don't really want to go."

"Why not?" asked one of the other puppies, "You'd make a great guard dog."

"Freedom," answered Thunder, scooting under a pile of logs, "I've got to be free. Free to run and explore and chew and besides, she wouldn't love me enough, maybe not at all, and I won't stand for that."

"Gotcha!" exclaimed J. Pierpont, seizing Thunder by the scruff and hauling him out, "Now, settle down. You're one of the lucky ones. You'll have a job to do and a nice big doghouse."

Holding Thunder up to the large lady, he then said: "Grip him under the arms while I stuff him into a cardboard box for you."

"Alright," replied the large lady, "I got him; he isn't going anywhere now."

Thunder twisted and struggled to no avail while J. Pierpont hurried off for a box. Gaining confidence, the large lady chuckled at Thunder and said to him: "I raised a husband and four boys; I guess I can handle the likes of you."

This annoyed Thunder of course, and hurt his pride; so, quick as lightning, he devised a plan. A plan that was crude, but clever. He simply stopped wriggling and started licking her wrist.

"Oh, ho," she chortled, pleased, "Like a firm hand, do you? Like knowing who's boss? You'll do fine after all."

Enjoying her triumph, charmed by his submission, she then made the mistake of bringing him up to her face for a nuzzle, and that's when it happened. He glared at her with pure malevolence, which froze her in shock; then he peed all over her neck.

Staggering back in horror, she flung him away screaming, "You pig! You dirty pig!"

"Takes one to know one," chuckled Thunder as he tumbled through space, before landing with a satisfying "Sploosh!" in a big gooey pile of mud.

"Here's the box," panted J. Pierpont, waddling up, "This'll hold him."

"Box!" shouted the large lady, "I'll show you a box!" Whereupon she inverted it over J. Pierpont's head, pushing him stumbling blindly backwards.

"Oh-oh, better shift position," decided Thunder hastily, as he scooted out of the mud pile just in time to give his spot to J. Pierpont, who landed with a humongous "SPLORP!"

"I'll get you for this!" sputtered J. Pierpont at Thunder, as the large lady flounced off to her car, "I'll get you good!" Fortunately for Thunder however, J. Pierpont was blessed with a great sense of humour and by the time he'd managed to wallow out of the mud pile on all fours, covered in goo from head to foot, he was laughing at himself. Laughing and laughing and laughing. Which met with Thunder's approval because Thunder too had been born with a sense of the ridiculous and appreciated it when he saw it in anyone else, human or otherwise. So, there they stood, on all fours, J. Pierpont and Thunder, nose to nose and covered in mud, lost in the joy of mutually-shared laughter.

"I'll keep him for myself," grinned J. Pierpont, "I'll keep this pup for myself."

"He's not such a bad guy," thought Thunder, "Too bad he isn't a girl. I want a girl human. Yup, it's too bad. It's really too bad."

"Hey you!" called out Angelica, jumping from a station wagon and running up towards them, waving a piece of paper, "You in the mud! I've come for a puppy! The puppy of my choice!"

"Bingo!" exulted Thunder delightedly, "Bingo! Bingo! Bingo!!"

Chapter Four

ANGELICA'S CHOICE

"A customer," thought J. Pierpont, rising squishily from the ooze, "A sure sale too, by the looks of things."

"Read this," bubbled Angelica happily, handing her paper up to the mud man.

"Looks authentic," nodded J. Pierpont, after inspecting the note carefully, "Yessir, it looks like my handwriting alright."

"Course it's authentic," said Thunder to himself, "She's the one for me; I can see that plain as day." And with that, in doggie glee, he dove back into the mud pile and rolled over and over in the goo, yapping happily, certain the little girl would dive in too for a good roll about with him, but to his amazement, she didn't. In fact she didn't even notice him.

Perplexed, he crawled out and looked up at her with a mixture of mud, disappointment, and a touch of resentment.

It would be unfair, however, at this point, to expect Angelica to realize he was the one, because she, being unfamiliar with dogs like Thunder, expected a puppy to be cute and fluffy rather than muddy and stinky, so she not only didn't notice him, she went over and began carefully inspecting his brothers and sisters and cousins instead.

One after another she picked them up, gradually narrowing her choice down to three. One was cute and round, a veritable butterball. One was cute and slim, with handsome markings. And one was cute and sleazy, licking her hand like a machine gun, sucking up to beat the band.

As she sat and inspected the three finalists again and again, Thunder began to get a little nervous, so he walked over to her, sat, cocked his head, and looked up at her quizzically.

Angelica's mother, fearing the wretched little mudball would mess Angelica's new birthday dress, nudged him away with a boot, saying: "Shoo! Shoo, you dirty thing!"

"Dirty?" puzzled Thunder, "Course I'm dirty. Who wouldn't be, given the chance?"

By now Angelica had narrowed her choice down to the butterball or the sleaze.

"I've got to do something, and I've got to do it quick," decided Thunder, so he scooted round Angelica's mother's foot and jumped on Angelica's lap.

"Yikes!" squealed Angelica, pushing him off her spoiled dress, before glancing up at her parents, nervous they'd be disappointed she was no longer clean.

Thunder sat down a few feet away and puzzled the problem.

"Hmmm," he thought, "She doesn't seem to care much about her clothes yet she checked out her parents to see if they were upset, which makes her a sweet girl, but it also means she isn't thinking clearly either, and that's no way to make an important decision like finding the dog you belong with. I'll have to ditch the mud to please the folks."

And with that, he raced over to a water trough and dove in, rolling over and over till all the mud was off his body; then he ran, dripping and happy, back to Angelica and her parents, to show how clean he was.

"She likes the fluffy butterball and the hand licker," reflected Thunder, "I can do both of those." And with that, he shook like crazy, showering water every which way, soaking Angelica thoroughly all over, and her standing parents up to the knees.

With a yelp both parents jumped back and Angelica flung out her arms to protect her face. When she looked down at him a few seconds later she saw a perfectly cute, fluffy puppy gazing up at her happily. A fluffy puppy that licked the hand she held out to him a few times before cocking his head to one side as if to say: "Ain't I it? Ain't I the real thing? Cute, clean, fluffy, friendly—the works?"

Glancing from Thunder to the other puppies, then back to Thunder, Angelica's heart positively exploded with recognition and joy. There he was, the puppy she wanted. A puppy who was smart and, judging from the friendly, mocking gleam in his eye, a puppy with a wicked sense of humour too.

Picking him up with slow and tender reverence, she kissed Thunder's muzzle gently and from the heart; then she put him on her forearm, head towards her hand, paws dangling, and, rising, held him up to J. Pierpont Huxtable.

"He's the one," sighed Angelica, "He's the only one. The only one in the whole wide world for me."

"W-e-e-ll," stalled J. Pierpont, scratching his head, "I was kinda goin' t' keep that one fer m'self."

"A deal's a deal!" barked Angelica, stepping back. "You read the note!"

"Feisty," thought Thunder to himself, "Ya gots t' love it."

"Course, it is," replied J. Pierpont, seeing she meant business, "All I meant was you got an eye for dogs. He's the best I ever saw."

"Are you sure you want *that* one, Angelica?" cautioned her mother nervously, picking up the butterball, "This one's really cute and it won't be nearly as rambunctious as..."

"Sorry," interrupted Angelica, showing an unusual disinterest in her mother's opinions and feelings, "This is the one and that's all there is to it."

"He's awful independent," added her father, "He'll have a

mind of his own, I'm afraid. Look, this other little licky one seems eager to please."

"He's a suck up," snorted Angelica scornfully, "He'll grow up to be a sneak, if he isn't one already; I can see that now. I've met the one I want. *He's* a dog. A *real* dog. The doggiest dog ever. He'll kill for me if he has to, Dad. Protect me for real; and I'll spend less time at the books, more time outside in the fresh air. I'll learn to run too. Run like the wind. Maybe go to the Olympics. Win a gold for Canada."

That did it of course. He'd never admit it but a part of her father had always wished his only child would be more athletic; do something to make her country proud, in a way he could understand. He'd never doubted, with her looks and brains, she'd go somewhere big but he was always just a little afraid he'd not be able to go there with her, not understand exactly what she was famous for—but an athlete—his little Angelica at the highest point of the podium, a gold medal round her neck, standing proudly at attention while *O Canada!** boomed and the Maple Leaf fluttered, filled him with parental satisfaction and bliss. She might even go on, what with her books and all, to become the first 'real' female Prime Minister of Canada. All because of this puppy. This damp little puppy balanced happily on her forearm, its paws dangling down both sides.

"He's all yours," sniffed her father, misty-eyed, "He's all yours. We'll call him Rex."

"No way!" thought Thunder, "My name's Thunder!"

"I don't think so, Dad," responded Angelica, with unusual disinterest in her father's opinions and feelings, "He's got a name already, I'm sure of that; all we got to do is figure out what it is."

"Exactly," chuckled Thunder to himself, "This girl is one sharp cookie."

"Ralph?" proposed her father. "Oggie-Doggie? Spot? Blackie?"

---

* p. 232

"No," insisted Angelica, "It isn't any of those; and there's no point in guessing."

Chapter Five

TURKEY SANDWICHES

$\mathcal{A}$s luck and fate would have it, Angelica's birthday happened to fall on the day after Thanksgiving, so her mother had made leftover turkey sandwiches for the picnic they would have after Angelica chose her puppy. Sitting in the rear seat with her as they drove away from the Pierpont Puppy Farm, on their way to look for a perfect picnic site beside a river or pond, Thunder began to smell something wonderful coming from a wicker hamper in the very back of the station wagon. For his whole life to date, all he'd ever gotten to eat were little dried pellets of Puppy Chow and the occasional milkbone, so as far as he knew, that was it—that was all anybody ate, even humans; but once he got a whiff of the contents of that basket he suspected a whole new world was opening up for him. A world in which he would soon find himself in trouble. Lots and lots of trouble, and very soon indeed, because from the moment he got wind of those turkey sandwiches he was a goner. A food fanatic for life. And his favourite food, he knew (until he ran into beefsteak and kidney pie a day later), would undoubtedly be turkey. Turkey sandwiches, turkey legs, turkey gravy—you name it.

He was, of course, too young as yet, to realize manners were involved in eating with people. Rules. So he innocently leapt over the back seat and, before Angelica knew what was happening, nosed up a flap of the picnic hamper and disappeared inside, rooting around for the source of that delicious turkey smell.

In a matter of seconds he trampled the chocolate cake flat; mooshed the potato salad about horribly after gnawing off its plastic lid; squashed open the drink container, spilling red raspberry juice everywhere; and bit into his first-ever bite of turkey sandwich.

Poking his head up through the other end of the hamper, eyes bulging with excitement, a turkey sandwich hanging out of his mouth, he stared at Angelica, willing and eager to share his wonder and joy.

Angelica, seeing his condition, burst out laughing, her father harrumphed paternally and her mother murmured, "Oh, dear. I hope he's an outside dog. We'll have to build a fence; one he can't tunnel under."

"Sure," chuckled Thunder, "Sure you do; and it'll work too— long as you stick it underground, halfway to China."

"I don't like that look in his eye," sighed Angelica's father to himself. "He's going to be a handful. A real handful."

Pulling over to the side of the road he turned to Angelica with a "We're going to have to set some rules around here, young lady. And the first one is he's a dog and can't sleep with you. We'll fix him a box in the basement and put a ticking clock in it for company, so he won't get lonely and yap the house down all night. Agreed, Angelica?"

"Agreed," conceded Angelica reluctantly, looking at her messy pup gobbling a second turkey sandwich.

"Not sleep with me?" puzzled Thunder, still gobbling, "Not sleep with me? I must be hearing things; that can't be right."

"I mean it," insisted her father, "He sleeps in a box in the base-ment and that's all there is to it. I'm firm on this point. Very firm indeed."

"He's serious," marveled Thunder in mid-swallow, "He's *ac-tually* serious. Looks like that one needs training; if he gets his way right from the start he'll wind up completely out of con-trol."

Chapter Six

FIRST WORDS

Since Thunder had more or less trashed the best part of a picnic, namely the entire contents of the food hamper, Angelica and her parents decided it would be wise to head straight on back home. This suited him just fine, for he was curious to see where he was going to live, maybe even check out the neighbourhood too. Having spent all of his life so far at the Puppy Farm, the big wide world also beckoned to beat the band, and the first thing he noticed as they cruised smoothly along was the weird way everything went past so fast without him needing to move his paws, because the big thing they were in seemed to be doing all the work. Farms flashed by, fields of corn, horses and pigs and sheep, ponds with ducks and geese, trees, hills, clouds—the works. Since it was a warm day, the windows were down and Thunder was able to smell everything too and everything smelled just great. So great, he got set to jump from the hamper and stick his head out a window, to feel the wind on his face and sniff in the smells even better but Angelica, glancing nervously at the rear of her parents' heads, suddenly shoved him back inside the basket, before fastening down its lids, sure as she was that if Thunder hopped all over the car covered in a mixture of potato salad, chocolate cake and raspberry juice, their good will would be stretched to the breaking point, and the one thing she *didn't* want was to hear a bunch of new rules before they even got home and she could clean Thunder up in the bathtub, with lots and lots of shampoo.

"Stay quiet in there," she whispered to Thunder. "Don't kick up a fuss and for heaven's sake, don't start whining."

"Whining?" puzzled Thunder. "Me? Whine? Never. Hey, I'm Thunder. Thunder the Wonder Pup. I can hold out long as she wants. Problem is; why does she want me in here? Has it got something to do with all this neat food all over me? Is it the same as that mud problem I had a while ago? I bet that's it. Yessir, I bet that's it. They don't want me to spread this stuff all over the place, for some reason. People are weird, that's for sure. They seem to be hostile to mess. J. Pierpont wasn't like that though; he loved the mud thing we shared. I guess families are different. Not as untidy as bachelors. I'll have to keep their house neat or they'll kick me outside or stick me in the basement sometimes, and then Angelica and I won't be together all the time and that won't do. That won't do at all."

After a few minutes Angelica and her parents became nervous about how quiet Thunder was and her father even suggested she peek inside to see if the little guy was all right; so she lifted one of the lids gently, to make sure he didn't jump out, and saw him all curled up in a messy ball, resting.

Her heart soared, looking at her sweet little pup like that and she sighed happily and whispered: "I love you. I really, really love you."

Opening one eye and looking up at her, touched to the very core of his soul, he said, silently in his heart, "I love you too, Angelica. I love you too; for always and forever."

With a gasp Angelica dropped the lid and looked at her parents in shock, open-mouthed and wide-eyed.

"Is he alright?" enquired her mother anxiously, fearful her little daughter's heart would be broken if he'd choked to death on something. "Is he alright?"

"You... you... you're not going to believe it," stammered Angelica, "but I heard him say he loved me. I actually *heard* him say 'I love you for always and forever.'"

"Dogs can't talk, darling," demurred her father kindly, "Not like people."

"I know," agreed Angelica, "But I heard him this time, right in the middle of my head; his exact words were 'I love you too, Angelica. I love you too, for always and forever.'"

"I'm sure he did," encouraged her mother, after exchanging glances with her husband, "I'm sure he did."

"It's called telepathy," continued Angelica reflectively. "He didn't actually speak out loud but I heard it and he heard me. Doctor Dolittle used to do it; and Indians in the old days, when they lived in nature. I read about it. It isn't just a story. It's for real."

"That's nice, dear," replied her mother.

"Think he'll do it again?" asked Angelica, too excited by the event to hear the condescending disbelief in her mother's voice.

"Sure. Why not?" chuckled her father good-naturedly, "Anything's possible."

Lifting the lid and looking in at Thunder again in awe and delight, she saw him take a big breath, exhale happily, and wink at her, once, before drifting contentedly into sleep, assured, once and for all, Angelica and he spoke with a single heart. Truly belonged together.

Chapter Seven

LOST AND LONELY

You'd think, after how well everything was going, Thunder would fit right in at his new house, but when Angelica's mother lifted the sleepy little pup out of the messy hamper and plunked him into the kitchen sink to soap him clean, he was so startled by the sudden dunking he bit her finger with his needle-sharp little teeth and jumped out the window, smack into an azalea bush, then scooted across the lawn, disappearing from sight; and by the time they'd looked about for a bit, then returned from taking Angelica's mother to the doctor for a tetanus shot, it was late afternoon, so there was very little time left to find Thunder before it was too dark to see him.

They searched of course. Searched and searched, and called and called and called, but to no avail; he was nowhere about. He wasn't next door on one side at Mrs. Witherspoon's. He wasn't next door on the other side at Mr. Grump's. He wasn't anywhere else on the street either.

"He's gone," thought Angelica's father, "Gone for good, I'm afraid. We'll have to get her another one."

"No he isn't!" snapped Angelica up at him. "We won't get another one! We've got to find him and that's all there is to it!"

"Must be something to this telepathy thing after all," reflected her father, glancing down at his daughter nervously, "I hope it isn't witchcraft. We don't want the devil nosing about our house."

"I'm not angry at him or anything, for biting me," assured her mother, "He didn't mean to; I just startled him, is all. We'll look for him tomorrow, all day, till we find him. You can stay off school and your father and I will take a day off work too. We'll find him, really we will."

"They seem to be more upset by all this than I am," mused Angelica, as her parents tucked her in for the night. "They must really love me."

Looking up at them, seeing the anxiety and vulnerability in their eyes, something she'd read sprang to mind. "'*Hostages to Fortune*,'" she said. "You are hostages to Fortune: My happiness is your happiness and my pain is your pain; isn't it?"

"Yes it is," answered her dad, "You'll find out when you have kids... Now, I'm going to look some more for him with a flashlight. I'll hunt all night if that's what it takes. Go to sleep if you can."

"OK, Dad," promised Angelica, "And try not to worry. He'll be fine, I'm pretty sure he isn't very far away. He's just scared to come back cuz he bit Mom."

"If you say so," replied her father doubtfully, snapping off the light. "Try to sleep, princess."

Closing the door gently, he turned to his wife and murmured "I've heard that frequently full-grown lost dogs are never found. If that's the case, a puppy..."

"I know, dear," sighed Angelica's mother, "But we've got to try. I'll phone all the neighbours while you're out looking, and hope for the best."

In the bedroom, Angelica, trying to be brave, scooted over to the window, opened it wide, and peered out into the night.

"Where are you, little one?" she said, "Are you OK? Watch out for cars, you hear me? Watch out for cars."

"It's a big world out here," thought Thunder from under a bush. "A big scary world, and I'm lost. Got to admit it. I'm lost and I'm lonely. Lonely for Angelica."

Chapter Eight

PETIE

*A*fter an hour or so under the bush, which was one street over from Angelica's house, Thunder began to get awful thirsty; so he sniffed about until he smelled water in somebody's backyard, trotted over to a little bowl, and started lapping it up like crazy— when suddenly a tiny creature came barreling through a little swinging door in a big door on a porch, flew down the stairs, and pounced on him, yapping furiously all the while.

"Must be some kind of dog," thought Thunder, flat on his back, paws in the air, his throat snugly held in a strong little mouth full of sharp little teeth, "If he ever lets go, we might become pals."

Instinctively, like all pups, he lay very still so the other dog wouldn't bite deep; and sure enough, when his assailant saw Thunder wasn't going to struggle, he let go, sitting back with satisfaction.

"It's not often I get to win a fight, cuz I'm so little," boasted the other dog. "What's your name? Mine's Petie. I'm a Chihuahua."

"How cum your so small?" asked Thunder affably, grateful for the company. "Got any food? I'm particularly partial to turkey."

"Why, you're just a pup," observed Petie, disappointed. "Guess that means I didn't really win. It doesn't count unless you're full-grown. You shouldn't be out all alone like this. It's dangerous."

"I bit a human," confessed Thunder, a little guiltily. "I didn't mean to but I bit one and now I'm scared to go back to wherever I live."

"Biting a human is real serious," cautioned Petie, worriedly. "You can get the death sentence for that."

"The death sentence?!" choked Thunder, aghast. "The death sentence?! All I did was nip her finger by accident cuz she dumped me sudden into a bunch of soapy water when I was half-asleep!"

"All the same," confirmed Petie, "It's a serious thing you did. A very serious thing."

"I don't even know where I live," sighed Thunder unhappily. "I was closed up in a picnic basket on the way to my new house; so I don't know what it looks like, even if I dared look for it."

"Hmmm," thought Petie. "Did you draw blood? See any red on her finger?"

"A bit," replied Thunder. "Just a drop, but I definitely saw red."

"Too bad," empathized Petie. "Maybe we should talk to Boris about it. He lives down the street. Boris is big. Huge, actually, but really nice. He's a Russian wolfhound; my best friend."

"I wouldn't object to being your friend too," offered Thunder. "I'd be nice to you; even when I get big."

"How big?" asked Petie nervously, "Most big dogs have a way of being mean to me sometimes."

"I won't be," assured Thunder, "That's a promise. As for how big I'm going to be, check out my paws. Look how giant they are. That means I'm going to grow like crazy. And fast too."

"By the looks of them you're going to be even taller than Boris," chuckled Petie. "In fact, you're going to be the tallest dog in the whole neighbourhood."

"Let's go find him," decided Thunder, "I'm kind of curious to see how huge I'm gonna get."

"OK," agreed Petie, "But stick close. It's dangerous outside after dark. Lots of bad things can happen to a new dog in a neighbourhood, especially a pup. I won't feel safe myself until we hook up with Boris. It pays to have friends in high places."

"High places?" enquired Thunder.

"Yes. High places. You know—high?—a tall dog? Get it? A big, high dog? ... never mind. You're too young to have a sense of humour."

"Think so?" retorted Thunder, with a grin, "I haven't laughed at your big bulgy eyes or your funny little bum, have I? And I want to. I really want to."

And with that, he pounced on Petie and they rolled all over the yard in a happy tangle, each as pleased as the other to have made a new friend.

Chapter Nine

BORIS

$\mathcal{P}$repared as he was to be introduced to a big dog, it proved nonetheless quite the shock for Thunder when he met Boris, because he was so tall Thunder had to lean way, way back to see the Russian's long pointy head, which tumbled him over on his back, making Boris look even taller still.

Fortunately, Petie was right; Boris was a sweetheart. A humdinger of a dog. Brave, regal, gentle, and blessed with a truly heartfelt, amiable, Russian sense of humour and hospitality.

"Borscht?" offered Boris, looking down at Petie and Thunder kindly. "Would you comrades care for a bowl of borscht?"

"What's borscht?" whispered Thunder to Petie.

"Beet soup," whispered Petie back, with a grimace. "Cold, beet soup."

"Yuk," gagged Thunder, shivering horribly. "Yuk, and double yuk."

"Of course we would, Boris," said Petie, lying his head off. "Can't hurt his feelings," he whispered to Thunder. "If we do he's liable to blame himself. And if he does, he'll howl the whole neighbourhood down with soulful lament. He'll break out the vodka and get royally drunk too—then he'll start singing and dancing till sunup and beyond. By then our hearts'll have broken with the beauty of his performance. I've not been the same since I heard it but once, and you, being just a pup, would never survive the sweet melancholy it inspires in the soul. You'd spend the rest of your days in sad lament, spouting poetry."

"All that from just hurting his feelings a bit?" puzzled Thunder.

"Yes," replied Petie, "I fear so. He's Russian, after all. A pure-bred Russian. Romantic as they come. Utterly impractical; but a friend, ah yes, a friend to the end and beyond."

"For that," spoke up Thunder valiantly, "I'd choke down a bowl of cold beet soup any day and twice on Sundays."

"Well said," chuckled Boris, his long, pointed snout suddenly separating the two whispering ones, "Well said. Let's pass on the borscht and celebrate our friendship with a drink. A finger or two, as they say, of vodka."

"A good idea," hastened Petie, "A noble idea, none better; but Boris, if I may, a word in private." And with that, he took a few paces off and whispered into Boris's large, drooping ear: "He's just a pup. Far too young for the hard stuff. And lost. Lost and tired and a wee bit frightened, I'm afraid; you see, he bit his mistress's finger shortly after adoption, then he cut and ran."

"Oooooh, the poor wee one," anguished Boris, his great Russian heart overflowing with compassion. "He didn't draw blood, did he? Tell me he didn't draw blood."

"I'm afraid he did," admitted Petie reluctantly. "Try not to break into soulful poetic lament, we've got to help the lad. Time is of the essence; by dawn he'll be found, impounded, and sentenced to death."

"We'll take him to Winston's," decided Boris, "He's ugly as only a bulldog can be but he's wise and tough as they come. If anyone can save him Winston can."

"Good idea," agreed Petie, relieved at Boris's restraint. "Maybe he'll have some leftover steak and kidney pie too. I just love steak and..."

"What's that?!" interrupted Boris, craning his neck high and peering over the hedge of his house. "Ah, it's a human, poking about in the shadows with a flashlight. Looking for a fugitive, I suspect."

Thunder, brave pup though he was, squealed in fear and flattened himself to the ground.

"There, there, my wee malchishka," soothed Boris, his long neck lowering his regal muzzle to the little shivering pup affectionately, "They'll not find you or my name isn't Boris Alexeievich Baryshnikov, linear descendant of the hounds of the Romanoffs, heir to the kennels of the Kremlin."

"Wow," exclaimed Thunder, impressed, like all North Americans, by anything blue blood, aristocratic, noble, "Wow, wow, wow, wow, wow."

"That's more like it; maybe everything's going to turn out all right after all," thought Petie, happy Boris wasn't going to get dangerously sentimental, and delighted by Thunder's restored confidence, as they poked their heads through Boris's hedge, looked left and right for humans, then set out for Winston's house, chatting amiably.

Chapter Ten

WINSTON

*I*f Thunder had turned right instead of left when he jumped out Angelica's mother's kitchen window hours before he might have wound up at Winston's house instead of Petie's because Winston lived on the same street as Angelica, right down at the very end.

Since fall was Winston's favourite time of the year, Boris and Petie were pretty sure they would find him in his backyard slobbering on a big beef bone or gorping down fish and chips because Winston, 'Winnie' to his closest friends in moments of invited intimacy (which was never), was as English as English could be. A Londoner through and through.

"He still thinks Britannia rules the waves," warned Boris, "Still thinks the sun never sets on the British Empire; so act accordingly."

"That's right," agreed Petie. "If it isn't from the Old Country, isn't from 'across the pond', it's second-rate; so if he starts singing *Rule, Britannia!* *, join right in. And if he gets homesick from that we'll have to sing *The Last Farewell* in its entirety. There's no escaping it, so don't even try."

"I don't know either one," sighed Thunder. "Think he'll notice?"

* p. 232

"We'll cover for you," assured Petie, "Don't worry about it; his eyes'll fill up when he sings and he won't see boo, except England in his head."

"Sentimental claptrap," sniffed Boris, with uncharacteristic abruptness. "Can't see it, myself."

"Oh, noooo," chuckled Petie, with gentle sarcasm, "You're a realist. Not a sentimental bone in your body."

"That's right," confirmed Boris innocently. "It's a failing of Winston's but he's a friend so we have to live with it. Have to pretend it isn't so. See the white house up ahead, Thunder? The one with wooden beams and a thatched roof? That's his place."

"It seems to be getting darker," thought Thunder aloud, looking up at a blackening sky. "What's happening to the moon and the stars?"

"Storm comin'," proffered Boris. "No doubt about it. There'll be rain, lightning, and thunder soon; you mark my words."

"Thunder?" quivered Petie, glancing up nervously. "That stuff scares the poop out of me."

"Can't say I'm all that partial to it myself," sighed Boris. "It's got a way of turning a full-grown dog into a snivelling pup; no offense, little fella."

"Well, personally I love it," enthused Thunder happily, "It perks me up an' makes me feel big, bouncy an' rarin' t' go."

"Very unusual," responded Boris, looking down at Thunder with respect. "Very unusual indeed. Pleasant previous-incarnational experience, I suspect."

"Could be," agreed Petie. "Could very well be. There's more to this young fellow than meets the eye."

"That's why I'm called Thunder," boasted Thunder, absorbed with himself. "I love thunder more than turkey, even."

"You like turkey?" enquired Boris. "You should have spoken up back at my place. Lots of turkey there. Tons of leftovers from Thanksgiving; why didn't you ask?"

"Petie said I had to eat borscht cuz your feelings would..."

"There's Winston," interjected Petie hastily, trotting ahead, "Hurry up, before it starts to rain."

Chapter Eleven

"I LOVE A RAINY NIGHT"

"*P*um. Pum, pum-pum,
Pum, pum, pa-pum, pum-pum.
Pum-Pum! Pum,
pa-pa, pa-pa-Pum, pum,
Pum. Pum. Pum!", pummed Winston, glancing up at the sky. "Looks like we're in for a spot of rain, what?"

Catching sight of Boris and Petie and a young pup approaching, he said to himself, out loud, as usual: "I say; company, what? A bit of the old palaver. Harrumph. Have to break out the brandy, I suspect. Snifters of port. Cigars too, of course. Nothing but the best for old Boris and Petie, what? Cute little nipper bouncing along with them too. Sprightly lad. Like the cut of his jib, I do. British, no doubt."

"Good evening, Winston," greeted Boris amiably. "How's the Queen? All well with the Royal Family?"

"Yes," added Petie. "How's the Queen?"

"Never better," assured Winston, pleased at their interest, "Never better."

"I'm Thunder," piped up Thunder, bouncing up and down with youthful zest, as the first few drops of rain began to fall, followed by a huge, jagged flash of lightning and a second later, a thunderous "BOOM!!" that levelled the others flat on the grass, legs extended cartoonishly to either side, like squashed turtles; then, before Thunder had a chance to laugh outright at them, they scooted into Winston's doghouse and pulled down the flap.

"FLASH!" went the sky. Then "BOOM!!" Then "FLASH!" then "BOOM!!" Then the heavens opened up and the rains descended like Noah's flood. All of this delighted Thunder of course because next to thunder and turkey, Thunder loved lightning and rain best of all; unlike Angelica's father, who, lost pup or no lost pup, went running past Winston's house, high stepping it all the way.

Thunder, recognizing who it was from the lightning flashes, seeing how silly he looked, couldn't resist bursting out laughing at him and rolling around on the grass. Hearing Thunder's merriment outside the doghouse, in the midst of the stormy din, made Boris and Petie and Winston feel downright sheepish, considering they were all-grown-up and he was just a lost little pup in big trouble, so they bravely poked their heads out the flap to address the problem. Winston, however, seeing the rain splashing about all over, grew immediately nostalgic.

"Just like Old Blighty," he sniffed. "Lots of rain. With luck we'll get some fog too, eh what?"

"How long have you lived over here, sir?" enquired Thunder.

"Beg pardon, old chappie?" replied Winston.

"I said, how long have you lived here in Canada, sir?"

"Canada?" puzzled Winston. "Oh, I say, you mean the Colonies. Why, six generations, my dear fellow. Six generations."

"That seems like a long time to be so crazy about England, sir." continued Thunder politely.

Petie and Boris gasped and looked aghast, at little Thunder's innocent *faux pas*.

"It's in the blood, old boy," responded Winston, "It's in the blood. And Winnie's the name, young sir. Winnie's the name, to some of my intimates, every now and again."

As Petie and Boris exhaled a startled sigh of relief, Thunder nailed down the permanence of a lifetime's friendship with Winston by asking him to sing *The Last Farewell* for him, so he could learn the words.

"If you step inside I'll do better than that," encouraged Winston happily. "I'll play a human singing it for you on my phonograph. His name's Roger Whittaker; listen and weep, no creature does it better." (p.234)

When the song, one of the most poignant of all audile nostalgias, was over, Thunder began to cry like the heartbroken little pup he was.

"I—I want to go home too but I can't. I bit Angelica's mother's thumb and I'll be killed even if I find out where she lives."

"Stuff and nonsense," snorted Winston, "Stuff and nonsense, I say. Angelica's the biggest dog lover there ever was and her parents dote on her. Positively *dote* on her. If *she* loves you *they'll* love you; won't be able to help themselves. Who told you such nonsense? Who, I say? Whoever it was I'll give 'em a shank savaging they'll not soon forget. Frightening a brave little pup. No excuse for it. No excuse at all. Harrumph!"

With that, Petie and Boris backed up nervously, protecting their shanks as best they could.

"It wasn't our fault," protested Petie. "He didn't tell us he was *Angelica's* pup."

"That's right, he didn't," added Boris. "We made the best judgment we could, under the circumstances. Erred a bit on the side of caution perhaps but better safe than sorry. Besides, our final decision was to seek out your council, Winston, and act accordingly."

"Quite right," agreed Winston, mollified, flattered, and proud. "Quite right indeed. A moment, please."

Opening a trunk, he reverently removed a British magistrate's wig and placed it regally on his head. Festooned with this traditional piece of British pomp and ceremony, he then turned back to his friends, harrumphed once, and gave his final judgment.

"Young fellow," he resumed, looking down fondly, but with dignity, at Thunder, "You must fetch yourself off to Angelica's house forthwith, escorted by these overzealous but essentially well-meaning, stout-hearted fellows, and scratch politely on the front door thrice. It's a magical number and sufficient to rouse alerted parental attention. Don't wiggle overmuch when they pick you up, look slightly contrite, and await developments. And for Pete's sake don't shake drops all over the place if they put you down."

"*'Been there: Done that.'*" confirmed Thunder happily. "Can we go now?"

"Certainly, young fellow," replied Winston, "But do come back soon, old chap. You will come back soon, won't you?"

"I certainly will," promised Thunder. "And I'll bring Angelica too."

"See he comes to no harm, fellows," cautioned Winston, turning to Boris and Petie. "See he comes to no harm, and for heaven's sake don't let them spot you bringing him back. A wet, shivering puppy on the porch all alone is a heart squeezer *par excellence*. He may well wind up sleeping on Angelica's bed instead of some lonely box in the basement. Got that, chappies? Have you got all that?"

"Ten-four," assured Petie and Boris, "Ten-four. Over-and-out."

"Righty-o! is the term, I believe," growled Winston, with a touch of temper. "Righty-o!"

"Righty-o!, guv'nor," responded Petie and Boris in unison and in haste. "Righty-o!"

And with that, they went off with their charge, flanking him on the last stretch of his journey home.

Chapter Twelve

BACK IN THE FOLD

"*H*e's out there somewhere," thought Angelica to herself, sitting up in bed and looking out the window. "He's out there in the cold and the dark and the wet."

"I should *never* have let him jump out the kitchen window," insisted Angelica's mother, going over and peering through the glass in the front door, at the rain. "If it was a child I'd have grabbed him as soon as he left my hands. What kind of mother am I?"

"Stop beating yourself over the head, Evelyn," commiserated Angelica's father, putting an arm around her shoulder and looking out into the night too. "It doesn't do any good. Nobody blames you, except you."

"I'd feel a little better if somebody did," sighed Angelica's mother. "That way I could defend myself. Feel a little bit resentful even, but as it is, oh, I don't know, I just feel dreadful. Guilty. Guilty, guilty, guilty."

And with that, in the perfect timing which comes only to the innocent or the wise, Thunder scratched three times politely on the door.

In a flash, Angelica's mother whipped it open, scooped up the little wet puppy, raced for the bathroom, towelled him fluffy, ran to Angelica's bedroom, flung open her door, hastened over to the bed, dropped Thunder into Angelica's lap, grinned at her stunned daughter, and withdrew, without spoiling the occasion with so much as a single word.

Chapter Thirteen

CONFIRMATION

"*I* was OK most of the time you were lost," confided Angelica, looking down at the sleepy, slightly-damp puppy on her lap, "except when there was thunder."

Hearing what he thought was his name, Thunder perked his ears up.

"Dogs are always afraid of thunder, aren't they?" she continued. And with that, Angelica saw Thunder perk his ears up a second time; and then she knew.

"Your name is Thunder, isn't it? Thunder, Thunder, Thunder, Thunder, Thunder."

"Yap, yap, yap, yap, yap," responded Thunder in agreement.

"I bet you even love real thunder, don't you?" laughed Angelica in surprise.

"Yap!" replied Thunder.

"Does 'Yap!' mean 'Yes!' this time too?" asked Angelica.

"Yes, it does," answered Thunder, right in the middle of her head.

"Did I just hear you speak telepathy again?" gasped Angelica, surprised, hopeful, and delighted. "Did I?"

"Petie," confirmed Thunder: "Petie and Boris and Winston."

BOOK TWO

THE BIGGEST LIAR IN COUNTY CORK

Chapter One

PLUM DUFF BRÛLÉ

*W*hen Angelica finally nodded off to sleep on the night of her ninth birthday neither she nor her brand-new pup expected to dream all that much because, although both were excellent dreamers in their own right, the adventure of picking each other at the Pierpont Puppy Farm; the fiasco of Thunder's innocent consumption and trashing of the family picnic basket; and his nipping of her mother's finger, resulting in his subsequent loss and recovery hours later, had exhausted them into a delicious down-filled stupor shortly after they went to bed and discovered they could actually talk to each other whenever they wanted, rather than it being merely an occasional, albeit extraordinary and delightful, occurrence.

When they awoke the next morning however they awoke with a start, nose to nose and eyeball to eyeball; and they awoke in such fashion because they'd had the same extraordinary dream. It wasn't a complex dream, didn't require any experts to give divergent interpretations of its meaning, wasn't the kind of dream Angelica usually had: like the one last Easter, when she'd experienced a delicious Smarties sun shower in the company of a giant white bunny holding a big basket full of decorated chocolate eggs; prior to climbing a yellow jello mountain with him and sliding together down the other side into a dazzling, sprinkles lake. No, it wasn't that kind of dream. And it wasn't the kind of dream Thunder usually specialized in; dreams in which he ran all night under the moon, cavorting with anyone who would play: wolves, foxes, bunnies, cats; it didn't matter to him, as long as they, like himself, never got tired of running and pouncing and rolling about in a tangle.

So, what kind of dream was it? Well, it was a rare dream. A dream grownups call a prophetic dream. A dream that quite literally gave them a taste of their future. A dream in which they suddenly found themselves sitting at a pleasant little table beside a pleasant little fire in a pleasant little Irish pub full of pleasant little people, all of whom immediately stopped whatever they were doing and stared in surprise at the lovely little girl with the handsome black pup, that'd suddenly appeared in their midst.

Such an occurrence in just about any other place in the so-called 'civilized world' would have caused a great stir indeed, but fortunately, the Irish, being who they are, are used to experiencing magic in one form or another on almost a daily basis, so no photographers and reporters suddenly pounced on them and no lawyers appeared with pens extended in one hand and an exclusive contract in the other. No indeed. What did happen was much more pleasant. A large, plump, wonderfully cheery woman dressed in a bonnet and skirts, with a very attractive apron tied snugly round her ample middle, spoke up. "Me manners," she said, "I seem t' have lost me manners."; and with that, she scooted out from behind the bar and bustled towards them, holding up a silver platter bearing what seemed to be half a bowling ball.

"If I have to eat that, I'm dead," shuddered Angelica to herself. "I hope I waken first."

"Ditto," agreed Thunder, looking up at her with a grin.

"Neat," thought Angelica, "Thunder's in my dream too."

"Maybe so," conceded Thunder, "But the fact is, I think *you're* in *my* dream."

"If that's the case," replied Angelica, with a wicked smile, "*you* have to eat that stupid bowling ball."

"Bowling ball?" interjected the cheery woman, suddenly much closer than Angelica, embarrassed, thought she was, "Bowling ball? No dear, 'tisn't a bowling ball. 'Tis me world-famous plum duff brûlé." And with that, she plunked it down before them and lit it with a match, that just seemed to be there in her hand.

Instantly the 'bowling ball' went "Foomf!" and burst into flames. Delightful flames. Mystical flames. Purple flames. Flames so beautiful and transparent the 'bowling ball' was transformed into what it was intended to be; a culinary masterpiece. Like cat-sup with fries and icing on cake, it couldn't be itself at its best un-less the two went together; and *boy* did fire and plum duff brûlé go together. Mmm-hmn, talk about *tasty!*

The long and the short of it was, Angelica and Thunder ate it all; and that's when the magic occurred. You see, after they'd stuffed themselves on the plum duff brûlé, politely and simul-taneously licking the last crumb off their plates, they suddenly awoke with a start, back in their bed, thousands of miles away from Ireland, way, way off in Canada, and they awoke hungry; hungry for bacon-and-eggs and toast and milk and tomato slices and the adventure of their first whole day together, despite the fact, moments before, they were absolutely bursting with plum duff brûlé.

Chapter Two

BREAKFAST

*W*hen Angelica and Thunder raced into the kitchen minutes later, Angelica's parents, about to be seated, were startled to see their normally quiet daughter bouncing with life.

"There's no way I can go to school today," announced Angelica, "Thunder and I simply *have* to spend all of our first whole day together and that's all there is to it. It's sunny and warm outside and there's all kinds of things we simply *have* to do."

"Like what?" asked her father, "It's not like you to not want to go to school. Weren't you looking forward to giving a book report on *War and Peace* today?"

"I was and I will," confirmed Angelica, "but not today. No sir. Today is too special for books."

"Too special for books?" puzzled her mother, concerned, "Too special for books? I thought you loved books more than anything. Are you running a temperature, dear? Do you have a fever?" And with that, she put a soothing hand on Angelica's forehead; only to discover her beloved daughter was cool. Cool as a cucumber.

"We want what you guys are having for breakfast," said Angelica, "We want bacon-and-eggs and toast and milk and tomato slices."

"Not cereal?" enquired her mother, surprised. "Don't you want your usual little bowl of cereal?"

"No," replied Angelica. "Today we need a truck driver break-fast. Lots of protein. Something that'll fill us up and last and last and last. Can I eat it on the floor too, with Thunder? Can I? Or can he sit on the table just this once and eat his beside me?"

"Of course not," snorted her father, "he's already sleeping with you and that's enough. More than enough. He's just a dog, Angelica. He's cute and he's smart, no doubt about it, but he's just a dog."

With that, Thunder eyeballed Shawn's slippered ankle and contemplated pouncing on it for a gnaw, but Angelica, remem-bering the tetanus shot her mother had to receive the evening before because of the nip Thunder'd accidentally given her, put the kibosh on his musing with a, "Don't you dare. Don't even *think* about it."

"Think about what?" asked her father, curiously.

"W-e-e-e-ll," hesitated Angelica, concerned about the conse-quences but reluctant to tell a first-ever lie, "Thunder was think-ing about pouncing on your ankle for calling him 'just a dog.'"

"Surely not," said her mother, "After all we went through yes-terday? Surely not."

"Consider yourself lucky," chuckled Angelica at her father, "If your legs weren't so long he'd have probably bit you on the butt."

"Angelica!" gasped her parents in unison, "Angelica!"

"Well, it's true," continued Angelica, "You might as well com-prehend right from the beginning that Thunder is very, very spe-cial. He not only understands everything I say, he even under-stands everything I think—and vice versa."

"Angelica," cautioned her father, "we're very, very pleased you love Thunder so much but you've always been a sensible girl and you simply can't go about telling people such things. They'll think you're a little bit..."

"Mental?" responded Angelica. "Crackers? Round the bend? Bonkers?"

"Well ... yes," replied her father. "I'm afraid so."

"Care for some proof, Dad? Want me to prove it?"

"Now, dear," warned her mother, a plate of bacon-and-eggs in each hand, "It's unwise to back yourself into a corner like that."

"If I prove it, can Thunder eat his bacon-and-eggs at the table with me just this once? Can he?"

"Darling," chuckled her father, reaching for his shoes, "if you can prove he understands your thoughts and words, he can not only eat his breakfast at the table, I'll give you twenty bucks to spend on treats as well."

"Deal!" agreed Angelica. "What do you want him to do?"

"Hmm," thought her father. "OK, tell him to go over and scratch at the door."

"Too easy," rejected Angelica. "Make the test unmistakable. If he does only that you'll say it was a coincidence. You'll say he just wanted to go outside."

"Fair enough," said her father. "I was only trying to be nice. I hate to shoot you down but you asked for it. Tell him to go over and scratch at the door, then tell him to come over and untie my *left* shoelace, then have him go over and offer your mother a pawshake."

And sure enough, no sooner said than done, Thunder did all three—zip, zip, zip.

"Impossible!" blurted Angelica's parents simultaneously, eyes bugging out, "Impossible!"

And with that, Angelica patted her lap and Thunder bounced up on it, gave her nose a quick affectionate snurf as she bent her face down to him, then jumped the rest of the way up onto the table and sat staring patiently at one of the plates in Angelica's mother's hands.

Bewildered, the poor woman looked over at her equally-bewildered husband, then put the plates down before Thunder and Angelica; who dove on them immediately, with gusto.

"That wasn't really possible," protested her father, with failing conviction, after sitting down and peering back and forth at Angelica and Thunder munching happily away. "That wasn't really possible, you know. You do know that, don't you?"

"Nothing like bacon-and-eggs and toast and milk and tomato slices for breakfast," replied Angelica, kindly refraining from rubbing it in. "Nothing like it when you're starving and have lots to do."

Chapter Three

THUNDER'S ADVICE

"*M*ake sure you come back for lunch," insisted Angelica's mother, as the little girl and pup scooted out the front door. "Make sure you come back for lunch; at twelve o'clock!"

"And don't spend that twenty all at once!" added her father from the doorway as the two disappeared around the hedge, "Don't spend it all on candy or anything!"

"He's got that half-right," chuckled Angelica to Thunder, "I'm only going to buy a box of Smarties, some licorice whips, and a Snickers bar, for me, but I've got to spend the rest on presents for Petie and Boris and Winston. What do you think a Russian wolfhound and a British bulldog and a Chihuahua would like, Thunder? Got any ideas? They were my best friends till you showed up, you know."

"Milkbones," replied Thunder, "A giant economy-size of milkbones for each of them, the assorted kind: liver and chicken and beef and fish. It's the one thing all dogs have in common; we *love* milkbones!"

"Milkbones it is," agreed Angelica happily. "They've got them at the variety store at the corner, near Winston's house. Mr.

Chan's real nice; he'll gift wrap them for us too I bet, just you wait and see."

Chapter Four

TEATIME

*A*t the very moment Angelica and Thunder entered Mr. Chan's establishment, Petie and Boris paused outside Winston's house just down the way. They were a bit nervous about dropping in on him unannounced, in case he was in one of his moods, and as they approached, if one were to judge the situation by the sounds they heard from inside, it's little wonder their nervousness turned to apprehension, on the spot.

"Where is it?!!" roared Winston, from within, "Where's my blessed Brown Betty?!! Can't make a decent cup of tea without a Brown Betty and that's a fact!! A stone, cold, blessed, *fact!!*"

"We better leave," quivered Petie, looking way up at his towering wolfhound friend, "We better leave and come back another time."

"We'd lose the moment," responded Boris mournfully, looking down at his little big-eyed buddy. "We'd lose the moment for ever and ever and ever. I simply can't bear it." And with that, his great Russian head lowered in such a melancholy way on the poetic curve of his long slender neck the sight of it was more than a sensitive soul could endure, even without the large salty tear rolling from his anguished eye straight down his long woeful muzzle.

"Got to think of something quick," thought Petie, glancing nervously about, "If Boris starts bawling and spouting poetry about the sad side of life we'll all be in the soup. Winston is very short-tempered before his first pot of tea in the morning and he may not be as patient as he usually is when Boris gets like this."

"Ah, ha!!" bellowed Winston inside, with triumph. "*Now* I remember; I left it by last night's fire, under the mulberry tree!"

"Thank god," murmured Petie, sitting down relieved, as Winston bulldogged his way past the flap of his doghouse, stepped outside into the sunshine, scratched his hindquarters with satisfaction on the grass, and looked about contentedly.

"Comrade," greeted Boris, with a loving embrace of a smile, "Comrade, Comrade, Comrade, was there ever such a morning as this; outside of Russia, that is?"

"Russia?" poohed Winston, without having ever been there. "Russia? Why, what's Russia to England? No offence, old chap, but punting on the Thames..."

"Sailing on the Volga," interrupted Boris indelicately.

"Dropped scones and raspberry treacle," scowled Winston.

"Caviar, radishes, boiled potatoes and tea," replied Boris regally.

"Bangers and mash," snorted Winston triumphantly, as if that was the end of the matter. "And *real* tea. English breakfast tea. Orange Pekoe."

"No offence," piped up Petie, "but since we're talking tasty, I defy anyone to surpass shrimp cocktails, burritos, tostadas, and beans – refried of course."

"The boiled beef of Merry Old England!" enthused Winston, caught up in the joy of the moment.

"Sturgeon!" ecstaticized Boris. "Sturgeon and borscht!"

"Water!" shouted Petie, to make himself heard.

"'Water?'" enquired Boris and Winston in unison, looking down at their little buddy in puzzled bemusement, "Don't you mean cerveza?"

"It's boiling," said Petie. "See? I put it on the coals, for tea, and it's ready."

"Just the thing," approved Winston, very pleased indeed, "Just the thing; I haven't had a spot all day, and it's halfway to noon."

Chapter Five

MILKBONES

*L*ike everyone else, Winston possessed his faults, but anyone with the good fortune to sit down to a tea lovingly prepared by the old royalist would have to say his merit as host wasn't one of them. "Warm the pot," he'd say, "Warm the pot first then spoon in the tea—no bags of course, they're an insult to the palate—add boiling water, cover with a cozy and sit back and wait. Never stir. When it's ready to pour, strain it into thin cups—the thinner the better—but always add it *to* the milk, never the other way round. Nothing worse than milk added to tea I always say, nothing worse, and that's a fact."

While all this preparation was going on, disaster loomed. Why disaster?—Because, unbeknownst to Winston, he was fresh out of biscuits. Fresh out of the Peek Frean's "By Appointment to Her Majesty" vanilla-and-chocolate wafers that were, next to milkbones, the biscuit of choice of both Winston and the Queen Mum herself; the oldest of the Royals and Winston's personal favourite.

As is so often the case however, things weren't as bad as they seemed, because before Winston could discover his embarrassing lapse as host, Angelica and Thunder suddenly appeared with big grins, carrying even bigger parcels; each beautifully wrapped by Mr. Chan.

"Well now," chuckled Winston, pleased, as always, to see Angelica, "A double treat; my oldest, and my newest friends, all gathered together. What a fine day this is turning out to be. If you and Thunder would care to sit yourselves and join us for tea I'll nip inside and fetch my biscuit tin."

"You don't have to, sir," offered Thunder, "Angelica bought everybody treats. See these parcels?—they're presents for you guys."

"For us?" gasped Winston, touched to the quick. "Those beautifully-wrapped presents are for us?"

"Yessir," replied Thunder, "Guess who gets which?"

"Well," mused Winston, "I'm kind of attracted to the one papered in the Union Jack, god bless it. Is that one for me?"

"It certainly is," laughed Angelica, placing it before him on the grass. "This one is specially-decorated just for you."

"Well now," responded Winston, "What more could a body ask for than such a splendidly-prepared gift?—Nothing, I'm sure. Nothing that I can think of, that is."

"It's certainly splendid," spoke up Petie, "Very splendid indeed but I must say I'm attracted to the one wrapped like a desert, with cactuses and pretty little lizards all over it. Is that one, by any chance, for me?"

"It certainly is," smiled Angelica, placing it before him on the grass.

"I don't know what to say," said Petie, eyes filling with joy. "I'm so happy I simply don't know what to say."

"I guess the last one's mine," sighed Boris, stricken by the knowledge he'd not a present to give in return. "I guess that one with marvelous pictures of my beloved Russia all over it is mine."

"It certainly is," confirmed Angelica, placing it before him on the grass. "What's wrong, don't you like it?"

"Nooo," groaned Boris in despair, responding to her concern rather than her words. "Oh, noooo, I love it so much more than I can say, but I haven't a gift for you in return. I haven't a gift for you or Thunder and it's breaking my heart." And with that, he began to look like he was gearing up for one of his legendary mournful howls. Howls that can only be safely enjoyed by a breast poeticized by a full moon married to a starry night.

Angelica, having been on the receiving end of one of his daylight anguishes, recognizing the danger, did what any sensible soul would do; she spoke to Boris, from the heart.

"A hug, Boris. If you were to give me one of your wonderful Russian hugs I'd melt inside like a pound of butter in the sun; and *that* feels better than any silly box of milkbones ever could."

"Milkbones!" shouted Petie and Boris and Winston in unison. "You bought us milkbones?! The giant economy-size?! The assorted kind with liver and chicken and beef and fish?!" And with that, they pounced on their presents and savaged them open in a manner they would afterwards find embarrassing but which, at the time, gave Angelica and Thunder greater pleasure than the normal restraints of good manners permit.

Chapter Six

THE CONFAB

"*T*hunder and I had the most extraordinary dream this morning," said Angelica, delicately sipping her tea. "We suddenly appeared in a pub in Ireland and a sweet, plump little old lady gave us one of her world-famous plum duff brûlés to eat and we did and it was great. Then, *poof*, we woke up in bed back here, even hungrier than before we ate it."

"Very unusual," mused Boris aloud, glancing at Winston, "Very unusual indeed."

"I couldn't agree more, old chap," confirmed Winston, teacup arrested halfway to his lips. "I'm afraid these youngsters are heading for an adventure; one that could prove perilous."

"Perilous?" enquired Angelica nervously, "Did you say perilous? Thunder's awfully young for a *perilous* adventure, don't you think?"

"Yes," replied Winston, taking a sip, "he is. However, he isn't cut from normal cloth, as they say: he's black as pitch, unusually alert, and, more importantly, less afraid of thunder than any creature, ever. If that isn't a rare combination of gifts my name isn't Winston and England isn't the crowning achievement of God's wondrous hand, in a universe too vast for contemplation."

"You mean, I'm destined for greatness?" spoke up Thunder proudly. "I'm really *that* special?"

"Of course you are," enthused Angelica, looking down at him fondly, "Didn't we prove how special you are to Mom and Dad a while ago? Didn't we prove you could understand all my thoughts and words?"

"Whaaaaat?!" gasped Winston, dropping and shattering an irreplaceable bone-china teacup emblazoned with the coronation of Edward VII. "You did what?! You *proved* he could understand human?! Oh dear. That's bad. That's very, very bad indeed."

"No it isn't," protested Angelica, "We even won twenty bucks from my father for betting it was true."

"Don't you know what that means?!" exclaimed Petie, in agitation, looking as concerned as only a big-eyed, shivering Chihuahua can. "Don't you know what'll happen?!"

"Doomed," moaned Boris. "We're all doomed now; nothing will save us."

"Here, here," cautioned Winston, "level heads prevail. Perhaps it's not too late. What did you do to win the bet, Thunder?"

"I scratched on the door, untied Angelica's father's left shoe, and gave her mother a pawshake."

"Oh, no," squeaked Petie. "You did t*hree* things? You actually did *three* things?"

"Yes," replied Thunder, getting a bit nervous, "Was that too many?"

"I fear so," sighed Winston. "Our only hope now is, they will find it so hard to believe they'll deny the facts. Humans are good at self-deception." And with that, Winston leaned forward and spoke to Thunder, with great solemnity.

"Thunder, my boy," he said, "You must never, ever broadcast your talents about indiscriminately."

"Why not?" enquired Thunder, "We already used it to win twenty bucks. Aren't there tons of people out there who'd pay to see me do tricks?"

"Yes," agreed Winston, "there are; but they'll hound you to death if you do them too well. At the very least, they'll take you away from Angelica; maybe even cut you open, to see what makes you tick. And that's if you're lucky. If you're unlucky you'll be stoned to death for being a witch or something."

"No!" gasped Angelica, appalled, "They mustn't do that; what can we do?!"

"First of all, you must stay calm," advised Boris, "It's important to stay calm in a crisis. Emulate me, young lady. Follow my example in such instances and you won't go wrong."

"Oh, sure," snorted Petie. "Do you want her to howl and snork and snivel at every little thing? Is *that* your answer to this dilemma?"

"I've never bitten a Chihuahua," warned Boris, "None of you are large enough to give my jaws a satisfactory crunch."

"Oh yeah?!" challenged Petie, hopping up and down, "I bet if I chomped you on the fetlock it'd cut you down to size!"

"Now, see here, chaps," interrupted Winston, "Much as I'd love to join in and give you both a sound thrashing, we've a problem to solve and we've got to solve it forthwith."

"How about if I pretend I can't do it, the next time they ask?" piped up Thunder. "Would that work?"

"It might," said Petie, "It might; what do you think, Boris?"

Boris, mollified at being consulted for his opinion, forgot he was irritated at Petie, lowered his great head down to Chihuahua-level, and looked deeply into Petie's eyes.

"I hope so, my friend. I really do hope so. I don't think my heart could stand the loss of this splendid young fellow. I really don't think it would ever manage to heal itself again."

"Well said," responded Winston gruffly, moved in his depths as only the British can be, "Very well said indeed."

"I'm scared," worried Angelica, "I'm not sure we can pull it off; my parents are pretty smart."

"*I'm* not scared," chuckled Thunder with confidence, "I can be as dumb as a post if I want to."

"That has its advantages sometimes," confirmed Petie, "I've used it myself to get out of trouble, but don't overdo it. If you do they'll smell a rat."

"That's right," added Boris, "Take the middle path when dealing with humans, it's the safest way, unless they're very, very special, like Angelica. And as for you, Angelica, you mustn't let people know you now speak canine either; it's just too risky."

And with that, he glanced up at the sky to confirm what the grumbling in his stomach had already told him despite the half-dozen milkbones he'd so recently wolfed down; it was almost noon.

Chapter Seven

LUNCH

*A*ngelica, normally, wouldn't even think of being frightened of her parents but as she approached her home on the way back for lunch, despite Thunder's confident belief they could con the grownups, she found herself becoming more and more nervous; a nervousness she knew they would spot if she didn't manage to get a grip on herself real quick. The problem was, she wasn't having much success at it because, like most deceptions, there were just too many factors involved she couldn't control. Like for example, being a rank amateur at lying, she wasn't all that sure she could do it without blushing and being unable to look her folks in the eye. Also, instead of just her parents' car in the drive-way, it was crammed with jeeps and vans and trucks she'd never seen before, with lots more double-parked in front of the house. A helicopter was circling overhead too; and, worst still, as she got closer, she noticed her father standing outside on the porch, wav-ing his arms about, with an idiotic grin plastered on a face she'd always thought handsome before. *Then*, even worse than *that*, she spotted her mother all luridly painted up and tottering about in an evening gown and extra-high heels, sinking and wobbling all over the lawn; with hundreds of people watching! Literally hundreds! How embarrassing!

"She doesn't smoke," thought Angelica to herself, "so why is my mother puffing away on a cigarette stuffed into the end an absurdly-long cigarette holder? Come to think of it, she doesn't drink either, so why is she sloshing a brandy snifter all about, one the size of a respectable goldfish bowl?"

All of these questions and more were answered as soon as someone in the crowd spotted Angelica and Thunder, and everyone stampeded towards them.

"There she is! There's the little girl with the talking dog!"

"Talking dog?" puzzled Thunder, as he and Angelica were suddenly and expertly surrounded by a ring of policemen, who escorted them safely up to the front door, "Talking dog? Me? I only talk to Angelica and I only do that in her head—what gives?"

"Make him say something!" shouted a voice. "Make him say something and I'll give you a thousand bucks! I work for Geraldo! Don't sign with anyone else! We'll put you on TV!"

"Forget it!" shouted another. "I work for Oprah; we'll give you ten thousand; and that's just for starters!"

"Peanuts!" shouted yet another. "Current Affair will pay you..."

"Letterman!" shouted somebody else, even louder.

"Ricki Lake!" shouted another, louder still; then the voices all blended into a general, muted roar, as the family stepped inside and closed the door—but not for long; a select, yet still numerous group of hucksters: clergymen, lawyers, merchandisers, politicians, psychiatrists, sociologists, zoologists, and so on and so on, ones who'd already greased Angelica's parents' palms with cash in order to get inside, surged forward and noisily surrounded them as they entered the living room.

"Back!!" roared a burly cop. "Back up and give the little lady and the pup room to show what they can do!"

By this time, of course, Angelica was more or less paralyzed with concern and indecision, but not Thunder. No sir. Seeing how worried she was for him however, Thunder forgave her for spazing out in a crisis and immediately went over and scratched on a cabinet door, undid her father's left shoe, and offered his paw to Angelica's mother.

"What are you doing?! Are you crazy?!" thought Angelica at Thunder, her face bug-eyed with shock and her mouth hanging open. "We're supposed to pretend you *can't* do it; not that you *can* do it!"

"I am," thought Thunder back at her. "Watch and see," and sure enough, after the cheering had settled down, a big round fellow in a cowboy hat stepped forward to challenge Thunder's veracity.

"Now look here," he said, hands on his waist and puffing up even bigger, "I'm from Missouri y'know, an' I wasn't born yesterday, no sirree bob. Mind if I smoke?" And with that, he lit up a big smelly stogy; scraped the dirt from his boots, on the fireplace grate; and proceeded to launch into his interrogation, pleased as punch at the figure he made and the attention he was getting.

"Y'all might be able t'sucker them there Canadian yokels outside but south a' th' border we've seen it all an' most of it, beggin' yer pardon miss, is crap. That's right, I said 'crap'. Now that ain't a p'lite word an' I apologize in advance if you an' that there pup turns out t'be th' real thing but I've got serious doubts. Serious doubts indeed."

"What can I do?" asked Angelica, amused, despite her fear. "What can I do, I'm just a little girl?"

"That's more like it," thought Thunder to her, with approval. "They're all acting like a bunch of bozos. We can buffalo this lot, no sweat."

"But you've already blown it," thought Angelica back at him, "You were supposed to ... aaah ... I get it!"

"Excuse me, little missy," continued the big man from Missouri in a cowboy hat, "but time's money an' I gots me a country 'r two t'buy 'r sell b'fore m'supper so I'll lay m'cards down on th' table all neat an' up-front, th' good ol' American way. You have that there pup of yers run 'round me three times then hop up in yer lap an' bark twice an' I'll give ya a cool ten million fer him—no strings. No ands, ifs, buts 'r maybes; that's not m'way. You have yer pup do them three things an' I'll give ya this fer him." And with that, he summoned somebody out of the crowd, with a finger snap, and a little bald fellow scurried forward, slapped a suitcase down and popped open the lid; and there it was, a cool ten million, all in brand-new thousand-dollar-bills.

"Oh, we're rich! We're rich!" squealed Angelica's parents, bouncing up and down, clapping their hands excitedly over and over. "We're rich! We're rich! We're rich! Oh, we're rich, rich, rich, rich, *rich!*"

"Watch close," thought Thunder to Angelica, "Watch real close; and try not to laugh." Chuckling, he then ran over and scratched on the cabinet door, undid her father's left shoe, and offered Angelica's mother his paw.

"Jest as I thought," snorted the Missourian, albeit slightly disappointed. "Jest as I thought—'nother 'miracle'." And with that, he snapped his fingers at his flunky once, who shut the money case closed with a click and followed his boss, already heading out the door.

What happened after that? Well, in less than five minutes the street and the sky were as empty as Angelica's parents' daydreams.

"I knew we should have run a couple of checks first," sighed Angelica's father ruefully. "Now I feel like a damned fool."

"Do you realize what you just about did, Dad?" said Angelica, with considerable restraint, considering the situation. "You just about *sold* Thunder. Not a 'pup', do you understand? Not some 'dog'; you just about *sold* Thunder. Are you out of your cotton-picking *mind?"*

"Well," confessed her father, looking sheepish, "I guess maybe I was."

"Me too," agreed her mother, slipping off her high-heels with a grateful groan. "Imagine thinking a dog could understand English. Think the girls will laugh at me at the mall and the hair-dresser's?"

"Mother!" barked Angelica, stamping her foot in exasperation, "That *isn't* the point! You were going to *sell* Thunder!"

"Surely not," doubted her mother, "Oh, surely not. We weren't going to do *that...*"

"Ask Dad," insisted Angelica. "Go ahead; *ask* him."

"W-e-e-e-ll," hesitated her father, looking down and scuffing at the floor with a shoe, "ten million dollars is a whole lot of shinola."

"Would you sell Mom or me for ten million, Dad?" grilled Angelica, driving the point home. "Is there a price tag on us too?"

"No sir," shot back her father, "You're both priceless to me and that's a fact."

"Well, *Dad,*" continued Angelica, looking up at him, "That's how *I* feel about Thunder, and *nothing* or *no one* will *ever* change it."

"I see," responded her father. "Well, if I'd known that I wouldn't even have considered..."

"You went gold crazy, Dad," interrupted Angelica, "And you've got to admit it or you'll do it again."

"W-e-e-e-ll, alright honey, I admit it. I went loco, as they say. Plumb loco, and so did your mother; right dear?"

"W-e-e-e-e-ll, I wouldn't go so far as to say that," demurred Angelica's mother, wrapping herself in the tattered remnants of her dignity. "No, I wouldn't go so far as to say that."

"Look in the mirror, Mother," demanded Angelica, "You've got makeup troweled all over your beautiful face, you're drinking brandy at noon out of a fishbowl, and you're smoking a cigarette stuck in the end of an old plastic straw; what more proof do you need? ... What's that, Thunder? ... Oh ... OK. Thunder wants us to forget the whole thing and just have lunch, could we do that?"

"Sure," agreed her dad gratefully, "Sure we can. Anything in particular the little fellow wants?"

"I don't know, I'll ask him," replied Angelica ... "Grilled cheese, Dad. He wants grilled cheese, with catsup on the side, same as me."

"Sure he does," chuckled her father, winking at his wife, "Sure he does. Two grilled cheese with catsup, comin' up."

Chapter Eight

THE TRIGGER

"*I* really don't think Thunder should eat his sandwich on the floor today, Mother," hinted Angelica, "With all those people tramping about in our house a while ago I bet there's all kinds of germs and such down there; don't you think so?"

"Well, yes, I guess you're right," agreed her mother, a plate with a grilled cheese sandwich and catsup in each hand, "I guess he could sit on the table just this once."

"Hear that?" said Angelica to Thunder.

"I sure did," thought Thunder back, springing up on her lap and giving her snout a snurf in passing as he hopped up onto the table. "I've never had a grilled cheese before, but I know I'm just gonna love this one."

"Look!" squealed Angelica's mother, "Look! He does..."

"Now, now, dear," cautioned her husband, "let's not get all carried away again. My guess is it's the tone in her voice he goes by. I bet that's it. He knows what to do by the tone."

"W-e-e-e-ll," hesitated Angelica's mother, before, as usual, surrendering to the more flawed perspective of her husband's logic, "I suppose you're right."

"Course I'm right," responded her husband, gratified, however erroneously, by her deferment, "Course I'm right. Cute as buttons, aren't they, munchin' away on their sandwiches; let's take a polaroid for the family album." And with that, he took a snap and laid it on the table to develop. Thunder, biting bits of his grilled cheese off and dipping them in catsup before chewing expertly and gulping them down, already predisposed to consider full-grown humans odd, was perplexed to see Angelica lean over and stare at the black square as curiously as her parents.

"She's going to need some watching," he thought, "Staring at a boring black square like it meant something."

"No, silly," said Angelica with a grin, "that's just the start. Keep looking, it's magic." And sure enough, to Thunder's astonishment, the little black square gradually turned into a miniature version of himself and Angelica, frozen in time. A permanent visual memory of moments before.

"Wow!" exclaimed Thunder, really impressed, "That's *amazing!* What's it called again?"

"It's called a polaroid—a photograph."

"And what's a family album?"

"That's where the photographs are mounted. You can see all of my family in it at different stages of their lives, even people from far away, and those who lived long ago. Our picture will be the last to go in it, right after lunch; the very last of all, until we add new ones nobody's taken yet."

"I've got to see that," enthused Thunder, "Right after lunch I want to see the family album; are we allowed?"

"Mother," asked Angelica, "Thunder wants to see the family album right after lunch, is that OK?"

"Sure," replied her mother, smiling fondly down at the two of them, before glancing over at her husband with a wink. "Sure you can. If that's what Thunder wants to do it's fine with us."

Chapter Nine

THE FAMILY ALBUM

*V*iewing the family album proved a great treat for Thunder; especially the snaps of Angelica as a little baby, a toddler, and then gradually growing big as now. There was, however, one oddity—a blank space where a picture used to be.

"Why's one spot empty?" asked Thunder, nosing the pages from back to front till he came to the right place.

"Well," answered Angelica, glancing up at her father, "That's where one of my father's clan used to be, but he's kind of the family black sheep."

"I want to see what he looks like," said Thunder, "Is his image still around somewhere?"

"Yes," replied Angelica, flipping to the back cover, pulling a big black-and-white photograph out of the flap, and placing it before Thunder. "His name's Shamus. 'Shameless' Shamus O'Shaughnessy. He lives somewhere in County Cork in Ireland, nobody knows quite where, he just pops up occasionally and lies his head off for a while then disappears."

"Lies his head off?" wondered Thunder curiously, looking down at a big, bald-headed, friendly face, "What lies does he tell, and why is there a little golden glow all around his head and shoulders?"

"What golden glow?" enquired Angelica, leaning forward and peering down at the photograph. "I don't see any golden glow." And with that, she and Thunder suddenly disappeared, right before her astonished parents' eyes.

Chapter Ten

THE HAND OF DESTINY

*W*hile Angelica's folks were gawking in slack-jawed, catatonic amazement at the spots where Angelica and Thunder had been moments before, Angelica and Thunder suddenly found themselves seated back at the pleasant little table by the fire in the pleasant little Irish pub they'd been in during their 'dream' earlier that morning; only this time everyone there was frozen like a statue, staring at a little white-haired man seated at another little table on the other side of the fire, who rose as they appeared and burst into song.

"'*Oh Danny boy, the pipes, the pipes are calling,*
From glen to glen, and down the mountain side,'" (p.235)

"What a beautiful sound," whispered Thunder. "I had no idea humans could make such a beautiful sound; but why's everyone frozen? Do beautiful sounds turn all grown-ups into statues, or just the Irish? Good thing Boris isn't here, his heart'd break in more than half, that's for sure."

"No kidding," whispered Angelica back, as touched as Thunder by the haunting sweetness of the little man's voice. A sweetness that seemed to be casting a spell on all about. "Think they'll move when the singing's over or just stay where they are?"

"Dunno," replied Thunder. "It's a mystery to me."

What neither of them understood yet was there's a lot of ways to stun an Irishman. You can crack him on the head with a shillelagh (preferably from behind), you can present him with a gift of single-malt Scottish whisky pre-poured into an empty bottle of Irish whiskey, you can fill him up with a bowl or two of Mulligan stew in a cozy kitchen on a wet winter's day; but if you want to coldcock a whole bunch of them at once all you have to do is sing, *a cappella* or no, in a tenor sweeter than a violin (especially by a fire in a pub), either *Danny Boy* or *Mother Machree*. Yessir, nothing like those ballads for turning the hurly and burly of a packed room of Irishmen into an oil painting, a Madame Tussaud's, a frozen tableau of soul-squeezed contentment.

"They really are as sentimental as Boris," thought Angelica with a grin, as the enchantment ended, observing a tear in every eye. "Just a bunch of sweeties."

"I wouldn't tarry there if I be ye," cautioned the little singer, resuming his seat and taking a quaff of ale. "That there's th' table only one person e'er occupies."

"May I ask who?" enquired Angelica politely.

"Why, that be th' table o' Shameless Shamus O'Shaughnessy, th' biggest liar in County Cork," replied the amiable little chap. "Better come o'er an' sit with me, in case he shows up an' starts bendin' yer ear with his nonsense."

"But we want to meet him," protested Angelica, "He's a relative of ours. Surely he can't be that bad, can he?"

"Well," began the little old fellow, but before he could finish, a giant of a man in leprechaun garb, six-foot-five if he was an inch, and bald as a cantaloupe, burst in through the door and strode towards them – like a typhoon – a crack of thunder – the Hand of Destiny itself.

Chapter Eleven

SHAMELESS SHAMUS O'SHAUGHNESSY

"We'd love to stay and chat with you," dissembled Angelica, rising nervously as the giant plunked himself down on a chair facing her, "but we got to get back to Canada somehow, and right away. We just 'disappeared' and my folks will be worried sick."

"'Tis n' problem," sighed the giant, putting his elbows on the table and supporting his huge bald head with his hands. "No sir, 'tis n' problem a'tall. If it's a problem yer after I've got me a doozie; ye see, I be a leprechaun, th' biggest leprechaun in th' whole o' Ireland, then an' now, an' I'm doomed. Doomed t' grow an' grow till someone believes I really *be* a leprechaun."

"I believe you, sir," offered Angelica kindly.

"Ye do?!" gasped the giant, surprised. "Ye do?! Why 'tis wonderful! 'Tis wonderful! A thousand year I've waited t' hear that! A thousand year! Bless ye, child! Bless ye o'er an' o'er! ... Am I gettin' any smaller? Can't feel meself shrinkin' down t' respectable leprechaun size yet, guess maybe it'll take a minute 'r two, care fer a whiskey?—Irish malt, o' course."

"No thank you, sir," demurred Angelica politely, "I'm only nine."

"Only nine?" repeated the giant, startled, "Only nine? Well now, 'tis surprised I am, an' no mistake."

"But look," said Angelica, rising again, "See?—I'm only this tall."

"Don't mean a thing," snorted the giant. "Ye be taller already than that little disbeliever o'er yonder whut just exhausted half his repertoire, an' twice th' size o' yer average leprechaun, most o' whom be old as th' hills."

"This is all very interesting," responded Angelica dubiously, "but we really have to go now—get back to Canada somehow; my folks will be frantic."

"No they won't," insisted the giant, "Ye've already dipped yer sleeves in th' tears o' a century o' me woe, soaked inta this very tabletop. Ye be in faerie time now."

"Faerie time?" enquired Angelica, glancing at her damp cuffs, and then sitting down once more, "What's faerie time?"

"Well," replied the giant, keeping it simple, "Each hour o' faerie time be 'bout a second in normal time; an' a good thing too, at present, for 'tis clear t' me, since I haven't shrunk, ye're th' biggest liar at this table, by far; howe'er, I'm optimistic a few hours is all I'll need t' convince ye I be in fact a leprechaun—then I'll send ye back home. An' ye'll do so bearin' gifts—great treasures."

"But," protested Angelica, "if I'm gone for a few hours my parents will freak."

"Aaach, no they won't, me dear; yer not listenin'. 'Tis n' more than seconds ye'll be missin', far as they can tell: they'll still be rubbin' their disbelievin' eyes when ye pop back inta place—I promise ye."

"I have to say, sir," confessed Angelica, rising again, "I don't believe any of this."

"Well, yer pup does," nodded Shamus with a grin, looking down at Thunder. "Th' wee fellow believes me every word."

"It's true," confirmed Thunder, recovering from the shock of fully comprehending a human other than Angelica. "I believe everything he says."

Chapter Twelve

BEEFSTEAK AND KIDNEY PIE

"You're really asking us to swallow a lot, Shamus," warned Angelica, sitting down and surrendering to the situation. "I mean, you're positively *huge* but you claim to be a leprechaun *and* you say you're a thousand years old."

"A thousand year old? Pish! I'm not a thousand year old. What nonsense; how could anyone believe such a thing? I'm as old as Time itself, if I be a day. Have a hot chocolate with cream an' marshmallows an' I'll give ye th' straight o' it; all I ask is ye keep an open mind."

"An open mind?" enquired Angelica, as the pubmaster, with a sympathetic smile, mutely plunked steaming mugs of hot chocolate before her and Thunder, prior to poking up the fire and disappearing down a trap door, heading for the basement pantry.

"Yes indeed," replied Shamus, "An open mind. Nothin' worse 'n a closed mind; no room fer improvement."

"It's true," agreed Thunder. "I've only been in this world a short time but I've learned that much anyhow. By the way, what *is* a beefsteak and kidney pie?—it sounds delicious."

"What made you say that, Thunder?" asked Angelica.

"Well, that nice little old lady who gave us the plum duff brûlé this morning was wondering if we'd like one and I thought 'Yummy!' at her, 'How 'bout two?' and she just told her husband to fetch us a couple from the pantry in the basement."

"I was wondering why he disappeared down into the floor like that," mused Angelica. "Hey! You talked to her too! That's amazing!"

"It's very handy," said Thunder. "It saves you having to repeat everything I want people to hear."

"'Tis me gift t' ye," smiled Shamus, scritching Thunder's ears pleasantly. "Yer 'treasure' in advance, as 'twere. Hereafter, all can understand ye; shake a paw."

"Hey!" responded Angelica, surprisingly suspicious and jealous, as she watched the two shake. "Thunder talked to me first! How do you know he wasn't learning to do it all by himself?!"

"A good point," replied Shamus with a chuckle. "An excellent point, but haven't ye noticed his coat now? Look at them delicious little flashes o' rainbow dancin' about all o'er it. They go with th' territory fer a talkin' animal, they do. 'Tis a great thing, not just a beautiful thing; there be precious few about nowadays, I'm sorry t' say. Common in th' old days though, when unicorns an' such abounded."

"It's just the firelight reflecting on his fur," insisted Angelica, still a bit jealous and suspicious. "We won't see it when we go outside."

"Ye wouldn't be from Missouri now, would ye?" laughed the giant. "Related to a big fat guy with a cowboy hat an' lots o' money, be ye, by chance?"

"No!" barked Angelica, getting really steamed in spite of herself, "He's an idiot and so are you!" And with that, the giant rose; pounded the table hard, once, to startle Angelica into alertness; bellowed, "Bla-Blek-Neth-Reth!!"; made an unrepeatable gesture with his hand; and instantly everyone in the pub, then the pub itself, vanished in a puff of smoke, till Angelica and Thunder found themselves standing outside on a beautiful sunny day, staring at a nearby castle—a castle streaming with colourful pennants—a castle ringing with the shouts of a joyous throng cheering on their favourites, to the clash of arms and the pounding hooves of great war horses. A tournament, clearly, was in progress.

"Where are we?!" shouted Angelica up at a beautiful, crowned youth in red-and-gold-emblazoned armour, on a startled, rearing white charger festooned in comparable splendour.

"Camelot!" he shouted amiably down at her, "Me name be Arthur, if ye care! Arthur—king of all the Britons! An' I'm late for me own blessed joust!" And with that, his steed came crashing back to earth and they thundered off in a glorious clatter of flashing, silver hooves.

"Where's Shamus?!" exclaimed Angelica to Thunder. "I believe him now! I believe him now!"

"Too late!" shouted Thunder, "He's nowhere about but others are! Look!"

But before Angelica could turn and see the huge, ugly trolls advancing on them with spears at-the-ready, hungry as they always were for a tasty meal of little girl and pup, the heavens cracked with thunder and the great voice of Shamus boomed out "Reth-Neth-Blek-Bla!!" and, *poof*, they were back at their little table in the pub, looking down at ample portions of beefsteak and kidney pie steaming on platters before them.

"Eat up!!" roared Shamus, shaking with laughter. "Eat up, me little travellers; nothin' like an adventure t' perk up th' appetite, an' nothin' like beefsteak an' kidney pie t' wrestle it t' its knees."

"No problem there," chuckled Thunder, digging into his dinner, "I'm *starving*. How about you, Angelica? Angelica? Aren't you hungry? Why are you just poking at your pie?"

"I was just wondering which part was kidney," replied Angelica, with a shudder. "Is it the big round hard stuff my fork doesn't want to go into? Is that part the kidney?"

Chapter Thirteen

THE CURSE

"*W*hy ain't I shrinkin' yet?" asked Shamus to the air.

"Well," answered Angelica, in the process of scraping her un-eaten kidneys onto Thunder's plate, "I'm afraid I still don't believe you."

"An' why not?" enquired Shamus.

"For one thing, Camelot wasn't in Ireland, it was in England or Wales. And for another, there wouldn't be any trolls that close to the castle, because the Knights of the Round Table would have chased them all away; and for another, you might have just hypnotized us; and for another..."

"Enough," sighed Shamus, with resignation. "Ye be a tough nut t' crack, as they say; probably a Brazilian, in previous incarnation."

"I believe you," offered Thunder, "Isn't that sufficient?"

"Sadly, no," replied Shamus. "'Twas a human put th' curse on me, 'twill take a human t' lift it."

"What human cursed you?" asked Thunder, curiously.

"A wench: a handmaiden o' that great an' treacherous sorceress, Morgan le Fay."

"Isn't Morgan the one who imprisoned Merlin in a crystal cave so long ago?" responded Angelica.

"Th' selfsame one; an' 'twas her equally-treacherous hand-maiden proved me doom. If there be anyone more vindictive than an ambitious beautiful sorceress I've yet t' meet 'em."

"What did you do to make her mad?" continued Thunder.

"Well..." hesitated Shamus, glancing over at Angelica, "Angelica's a wee bit young fer me t' elaborate but suffice t' say 'twas not entire her fault or th' spell wouldn't o' worked; ye see, I was younger then an' a titch rash, but I think I've paid me dues by now, an' then some."

"Could you take us to where Merlin is?" enquired Angelica skeptically. "I'd really like to see him, frozen or not."

"That I cannot do," apologized Shamus sadly. "I've more powers than most but I be no match fer Morgan, an' besides—I don't think Merlin'd take kindly t' bein' gawked at by th' likes o' us. Just cuz he's froze don't mean he can't turn us inta mice 'r somethin'. Personally, I wouldn't care t' risk it."

"Very convenient," snorted Angelica, with even more skepticism. "How about St. Patrick? Ever have any dealings with him?"

"Funny ye should ask," brightened Shamus, "I knew him well in th' old days. Very well indeed, an' I'll tell ye this; like just 'bout ever'body else, he wasn't what he seemed."

"Ye'll not be spinnin' *that* old one, will ye?" chuckled the little fellow from the other table near the fire, in obvious derision. "Hear that, ever'body? He's goin' t' sail that old 'I knew him when' thing past th' wee innocent child." Then he burst into a knee-slapping guffaw, which triggered a generous bout of laughter from the general company.

"Pay them n' mind," advised Shamus tolerantly, "They think they know me well, but, as they say: '*A prophet is not without honour, save in his own land*', an' these dunderheads be no exception t' that sad rule."

"A prophet?!!" roared someone from the bar. "*Ye*—a prophet?!! Haw, haw, haw!! Haw, haw, haw, haw, haw!!"

"I hate t' repeat meself, despite, or perhaps because o', th' fact I've lived s' long, but their derision gives me n' choice," said Shamus, "S' once again, pay them n' mind. Now, where was I?"

"You were telling us about St. Patrick," hinted Thunder helpfully.

"Right," nodded Shamus. "Well, I guess ye've heard there be no snakes in Ireland. Ye have, haven't ye?—'tis common knowledge."

"I'm new here, so I didn't," replied Thunder. "Just about everything is new to me, in fact."

"Well, now ye know th' way o' it," smiled Shamus.

"Not quite," added Thunder, "What's a snake?"

"They be slithery things that scoot about on their bellies cuz they've n' legs. An' a goodly number can kill ye with a poisonous bite."

"Yuk!" responded Thunder, casting his eyes nervously over the floor.

"Some be s' big they can swallow a horse," continued Shamus. "Can ye imagine that?—a *whole* horse. Why, ye'd be n' more than an appetizer t' them—a wee little morsel."

"I think I'd like to go home now," urged Thunder, hopping over into Angelica's lap, "I've had enough adventure for today."

"You don't have to worry about it here, darling," soothed Angelica, "St. Patrick drove all the snakes out of Ireland long ago."

"Is that true?" said Thunder to Shamus. "Tell me it's true."

"Well," replied Shamus, sitting back and packing his pipe, "I fear 'tis not. Fact is, there be more snakes in Ireland than anywhere else on Earth."

"That's silly," scoffed Angelica, "Everybody knows nobody's seen a snake in Ireland since almost forever."

"Precisely," agreed Shamus, lighting his pipe, "An' 'tis why there be s' many o' 'em. Show th' average person a snake an' like as not they'll bash its brains in on th' spot. Why, I'll ne'er...

"Wait a minute," interjected Angelica, "Are you saying there's more snakes in Ireland than anywhere else because nobody's bashed one for hundreds and hundreds of years? That's ridiculous!"

"No," replied Shamus, sadly, "'Tis not ridiculous. 'Tis me fate. Me lies be believed an' me truths be not."

"That's the curse the sorceress put on you, isn't it?" piped up Thunder. "How come?"

"Well," sighed Shamus, glancing over at Angelica again, "I'm afraid I told her a wee bit o' a lie t' get what I wanted from her an' I got caught out after she basically 'succumbed to me blather', as 'twere, an' here I be."

"And the way you're going, that's where you're going to stay," snorted Angelica, "We've been at this for an hour now and I'm further away from believing you than when we started—snakes in Ireland, indeed."

"'Tis true, nonetheless," assured Shamus, with as much dignity as he could raise, considering the tidal wave of laughter that rolled over him from all and sundry, save Angelica, and Thunder—who was still looking nervously about for snakes.

"And I don't appreciate you frightening my puppy like this either," warned Angelica dangerously, "This 'story' of yours better have a happy ending, and soon."

"Well," continued Shamus, with confidence, "we be on th' right track at least. First o' all, there ain't, an' ne'er have been, any huge 'r poisonous snakes in Ireland, s' Thunder can relax now an' enjoy what I've got t' say. Another ale, Paddy, I'm parched from defendin' meself. Thank ye kindly. Now, where was I?"

"Ye were tryin' t' bamboozle this bright young lady," snorted the pubmaster, plunking down a tankard, "An' makin' th' same headway, I'm pleased t' say, ye've e'er made with we who know ye."

"Be that as it may, Paddy, if ye go 'bout yer business I'll continue with mine."

"Please do," encouraged Thunder, feeling safe and confident again, "I'm as interested as I can be."

"So am I," mocked Angelica. "I'm as interested as *I* can be."

"Ye're a tough one, Angelica," nodded Shamus, "but if there's anythin' I enjoy, 'tis a challenge. Fact o' th' matter be, afore he was famous, while Patrick was crammin' fer his saint exams, he decided—ye see, he was always a bit o' a politician—t' whip up one o' th' required miracles fer canonizin' by askin' all th' snakes in Ireland t' gather together an' lay low fer a while, s' word'd get out he banished 'em entire. A pretty good ruse, when ye consider Patrick wasn't even Irish—bein' Welsh an' all."

"Shamus," laughed Angelica delightedly, "you're full of the blarney. That's why you're so big; you need every inch you've got just to keep it from leaking out your ears."

"No he's not," protested Thunder. "He's telling the truth, I can feel it. You've got to believe him Angelica; so we can go home."

"I'd love to," Angelica chuckled, "I really would but I can't. I just *can't*."

Chapter Fourteen

BOILING WITH SNAKES

"*W*ell," warned Shamus, rising dramatically, "I hate t' do it but ye've left me n' choice. Be it on yer own head, that's all I c'n say. Be it on yer own head." And with that, he made an indecipherable sound while executing a strange little wrist flip of his hand, the trap door in the floor that led to the pantry in the basement suddenly leapt open with a *bang!* and right before Angelica's fascinated eyes a snake popped its head up, looked swiftly about, then ducked back down out of sight.

"Good one," laughed Angelica, "That was a good one, but it wasn't near as good as the Camelot thing; I wasn't even scared this time."

"That's what kindness gets a body," sighed Shamus, "Guess I'm goin' t' whistle."

"Go ahead," teased Angelica, "Whistle your brains out."

"So be it," said Shamus, "If it has t' be it has t' be." And with that, he whistled—once.

In a flash, Angelica screamed with terror and leapt up onto the table, with Thunder in her arms; and it was a good thing she did so because, in a moment, more snakes than a computer could count suddenly came pouring out the open trap door in the floor, until the entire pub was virtually boiling with snakes.

"I believe you!!" shrieked Angelica, dancing up and down as the level of snakes rose higher and higher till it lapped at the lip of her tabletop, "I believe yoooou, Shamus!! I believe yooooou!!"

Thunder, of course, nestled in her arms, positively bug-eyed with curiosity, stood up on his hind legs, put his paws on her shoulder, and looked about like a scientist. He could do this because he trusted Shamus totally and Shamus had told him there were no dangerous snakes in Ireland. The first thing he noticed was the depth of snakes had stopped rising at table level. The second thing he noticed was none of the snakes was casting a shadow. And the third thing he noticed was all the snakes were exactly the same size, shape and colour—exactly.

"They're not real!" he shouted into Angelica's ear, to get her attention. "They aren't any more real than the trolls and everything were last time!"

"Really?" panted Angelica, calming down, "He's just doing some more magic stuff again?"

"Right," confirmed Thunder, "If you weren't so scared of snakes you would have remembered the weird thing he did with his hand, and the sound he made."

"That's right!" exclaimed Angelica, laughing. "That's right! And the whistle he did wasn't an ordinary whistle either, was it?!" And with that, she stamped her foot on the table, going, "Shooo!", the snakes poured back down through the trap door ten times faster than it took them to come out, and in about three seconds, they all were gone.

"Nice try, Shamus," said Angelica, with a chuckle, as she, cradling Thunder, jumped off the table and sat down. "You really had me going there for a while; I actually believed you again."

"'Tis no use t' me," responded Shamus sadly, as he resumed his seat.

"Why not?" asked Angelica curiously, "I believed you twice now and you didn't shrink either time. Are you sure there's a curse on you; really sure?"

"Take me word fer it," sighed Shamus unhappily, "There be a curse on me, right enough."

"Then why didn't you shrink when I believed you those two times? Does it take more than two times? Does it take three? Is that the magic number? If it is, all you have to do is scare me one more time and you'll break the curse and shrink down to normal."

"Ah," replied Shamus, "If 'twere only that simple I'd be normal long ago; scarin' folk be easy as pie. Y'see, th' problem be, there ain't just faerie time an' normal time; there be also faerie place an' normal place, an' they tend t' live atop each other, as 'twere. That makes it easy fer me t' go back 'n forth, an' even take special people an' creatures; but ye've got t' believe I be a leprechaun in 'normal' time an' place, not 'faerie' time an' place, an' ye don't—an' it looks like ye won't. 'Tis doomed, I be. Doomed by a curse from an old 'indiscretion' o' me youth. Doomed, it seems, forever." And with that, he rose like a creaky old man and began to walk slowly away, his great shoulders and head slumped to the point of heartbreak—the very picture of sadness and surrender itself.

Chapter Fifteen

HOPE AND RESIGNATION

"Come back!" called Angelica. "Come back! Just because I don't believe you doesn't mean we can't be friends!"

"That's right," added Thunder, "A person can't have too many friends. I've got four already and I'd certainly like you for five."

"Really?" responded Shamus hopefully, turning around and straightening up. "Ye really want t' be me friends?"

"We already are," encouraged Angelica, "If you'll let us."

"Can't think o' a time I've e'er been this happy," grinned Shamus, "'Tis been s' long since I had a real friend I'd forgotten how good it feels."

"Who was he?" asked Angelica curiously, as Shamus resumed his seat.

"Shakespeare," replied Shamus shamelessly. "William Shakespeare."

"Shakespeare?" queried Angelica, with a little quirky smile, "The Bard of Avon? The guy who wrote all those plays?"

"Th' selfsame one," confirmed Shamus. "I'm surprised a kid yer age would know 'bout a fellow from four hundred year ago."

"I've read all his stuff," enthused Angelica, "He's the greatest writer ever."

"Yes, he was," agreed Shamus, leaning back comfortably and tamping down his pipe. "All he needed was a wee bit o' help, an' I was glad t' give it."

"Help?" doubted Angelica with a laugh. "What kind of help?"

"Well, fer one thing, he was goin' nowhere here in Ireland, I'm sad t' say, so I told him t' move t' London, build a theatre, an' put on his own plays, an' when he did his career took off like a shot. He ne'er looked back."

"Are you saying he was Irish?" chuckled Angelica.

"He was indeed," asserted Shamus, "'Tis common knowledge hereabouts."

"How else did you help him?" piped up Thunder. "Did you only tell him to move to England or did you do other stuff?"

"Well," paused Shamus, putting a match to his pipe and giving it a puff, "I also gave him a few gold coins from me pot o' gold, t' get started; an' I helped him a bit with th' faerie stuff in *A Midsummer Night's Dream*, but..."

"I love that one," interrupted Angelica, "It's my favourite, next to *The Tempest*."

"Yes," affirmed Shamus, shaking his head with a touch of sadness, "'Tis a good one all right."

"Why so sad?" enquired Thunder. "Did you and Shakespeare have a disagreement or something?"

"No, no," replied Shamus, "Not a disagreement, but, I'm sorry t' say, we did come eventual t' a partin' o' th' ways."

"Why?" asked Angelica curiously.

"I'm reluctant t' tell ye," hesitated Shamus, "fer fear o' bein' disbelieved."

"No problem," assured Angelica, "I don't believe you anyhow but I don't care anymore; I love your stories now."

"'Twas actual *Th' Tempest* ended our friendship," continued Shamus, slightly wounded by Angelica's remark. "'Twas your favourite play he 'wrote'. Ye see, I didn't help him with it; I penned th' whole blessed thing."

"That's great!" laughed Angelica, clapping her hands in delight. "Christopher Marlowe, Francis Bacon, and now, Shameless Shamus O'Shaughnessy; all claiming to 'be' Shakespeare."

"I'm not claimin' t' *be* anybody," protested Shamus, with great dignity. "All I'm sayin' is I got him started, helped him a bit with one play—only th' faerie stuff—an' then I wrote *Th' Tempest*. He did all th' rest."

"Well," mused Angelica with a chuckle, "*The Tempest* certainly *is* different from the others; I'll give you that."

"'Tis more than that, Angelica," insisted Shamus, "'Tis faerie time an' faerie place like no one else has e'er penned it. No mere artist could write such a thing an' that's a fact an' that's th' end o' it. 'Tis a few seconds ye've been gone back home, an' time ye returned; any longer an' yer parents be liable t' drop dead from th' shock, we've already stretched it t' th' wire. I'll miss ye both an' I wish ye well: no hard feelin's." And with that, he rose, kissed them affectionately, and began a movement with his hand as his throat gave birth to a sound.

"Wait a minute!" hastened Angelica, jumping up, "Wait a minute!" Then she scrunched her eyes up real tight, made fists of her hands, and concentrated as hard as she could; before her eyes popped open, her fists returned to hands, and she looked him right in the eye.

"I believe you, Shamus," she avowed earnestly. "I really and truly believe you are a leprechaun, even though I don't believe you wrote *The Tempest*."

"Nice try," nodded Shamus, "'Tis a heart as big as all outdoors ye've got an' no mistake, but wantin' t'believe ain't believin' an' th' proof towers o'er ye. If anythin', I'm a titch taller than afore we met. Only a titch, but when ye live forever they all add up.

'Tis as high as a house I'll be one day, as high as a house an' there's naught t' be done 'bout it. 'Tis me fate; so be it an' God bless." And with that, he raised his hand to make the sign, and the sound began to rise again in his throat.

Chapter Sixteen

TURNABOUT

"*W*ait!" insisted Thunder, "Wait! What about Angelica's present; does she get one too or is it only me because I believe you?"

"O' course she does," replied Shamus, "I've already given it her; 'tis a surprise."

"Things don't feel right," sighed Angelica sadly. "Something's wrong and I don't know what it is; we can't leave yet."

"I don't see what's left t' be done," pondered Shamus. "Frankly, I'm at me wits end."

"Isn't it possible," suggested Angelica, brightening suddenly and turning to Thunder, "that you and Shamus 'think' he's a leprechaun because he 'used' to be a leprechaun, but he actually 'isn't' one any more? Couldn't that be possible? Besides, I don't see what's so special about being a leprechaun anyhow."

"'What's so special 'bout being a leprechaun?!'" gasped Shamus in astonishment. "What's so *special* 'bout it?! Why, we can pop up here, there an' ever'where, whene'er we want; we've mostly all got a pot o' gold 'r two; we..."

"But look," interrupted Angelica, "What's so hot about that? You've got all of that and more already: you're a whiz at sorcery; you don't have to worry about anybody grabbing you and demanding all the gold you've collected over the years, because nobody believes you have any; you're not *all* that huge, I mean, there's lots of people your height and even higher, basketball players and such, and besides, people are getting taller and taller all the time, even most of the teens *I* know have outstripped their parents, height-wise. I just don't see what the big deal is."

"How'd ye like t' ne'er be believed an' ne'er stop growin'?" growled Shamus, sitting on the floor and poking up the fire. "'Tis no bed o' roses."

"Has it ever occurred to you," continued Angelica, hands on her hips, looking down at him, "if you stopped claiming right-off you're a leprechaun, people *would* start believing you? I mean, let's face it, first impressions are important and if you open with 'I be a leprechaun' all the time you haven't a chance of being believed by anyone anywhere, you're so big it's just too ridiculous to accept."

"True," agreed Shamus, shaking his head. "That could very well be true; 'tis a wonder I ne'er thought o' it. Too close t' me own problem I've been, an' that's th' long an' th' short o' it. I don't know how t' thank ye, I really don't."

"A hug would be nice," advised Thunder, "I've noticed Angelica's particularly fond of them."

"A hug?" grinned Shamus, "I've forgotten what such a thing be." And with that, he spread his giant arms wide and enfolded them gently about Angelica, who melted into his embrace, like chocolate on a stove.

"You're a fine and loving something-or-other, whatever you are," sighed Angelica, contentedly stroking his shiny bald head. "And I tell you this; being hugged by a big bear like you must *surely* feel better than *not* being hugged by a little bitty nervous and suspicious thing, like a leprechaun all spooked about someone after his gold."

And then it struck her. The answer to Shamus' problem.

"Gotcha!" she exclaimed, suddenly wrapping her arms tightly around his neck. "Gotcha! Now you've got to give me your gold!"

"Aaaaaaagh," moaned Shamus, "Aaaaagh, me *poor* heart's goin' t' break. Treachery! Such treachery from one I s' loved an' trusted I cannot bear! Let me go, lass, let me go s' I can die, I've n' use fer life now: me gold gone, n' friends, n' hope; please girl, let me go s' I can die!"

"Nice try," chuckled Angelica, squeezing even tighter, "However, as you and I both know, a leprechaun will do *anything* to trick whoever's caught them into letting go, so they can vanish and keep their gold, but I'm wise to all that, I've read too many books to be fooled by the likes of you; now, give me your gold and be quick about it!" And with that, she squeezed him even tighter.

"I can't believe you're doing this," cried Thunder, shocked and horrified. "How can you be so mean to Shamus; he's our *friend?!*"

"Friend, schmend," mocked Angelica with a wicked laugh, "Gold is gold and he's got it and I want it and now it's mine."

"I don't want to be your dog any more," sniffed Thunder sadly, ashamed of Angelica for the first and last time in his life. "I never thought I'd say this but I don't want to love you any more." And with that, he turned and padded slowly towards the door, every bit the picture of misery itself; as sad a sight as anyone could wish to see: sadder even than Shamus had looked when he'd tried to leave a while ago, used as he was to loneliness.

"Your gold!" shouted Angelica, giving Shamus' neck a forceful twist, "Give up your gold and give it up now!"

"I will," moaned Shamus, "I will, I've n' choice; 'tis th' fate o' a leprechaun t' forfeit his gold if he be caught an' we're bound by it like iron itself."

"Where is it?!" demanded Angelica, still holding on tight, "Make the sign and the sound and summon it forth!" and Shamus, broken in spirit, wearily made the sign and the sound—but nothing appeared. No gold. No trace of gold—not so much as a single doubloon.

"'Tis impossible!" marveled Shamus. "'Tis impossible; I did what I must an' me gold's still in Faerie, still at me rainbow's end! How can it be?! How can it *be?!*"

"That's easy," said Angelica with a laugh, releasing her hold on his neck and giving him a big smacking kiss on the cheek, "You're not a leprechaun. Never were. Leprechauns *can't* grow tall. And there's no growing curse on you either; you're just a big guy, that's all. No wonder nobody believed you! Isn't it great?!"

"But... but, if I be not a leprechaun," stammered Shamus, bewildered, rising to his feet with Angelica in his arms, "what be I?"

"You're a sorcerer, silly," continued Angelica in delight, "A kind one, like Merlin; and one day, now that you know who you are, if you work at it, you'll be a great one, just like him. One so great, you'll be able to release him from his spell. And *then* think how much good the two of you can do in the world. Think of it! Just *think* of it!"

"A sorcerer," mused Shamus aloud, getting used to the idea and finding the concept delightful. "A sorcerer; who'd o' thought?"

"Me, for one," chuckled Angelica, "Now, lower away; I've got to scoot after Thunder before he gets lost, and bring him back."

And that, gentle reader, is exactly what she did: she raced for the door, which swung open to her like magic (Shamus' secret gift); swept Thunder up in her arms, as soon as she spotted him sitting forlornly all by himself by a rock; and marched back inside sniffing and snurfing her relieved little pup, who was able to read her thoughts once again, as soon as his wounded heart calmed.

Chapter Seventeen

A FEW SECONDS

"*N*o time fer good-byes," cautioned Shamus, as the youngsters reentered the pub, "Ye've been gone a few seconds back home an' we've not a moment t' lose. Farewell an' good luck."

And with that, he pulled himself as high as his upstretching arms would take him, hesitated long enough for Thunder and Angelica to see the emerald twinkle in his eye, then brought his huge hands crashing down with an indecipherable utterance, and the little girl and pup disappeared in a flash of purple fire, to the astonishment of all at the pub, able to see Shamus' magic for the very first time.

Chapter Eighteen

CLOSURE

"If you don't mind, Dad," suggested Angelica, feigning an innocence she no longer possessed, "I really think Uncle Shamus' picture should be put back where it belongs. It isn't right to hide him in the back cover; he is, after all, family."

"I... I don't feel very well," stammered her father, putting a hand to his forehead and sitting down at the table, before looking at his wife. "Do we have any aspirin, honey? Honey? Are you all right? You don't look very good."

"No, no dear, I'm all right," she replied, "Everything's OK."

"I think you better sit down too, Mother," cautioned Angelica, "your face has gone white."

"Yes, yes, I think I will, I do feel just a wee bit woozy."

"Thunder and I were planning on playing with Petie and Boris and Winston this afternoon but if you guys are sick we'll stay home and nurse you. Care for some soup?"

"We're OK," assured her parents, looking at e~ ˙ vously, then over at their daughter, "Just ˎ selves."

"OK," said Angelica happily, picking up 1 ing for the door; a door which swooshed open proached, and slid gently closed behind her as she disappeared into the hall.

In a flash both parents raced for the window, flung it open wide and leaned out at a perilous angle, just in time to see Angelica skip down the steps, but they weren't looking at her; they were staring in delight and awe at their beautiful white front door with its big brass leprechaun knocker, swinging silently closed behind her.

BOOK THREE

MERLIN

Chapter One

THE CURTAIN RISES

*T*hunder awoke from a deeply salutary slumber on the morning of his first birthday with the sense something profound was going to happen, but he hadn't a clue the seeds of the adventure about to come crashing in on him were sewn long ago by the subtle mind of the greatest of all sorcerers, the immortal Merlin.

Thunder's lack of knowledge on the subject of Merlin was forgivable: he was, after all, only a yearling; but History cannot wrap itself in so convenient a mantle of innocence, and thus, to some degree, this tale exists to redress a wrong. A wrong done to the sagacity of Merlin and the reputation of the greatest of all sorceresses: for the fact of the matter is, Merlin never 'succumbed', not even for a moment, to the 'ambitions' of his young protégée, the beautiful half-faerie/half-human sister to King Arthur himself, Morgan le Fay. No indeed. Right from the beginning he knew exactly what he was doing; and so, in all of its significant details, did she, after but a brief period under his tutelage.

Chapter Two

MORGAN
(THE EARLY YEARS)

*L*ong before Morgan became Morgan le Fay, she understood, even as a child, she was destined to be a shapechanger and mistress of spells. She understood this because, as an infant, much to the trepidation of her human father and delight of her faerie mother, she had no difficulty, untutored or no, in transmuting folk into frogs and frogs into folk. This made it extremely difficult to find a nanny for her, even in the *very* early days, and by the age of three, word had spread throughout the lands of Faerie and Earth that even a finger wag in her direction was a thoroughly risky venture indeed. This left her, for good or for ill, basically in charge of rearing herself when her parents were off at Court; which they usually were.

It must not be said however, despite her later reputation, that Morgan was precocious and cruel. When not annoyed by foolish humans into leaving them hopping confusedly about in a pond, she preferred making pretty shapes of clouds, and was often seen actively encouraging plant, fish and animal runts to flourish, despite the misfortune of their DNA inheritance (the existence and workings of which she was fully aware by the age of five, a good millennium-and-a-half before its fortuitous rediscovery in the mid-Twentieth Century). Which meant, of course, that, prodigy in biology and chemistry and such though she clearly was, there would be no Nobel for her, no celebrations in her honour by an astonished and grateful humanity, no pride in her as the centuries rolled on down to the future. No, in fact, what happened to Morgan, unfair as it was, lacking a good spin doctor or even the knowledge one was needed, was a pummeling of her reputation that exists to this day. And why?—well, as a twenty-year-old she committed an unpardonable sin: she put Merlin to sleep; and if there's one thing the world never forgives a person for, it's depriving it of a saviour – a leader – one who looks the part—everybody's daddy.

Chapter Three

MORGAN
(THE TEEN YEARS)

As an adolescent, it must be admitted, Morgan was somewhat of a hellion. It wasn't just high spirits which governed her; nor was it the fact she slid so easily between Earth time and place and Faerie time and place, both were the same to her. No, she was a hellion because she was intelligent and gifted beyond imagining: so gifted and so intelligent she was without peer, and thus, a very lonely creature indeed; which explains why, to fill those empty, boring years between carefree childhood and the responsibilities of maturity, she, quite simply, indulged in a period of harmless, but distressing, mischief. Cows gave purple milk, fish netted humans, rain fell up, and pants came down—in church. As her talents ripened, orators passed wind like a rhinoceros, at the pinnacle of triumphantly elevating a throng to awe of their erudition; amorous swains of dubious intent awoke with their privates in a painful and inexplicable knot; and grand old souls nodding by the fire, waiting for soup and peaceful death, suddenly found themselves reluctantly getting younger and younger—facing a repeat of the foolishness and toil of their middle years.

One could go on and on describing her ever more elaborate pranks, and, since they're so delightful, I will; but just for a little longer, because we've much to do and more people to meet before this tale closes with an award-winning, clever twist.

Where was I?—Oh yes—Morgan as an adolescent, amusing herself with pranks.

Parents paddled themselves and ordered each other to bed without supper; nutritiously-packed, school lunch-boxes suddenly turned into huge, teacher-distressing mounds of chocolate; and dogs chasing cats became cats chased by dogs, then back to dogs chasing cats, and so on, over and over and over every few seconds or so, until they all fell down and gibbered in mindless idiocy.

It was, therefore, as you can see, a very good thing that her parents, more or less at their wits end from the constant complaints of beings from both worlds, finally decided to apprentice her, at eighteen, to the great Merlin himself—*if* he would have her.

Chapter Four

TOGETHER AGAIN

*I*f one were to assume Morgan had to be dragged kicking and screaming into Merlin's presence, subdued by a worldly potion slipped into her mead by her father, then enmeshed in a net of spells by her mother, one would, as is so often the case, fall victim to the odds that weigh so heavily against any who speculate, regardless of expertise. By the same token, if one were to assume the aging Merlin would be reluctant to take on a young spitfire as apprentice, error would once again be one's overcoat. And why?—Well, they were made for each other, both figuratively and literally, by a Presence and a Place and a Time which antedates the world itself. Why again?—Because, like all true lovers everywhere, they were soul mates.

Chapter Five

A MEETING OF MINDS

$\mathcal{M}$erlin, being older in worldly time than Morgan, had scant difficulty in recognizing Morgan for whom she was, having suspected they were soul mates, since shortly after her birth, despite the fact he already possessed two hundred and eighty years to her one, at that point in time. Morgan however, being only eighteen in Earthly time, didn't recognize Merlin as her other and immediately set out to seduce him with flattery and beauty, eager as she was to gain all of his skills and more.

Merlin of course, although enchanted, as always, by Morgan's personage in whatever form it took, refrained from telling his 'apprentice' flirtations were superfluous to her destiny; which was to maximize her powers as expeditiously as was pleasant, in order to hurry him into the peace of a quasi-oblivion, for the good of his soul and aging limbs, since he'd recently, after a very long service indeed, assisted in the rise of Camelot to all its glory, then nursed it nobly during its inevitable decline. Thus, he was, quite simply, very much in need of a rest: a rest only she could give him; for only she, as a sorceress and his soul mate, could wed ambition to selflessness, without negative effect.

Chapter Six

MORGAN'S APPRENTICESHIP

*A*lthough it took her a year to awaken to it, the two years Merlin deemed necessary to 'train' Morgan to the full flowering of sorcery were as unnecessary as her flirtations. No exercises were required, no meditations, no pouring over dusty tomes. Merlin saw, from day one, she was capable, at eighteen, of assuming his mantle forthwith, but he refrained from telling her this and teaching her the one spell she couldn't master without his assistance. He did so because he feared she might, in her youthful exuberance, do some small harm to the world, like interfering with the full flowering of Christianity; and because he wanted to enjoy her companionship for a while before entering his great rejuvenating sleep.

Surprisingly, the impatience of her youth didn't wear on him, and the calmness of his age didn't wear on her, so those two years unfolded like a dream; but, like all dreams, no matter how pleasurable, their brief idyll soon came to an end and he found himself, shortly after the 'passing' of Arthur, teaching her that one last enchantment. By this time they were friends: comrades of the highest order; so when she uttered the fateful spell and made the sign that 'imprisoned' him in his famous crystal cave, it wasn't in the spirit of betrayal but in the spirit of compassion. Compassion for one of the grandest souls who ever lived. Compassion for a revered elder in need of a much-deserved rest.

Chapter Seven

LONELINESS

*I*t would be inhuman to expect, despite the charm of their friendship, Morgan wouldn't, for a brief period at least, enjoy the limelight for a while after her 'enchantment' of Merlin: after all, his was a very long and famous shadow to stand in indeed. She soon found herself however, feeling neither fish nor fowl, as Faerie increasingly faded from the world of man, Christianity having raised its sterner and sterner hand, till its presence, then visits from its denizens, became a rarity rather than the norm. Nymphs, the first to go, eventually stopped sporting altogether in the streams of Earth, preferring the less tangible but safer waters of 'not here'—then dragons, griffins, fauns, satyrs, goblins, elves, trolls, nature spirits, and finally, even unicorns, bade a silent farewell, until their very existence was considered but base superstition.

Alone in the world, and, paradoxically, in hiding for her life for having 'betrayed' Merlin—the greatest of all pre-Christian men—Morgan committed a final act of 'pique' before setting sail for Ireland: she befuddled the exact time and location of Camelot in the consciousness of all, and thus, made it the stuff of legend evermore. No sad remnants of its foundation and flourishing

would be found, to tarnish its glory in the mind of man. No broken lance mounts, no pottery shards, no forlorn shoe buckles.
Nothing would remain of Camelot down through the ages but
a memory of its wondrous rise and fall. A memory man would
take to the stars when he shook loose the bonds of gravity and
voyaged out into the galaxy and beyond. A memory we all need.
A memory that said, for a while at least, Glory and Justice existed
side by side on Earth; then faded, as all things must.

Chapter Eight

BRENNA

One hot afternoon, in her two hundredth year of solitude, Morgan, strolling by a stream in a pretty Irish dell, happened upon a tall, raven-haired, milk-white, naked Celtic maid cursing to beat the band. She was doing so because her beautiful hair, thick and long by any standard, had been cleverly entwined in the branches of a rowan tree by a bunch of mischievous crows with nothing else to do, while she napped in one of its forks. Her frustration at being unable to unravel it had led to an escalating anger, which, as is so often the case, had progressed to further entanglement, which in turn had resulted in fury, which tumbled her off the fork and left her dangling helplessly, in an even greater rage.

Now, when a person's in a rage, especially if their clothes are just out of reach, it's neither polite nor wise to laugh at them but Morgan, having not enjoyed such in over a century, was unable to refrain from doing just that.

"Cut me down, ye bitch!!" shrieked Brenna. "Cut me down an' we'll see who laughs th' loudest after I've pummeled ye inta a pile o' sobs!!"

"Gladly," replied Morgan, with an uncharitable chuckle. "I could do with a tussle an' I won't even use me magic, should our little roll-about turn 'gainst me favour." And with that, she made a pass with her hand and uttered the spell of disentanglement, which sent Brenna tumbling to the ground in a fetching flail of frustration and surprise.

In a flash, anger fled from Brenna as fast as her predicament and she flowed erect in a grace that would bring jealousy to the breast of a tiger.

"Your name?" she insisted, indifferent to her nakedness, as only the young can be.

"Morgan," boasted Morgan, "Morgan le Fay: master of Merlin and all of his arts."

"Right," affirmed Brenna, bursting into laughter, "I'm convinced: who wouldn't be?"

"'Tis proof ye're after, be it?" snarled Morgan, offended. "Very well, I'll turn ye into a frog; that way ye can hop up an' down while ye mock the most dangerous woman ever lived." And with that, she made the shape-change sign and uttered the spell, but to her bewilderment, nothing happened.

"How can that be?" she thought, perplexed. "How can that be?"

"Bribbit," mocked Brenna, pretending to be a frog by hopping about on all fours, "Bribbit! Bribbit! Bribbit!"—and then she fell over and rolled about, in an absolute paroxysm of laughter.

"A snake!" shouted Morgan, incensed, and a wee bit uncertain of her powers for the first time in her life. "I'll turn ye into a snake!" And with that, she made the sign and the sound—to no effect once again, other than being forced to view the insulting sight of Brenna wiggling about on her belly, going, "Slither! See?! I'm slitherin'! Ha, ha, ha! Ha, ha, ha, ha, ha!"

"It can't be," moaned Morgan, aloud and in shock, "It can't be. Only a pure soul be immune t' me powers. Only honesty incarnate, an' there's no such human—ne'er has been—ne'er will be. What can it mean?! Have I lost it?! Have I lost it all?!" And with that, for the first time in any of her lives that she could remember, she collapsed on the ground and blubbered like a child who'd lost its only ice-cream nickel.

"Aaaaach," empathized Brenna, running over and rocking her in her arms, "Don't be s' sad. I can't bear t' see heartbreak o'er s' trivial a matter as maidenly delusion. Let's be friends, shall we? Let's pretend ye *be* Morgan, I really don't mind; just as long as we don't lie 'bout it t' anyone. I can't handle lyin', ye know: E'en th' thought o' tellin' one has revolted me soul from birth."

"A lie?" puzzled Morgan, recovering in spite of herself. "Ye can't tell a lie? A human that *ne'er* lies? Is it possible? Can it be?"

"Nothin' difficult 'bout it," replied Brenna. "'Tis easy as pie. Give it a try sometime. It really fills th' lungs with air."

"That's why I can't spell ye!" shouted Morgan, leaping up with joy. "I haven't lost it! Ye really be unique! A truthful human! That's why me spells didn't work! I'm sooooo relieved!"

"I bet ye be," encouraged Brenna kindly, "Let's find us some supper, I'm starved."

"No need," laughed Morgan, "I'll summon a trout from the stream." And with that, she made a sign and a sound, and a beautiful glistening trout leapt from the water, arced towards them in the sunlight, and landed at their feet with a plop—dead (if you'll excuse the platitude) as a mackerel, before it flopped or gasped for air.

"Who be ye?!" exclaimed Brenna, in shock.

"Morgan," replied her companion contentedly. "Morgan le Fay."

Chapter Nine

AMENA THE HONEST

"The trout was superb, as ye cooked it, Brenna," praised Morgan, sucking her fingers. "I realize hunger an' friendship be the best seasonin's in any dish but I must say, beyond that, 'tis as fine a fare as any I've tasted."

"Teach me sorcery," grinned Brenna, motivated by appetites of a different kind, "I've a boyfriend needs smartenin' up an' a thirst fer knowledge in its own right. Can I be taught?"

"Yes," replied Morgan, the germ of an idea gestating in her brain. "Yes, I believe ye could, an' quickly too: ye're boundin' with health, alertness, courage an' will *an'* ye're honest t' the core. I'll teach ye. An' from this day forth ye'll be called Amena. Amena the Honest."

"What about me boyfriend?" asked Amena. "His name be Shamus, th' big bum, an' I just can't abandon him; th' sleazy rat has eaten his way inta me heart."

"Insurance," thought Morgan, "Two for the price of one, 'Twill be less risky when I join Merlin in the cave."

"Are ye listenin'?" enquired Amena, "Will ye take *him* on?"

"I'll have to," declared Morgan, "A divided heart be no use t' me nor anyone else. Does he possess any particular gifts?"

"Well," laughed Amena, "fer one thing, he be full o' th' blarney."

"Excellent," chuckled Morgan, "the opposite t' yourself. Together ye'll make a whole. An unbeatable team—where be he?"

"'Tis him way o'er yonder amblin' this way," replied Amena, pointing an affectionate finger at a dot in the distance. "I can spot th' shifty lout a mile off, usually chattin' up some gullible wench. I apologize in advance fer every lie he's bound t' tell ye."

"No fear," assured Morgan, the germ of her idea now in full flower, "He'll make a grand sorcerer an' even better husband; all we have t' do is teach him a lesson."

Chapter Ten

THUNDER'S BIRTHDAY

*W*hen Thunder flowed off Angelica's empty bed moments after he awoke he did so with the power and grace of a panther, despite the fact he was a canine; but oh what a canine he was. Fleshed out like a boxer in its prime, big as a Great Dane and fast as a whippet, with exquisite flashes of rainbow dancing in subtle, perpetual motion about his ebony coat, he was, clearly, the most magnificent dog that ever lived. Confident, alert, intelligent, and able to speak the thoughts and words of man, he stood equipped like no dog before or since for the great adventure awaiting him at the kitchen table; a table already encircled by Angelica and her parents, preparing his very first birthday treat: a treat which, delicious though it clearly was, would go unnoticed and untasted, because of the dramatic entrance of Shamus.

Chapter Eleven

AN ENTRANCE AND AN EXIT

"*What* are your plans today, darling?" asked Angelica's mother of her. "Are you and Thunder going to celebrate his first birthday with Petie and Boris and Winston? ... Angelica? ... Are you listening? ... Shawn, what's she staring at? ... Shawn?" But Angelica's father couldn't answer either because he too was staring, at a phenomenon he'd only read about. He was staring at the astonishing materialization of a magnificent six-foot-five sorcerer, with a strangely familiar face. Impressed already by the *fact* of Shamus' extraordinary entrance, height and radiance, he was positively in *awe* of the splendour of Shamus' new raiments: raiments which impossibly blended the essence of all four seasons and every part of the day and the night. And if *that* wasn't enough, Shamus' eight-foot staff, an ever-shifting tableau of magnificent snakes with disturbingly-watchful, bejeweled eyes, rendered the poor fellow both wordless and witless.

Turning, perplexed, to see what had affected her family so, Angelica's mother unfortunately did so a second before Thunder's entrance; so when the giant sorcerer flung his arms wide with a huge grin and bellowed, "Give us a hug!!" then stepped forward, she thought the hug was for her and fainted straight away, collapsing in a graceful cloud of peignoired chiffon and aproned housecoat.

"She's got th' knack," nodded Shamus, mistaking her condition, while stepping over the perfumed feminine pile, "T' fall asleep at will be a great blessin',"—then all thought of her vanished as Thunder, airborne, piled into his chest for a giant heartfelt hello. Such a leap, executed on most mortals, would have resulted in an instantaneous opportunity for further incarnation, but Shamus, clearly up to the task, spun a delighted Thunder around and around in circles of mutual joy.

"How ye've grown!" laughed Shamus. "How ye've grown; an' all in one short year! 'Tis wondrous! Merlin will be impressed indeed. Ready t' go, Angelica?"

"Go?" replied Angelica, beaming from ear to ear. "Go where?"

"So like a woman," chuckled Shamus, shaking his head in gentle mockery. "So like a woman; always answerin' a question with a question. 'Tis a fine sorceress ye'll make."

"Sorceress?" enquired Angelica, astonished. "I'm going to be a sorceress?"

"O' course, lassie," continued Shamus, tossing Thunder aside in a graceful, happy arc, "O' course. Ye've all th' prerequisites."

"Prerequisites?" echoed Angelica, delighted and confused.

"'Tis clear enough t' me," confirmed Shamus, hands on his hips: "Ye've a kind an' feisty heart—a must fer sorcery; 'tis in yer nature t' turn fear t' appropriate action 'r repose; yer intelligence be self-evident; an' yer knowledge considerable, fer yer years, thanks t' all th' books ye've gargled. But now, me dear, 'tis time fer action." And with that, he raised his great arms and dazzled the room with the infinite possibility of what was to follow.

"Wait!" shouted Angelica, stepping forward alarmed, "I can't leave them like this!"

"Who?" paused Shamus, lowering his arms curiously.

"Them!" replied Angelica, pointing with one hand at her stupefied father and the other at her collapsed mother. "They'll positively *freak!*"

"An' why be that?" asked Shamus.

"They thought you were a family joke," laughed Angelica indelicately, "Then you showed up with all your sorcery power and stuff and shocked the poop out of them. I mean, look at your clothes for example, and your staff."

"I thought it all looked neat," protested Shamus, checking out his snakes and wardrobe, "Ye wouldn't believe th' respect they get me back in th' pub in Ireland. Speakin' o' which, we be late already." And with that, he spun in a circle round and round, robes flowing and staff crackling with fire and sound, till, *bang!* he and Angelica and Thunder disappeared, in a thunderclap that revived Angelica's mother with a start, at the same time it overloaded Angelica's poor father, who hit the mat in a delicate, curved swoon; spiraling down, as he did, like a maid seizing an A+ in the art at a high-class finishing school.

Chapter Twelve

OLD FRIENDS

"*M*e arrivals be usually dead on," said Shamus with a grin as they suddenly appeared, seated at their table by the fire in his favourite Irish pub, "but ye held me back a second 'r two so it's too late t' stop him now, th' wee runt's 'bout t' warble." And sure enough, the sweet little old fellow who'd done justice and more to *Danny Boy* on their last visit, rose and broke into a consummate rendering of that greatest of all heartbreak melodies—*Mother Machree.* (p.235)

As before, the pub silenced, its denizens frozen in treacle. This freezing however, was slightly different from the freezing they'd experienced at the hands of *Danny Boy*, because this one included an occasional auditory response from the company; a response proclaiming the deepest of heartfelt, tender sorrows.

"Might as well snaggle me a brew," chuckled Shamus, rising and taking a tankard of ale from the unconscious, hand-held tray of a sculptured, sobbing pubmaster.

"That's stealing!" gasped Angelica, shocked.

"An' that's judgment," responded Shamus, taking a quaff. "Me gold's n' good here; he never lets me pay now. 'Tis one o' th' pleasantries accompanyin' respect an' a growin' reputation."

"Well," sniffed Angelica, "How was I supposed to know? I didn't have all the facts."

"Get used t' it," retorted Shamus, in gentle mockery, "'Tis commonly th' way o' it."

"OK," frowned Angelica, irritated by the obvious condescension in his tone, "What I meant was, I didn't have *enough* facts."

"'Tis always th' way," teased Shamus, enjoying their verbal joust and sniffing victory, "'Tis always th' way o' it when one leaps on an old friend, gavel in hand. Care fer th' full outfit?" And with that, Angelica's comfortable overalls were instantly replaced, with a sound and a flick from Shamus, into a judge's full red robes, complete with gavel and a curly white wig draped in the black cloth of a hanging offense.

"Cut it out!" shouted Angelica, banging the gavel soundly on the table with each word, before flinging the cloth, and then the wig, into the fire. "Cut! It! Out!"

"Yer gettin' th' hang o' it," laughed Shamus, "Sure ye don't want th' wig?—'tis no trouble fer me t' conjure up another."

"I'm being stubborn, aren't I?" confessed Angelica, tossing the gavel aside. "And it was so funny too. I mean, didn't I look absolutely silly?" And with that, she burst into laughter and collapsed sobbing on the table. "Ah, ha, ha! Ah, ha, ha, ha, Ha, ha, ha!"

"A sorceress lackin' a sense o' humour be a contradiction in terms," chuckled Shamus. "Ye're one o' us all right. Can't think o' anybody I'd rather laugh at than meself. Sustainin', it be. A great time-passer."

"Why are we here?" spoke up Thunder, looking about contentedly, then eyeballing a steaming steak and kidney pie bubbling on somebody's plate. "Is it time to eat?"

"'Tis indeed," confirmed the sweet little old pubmaster's wife, "'Tis indeed. Look, I've brought ye me specialty." And with that, she plunked two extra-large steak and kidney pies down on the table before them.

"Thank you," responded Angelica weakly, and with a shudder, remembering her fork prodding hopelessly and grossly at some stubborn kidneys last time, "Thank you very much."

"They be both for Thunder," said the little old lady, "for his birthday. But don't worry, your fare be comin'. Do ye like pickled pigs feet? ... brain cheese? ... blood pudding? ... crêpes with strawberries, cream an' just a trickle o' maple syrup?"

"Yes!" exclaimed Angelica, hungry and relieved. "Oh yes!"

"One, several, or all o' th' above?" enquired the goodly woman. "'Tis n' trouble t' mix th' lot t'gether even, if ye prefer."

"Are you kidding?!" replied Angelica, appalled.

"Yes," chuckled her little round tormenter, "Yes I was. 'Tis an Irish tradition when absent friends return. Loved, ye be, by all o' us. Missed—an' no mistake."

And with that, the pubmaster placed a just-right-sized platter of maple-syrup-dribbled crêpes swimming in strawberries and cream before Angelica, with a grin.

"Eat up," encouraged Shamus, "Eat up an' savour; I've much t' tell ye both."

Chapter Thirteen

REFRESHMENT AND SETTLING IN

"'Tis th' facts ye need now," began Shamus. "Th' facts o' who an' why an' when; then 'tis off t' Avalon t' minister Arthur's wound afore th' awakenin' o' Brenna, Morgan, an' th' great one himself: me master an' mentor, Merlin."

"Now, hold on," interrupted Angelica, a mouth-watering combination of berries and cream arrested in a spoon halfway to her mouth, "Who's Brenna and why Morgan and since when did you know Merlin?"

"Me tale wouldn't leap about like a rasp in a shredder if ye'd lay back an' listen with skill," responded Shamus. "'Tis me tale after all—though it clearly includes ye at th' end—our immediate future."

"I wouldn't care to wrestle with *that* knot," chuckled Thunder, taking a connoisseur's snap out of a wedge of his steak and kidney pie.

"Nor I," laughed Angelica. "Run with it, Shamus; we're all ears."

"Well," continued Shamus, settling in, "here's th' way o' it ..." And with that, he began his tale.

Chapter Fourteen

THE FACTS

"'Tis simplicity itself," said Shamus, leaning over and prodding the fire to life with his staff. "When Arthur fell with a mortal wound t' th' side, Merlin spirited him off t' Avalon, then Avalon off t' Faerie, where he lies today, healin' slowly in th' fullness o' time. Then he polished th' sorcery o' Morgan an' she gentled him inta his long rest. *Then* she met me girlfriend Brenna, now called, I'm chagrined t' say, Amena th' Honest, an' trained th' wench, an' me, in th' art as well, afore we uttered th' spell releasin' her t' join her sweetheart in his crystal cave.

Brenna, I beg yer pardon, Amena an' I, were then t' stand guard fer a spell, dwellin' in th' world an' enjoyin' it together till today's reawakenin', but me eye wandered overoft t' other lassies so she twisted me ear till I uttered th' crystal spell, an' she, with a final finger dance an' sound, joined Morgan an' Merlin—leavin' me wanderin' about as she vanished; wanderin' about saddled with th' foolish delusion I be a leprechaun under a spell, th' clever devil. Unwise be it, Thunder, t' annoy th' lady o' one's heart, for 'tis many a labyrinth they'll punish ye with till ye crawl back t' lave their instep—broken, penitent, an' eager t' try again. How I miss her, lad. How I miss her, now I know she's the one."

"Do you mean to tell me," marveled Angelica, "you've been wandering about like an idiot all this time just because you *flirted* with few *wenches?*"

"Yes," replied Shamus. "Cross a woman an' ye be chopped liver: Cross a sorceress an' ye're a clown t' boot. Still, I can't complain. Time passes when a body's obsessed an' I can't say I didn't have fun here an' there—she wasn't entire cruel, an' now I'm cured. Ready fer matrimony, I be, an' no mistake. Done yer treats?—'tis time t' voyage t' Faerie."

"How do we do it?" enquired Thunder. "Do we sail there in a misty, romantic ship?"

"'Tis one way," assured Shamus, "But there be quicker." And with that, he seized them by wrist and paw, uttered a sound beyond sense, and leapt with them into the fire.

Chapter Fifteen

SUSPICIONED

*T*here is no part of the good side of Faerie lacking in beauty; but Avalon, the mystical Isle of Apples, that happy realm dominioned beyond memory by Morgan and her kin, home of the healing arts, was blessed like no other—proof enough in itself, the great sorceress was naught but a force for good. All in Faerie knew this, of course, but few in the world, because when Merlin spirited Avalon to Faerie, its location, and then its very existence, was lost to the certitude of man; a loss which furthered human resentment for the role she'd supposedly played.

"'Tis risky enough t' hang out with a hero," said Shamus, as Angelica and Thunder soaked in the scene, "but hangin' out with Merlin be like cuttin' yer own throat—One way 'r another ye'll pay fer th' privilege o' it. Here, at least, howe'er, Morgan be revered. We can expect tumultuous welcome."

The denizens of Faerie, nonetheless, especially those guarding the helpless body of the Once and Future King, Arthur himself, weren't taking any chances, and they suddenly found themselves encircled by a forest of spears held at pricking distance, in the hands of the impossible—beautiful trolls.

"Make a spell," suggested Thunder, with confidence, "and shoo them away."

"Well, now," whispered Shamus uneasily, "'tis not s' simple in Faerie; all be enchanters here. We be as vulnerable t' th' best as any mortal on Earth."

"But they're so beautiful," marveled Angelica, "How could anything as beautiful as these trolls do us harm?"

"Did ye hear, lads?" spoke up a troll, revealing himself as their leader, "She finds us beautiful." And with that, they raised their spears in unison, plunked them into the ground, and instantly, each burst into a fragrant rose tree, which flowered exquisitely in one colour after another, until their heady bouquet and beauty rendered the travellers giddy—a giddiness progressing to the loveliest of swoons – swoons which dissolved them out from the entrance to Avalon and into the presence of Arthur, resplendent on his royal bier.

Chapter Sixteen

ARTHUR

"*Shoot*," said Angelica, looking down at the regalest of men, grown handsome beyond telling by the fragrance of the apples of Avalon, the slowest but surest healer of all ills to the flesh and the heart, "Shoot. If I only had my Polaroid I could really kick ass on show-and-tell day back home."

"That's healthy," opined Shamus, with a grin, "Nothin' like humour fer levelin' th' moment; 'tis proof, if e'er ye need it, beauty, past a certain point, be frightenin'. Snivellin', I'm told, has th' same effect, but it comes trailin' a fog o' embarrassment."

"I like that," chuckled Thunder, "Could I quote you?"

"Feel free," offered Shamus, "'Tis sure th' person I stole it from won't complain; he's been dust fer centuries. Besides, he owes me one."

"Shakespeare?" enquired Angelica curiously.

"Don't get me started," replied Shamus, "We've a wound t' tend, an' th' moment's solemn."

And with that, he bent forward, sweetly kissing the healing, pink rose of Arthur's wound, birthing a sigh from the youthening king; who smiled in his rest, as an onionskin of pain lifted, like a mask, from his face. An onionskin no one knew was there, so beautiful had he seemed before.

"Me," murmured Angelica softly, motivated by a female heart tortured by longing, "Me. I have to lessen his pain."

And with that, she kissed his wound, which altered noticeably and pleasantly as he sighed and smiled once more, another onionskin of pain lifting and dissolving, like breath on a frosty night.

"Now me," said Thunder stepping forward, the only one there who could still look upon the majesty of Arthur, without unbearable anguish of soul.

Lacking proper lips, Thunder couldn't kiss Arthur's wound but he could do something else; something that raised triple onionskins from the altar of Arthur's pain and multiplied his already impossible beauty accordingly—he blew on it thrice.

"'Tis all we can do," stated Shamus, keeping his back, like Angelica's, to the radiant Arthur, "'Tis time now fer Brenna, Morgan, Merlin, an' th' crystal cave."

"Not yet," insisted Thunder, "I want to look at his face just once more; I'll not be seeing it again for a thousand years and I want to remember the husk of what he will be."

"What's he talking about?" whispered Angelica to Shamus.

"He's caught up in th' seein'," whispered Shamus back, "His destiny's callin' an' he's feelin' th' breath o' its wings. Were I churlish, I'd envy him this moment; 'tis as rare in this world as any other. I've only had it twice meself: Once, when I gazed into th' eyes o' Brenna fer th' first time; an' once just after we three last met, when th' enchantment she laid on me broke, thanks t' ye an' Thunder, an' I 'membered her sweet face again an' th' spell t' take me to her. Cover yer ears, lass, 'tis death t' hear it untrained."

"What about Thunder?" asked Angelica nervously.

"We've naught t' fear," replied Shamus, "He's lost in th' resplendence o' Arthur." And with that, as Angelica covered her ears, he uttered the spell, fingers dancing secretly by his side, and the three vanished, on their way to Earth, and the crystal cave.

Chapter Seventeen

THE CAVE

$\mathcal{T}$he choice of a crystal cave on Earth to harbour Merlin's rejuvenation and peace was by no means because it possessed merely the virtue of seclusion, for some of its crystals were dragon's teeth; teeth from the great, slumbering earth-monster that formed the spine of 'Prospero's Island'—the dragon who'd become his fearsome mount when the great sorcerer fully rejoined the world, to battle Ignorance once again—since his destined work would not be complete until Faerie and Earth wed. Until Science, Religion, and Magic became indefatigable allies in the breast of wholesome humanity. Until his peers were numerous, his solitude over. On a practical level of course, crystals on Earth, in their natural state and abundant, are the subtlest and best-to-be-offered of all the world's healing ministrations because they, like the apples of Avalon in Faerie, rejuvenate slowly, and thus, to a depth and duration of body, mind and soul that mere medicaments, unguents, and glacial waters could ever do. Beauty and refraction were factors as well: beauty for his soul and aesthetic pleasure, and refraction to multiply his image ten thousand fold, should some malignant power discover his seclusion; for being unable to focus forthwith on the actual corporeality of Merlin, few would have the courage to violate the privacy of his sanctuary long enough to instigate any harm, before he summoned a surprise he'd kept even from Morgan.

The effect of all of this, its ambience, made the crystal cave, as one would expect, a very special place indeed; as our travellers discovered, when, to their surprise, they suddenly materialized into a void. A void so dark, all they could see were the flashing rainbows dancing on Thunder's invisible coat. Rainbows that, as they flashed, caused the crystals in the cave to ring with a pleasant delicacy, which gradually increased in timbre until our voyagers felt themselves to be nothing but triumphant, joyous sound. Sound beyond, but akin, to the exultant tolling of Christmas bells throughout a peaceful realm. Saturated by this exciting and harmonious ringing, the very personification of audile celebration, the three stood in silent, egoless awe and basked in a perfect marriage of serenity and bliss—then the crystals began to visually manifest, glowing at first with a delicate blue flame, that was never lost, but added to, by further subtle hues beyond normal human perception—until the cave was flooded with dazzling, euphoric light surpassing the glorious sounds which had given it birth, that gradually quieted, as it grew.

"I wish I had my Serengetis," spoke up Angelica, "First all I could feel was dark, then all I could hear was sound, and now all I can see is light. Is this the crystal cave?"

"It ain't Hoboken," quipped Shamus, with the sarcasm only a friend is permitted.

"I can see the real Merlin," observed Thunder, in a tone beyond awe, "He makes those two gorgeous women beside him look drab."

"Hey, now," growled Shamus, adjusting to the light and gazing in reverence at his beautiful Brenna, "Splendour be one thing but look at th' sweetness o' me beloved's hip, th' grace o' her elbow, th' perfect shell o' her ear."

"You're right," agreed Thunder, diplomatically, "How can perfection outstrip perfection?"

"Precisely," grunted Shamus, mollified.

"I can't see what you guys are seeing," complained Angelica, hand-shading her brows while peering into a field of light, "I can't... ooooooh, I see her. I see Morgan, she's ... ooooooh, I want to be her. I want to *be* her."

"No ye don't," responded Shamus.

"That's right," added Thunder. "If you were, you'd love Merlin and never get to marry Arthur."

"Marry Arthur?" gasped Shamus and Angelica in astonished unison.

"I think so," confirmed Thunder, still staring at Merlin, "That's the impression I got back at Avalon when you smooched his side."

"I *didn't* smooch it!" blurted Angelica, "I didn't even notice he was naked!"

"Sure," mocked Thunder, glancing at her briefly, "And I only eat beefsteak and kidney pie to be polite."

"Methinks I taste a titch o' jealousy in yer first foray down sarcasm's pleasant road, Thunder," warned Shamus, with a chuckle. "Ever'body has t' grow up, ye know; an' if e'er there be a place fer an accelerated course, 'tis here an' in Avalon. Methinks, truly, th' unthinkable has happened: both o' yer loves lie elsewhere. Friendship, I fear, be yer destiny."

"That's silly," scoffed Thunder, "Angelica's my heart."

"Think ye so?" grinned Shamus. "Then tell me, lad; why be a moment with yer eyes off Merlin part o' a diminished reality? Why, in all this splendour, be ever'thin' drab but his face?"

"Really?" puzzled Thunder. "Is that what's happening to me? Is it love, not power, that has me enmeshed?"

"Yes," replied Shamus, "But in a noble breast, th' two be one an' th' same."

Chapter Eighteen

THE AWAKENING

"*W*ho first?" asked Shamus, of Angelica. "Who do I disenchant first?"

"Morgan," answered Angelica promptly.

"And why be that?" he enquired curiously. "Why th' big hurry? Do ye figure she's th' one who's goin' t' teach ye sorcery, as she did Brenna an' I?"

"No," said Angelica, "I'm just being logical. If you do Amena first I'm liable to see something I'm too young to witness, when you two slobber all over each other. And even if you don't, I'd probably collapse from hunger pangs waiting to meet Morgan, once you get befuddled by Amena's navel or something."

"Right," agreed Shamus, "Can't argue with th' probable, much less fact. Morgan it be." And with that, he uttered the spell and made the sign, the crystals about his beloved Brenna melted like icicles at high noon, and she, droplets sheening her lovely face, silently stepped forth into his heart.

"Hey!" protested Angelica, "You cheated!"

"No I didn't," replied Shamus, eyes savoring Brenna's lashes, "Spells be like ever'thin' else; they've a personal will." And with that, he strode forward, swept Brenna into his arms and spun her

142

round and around, their lips locked together, in a timeless world of their own.

"We might as well sit down for a while," asided Angelica to Thunder, with a grin. "Too bad we didn't bring sandwiches."

"What if I gave it a shot?" suggested Thunder. "Think it would work?"

"Go ahead," encouraged Angelica hopefully.

But alas, despite a perfect rendering of the spell's auditory aspect, Thunder's paws were not equipped for the delicate finger dancing required for crystal cave magic and nothing changed, except the thrilling sight of Merlin's eyes suddenly shifting from a distant, alert passivity down to the gaze of Thunder, who sat in surprise at the effect of their curious nowness.

"Stand aside," commanded Angelica, making a treasure of the moment by ending it. "Stand aside for a pro." Then she made the sign and the sound, till, to her surprise, though not Thunder's, the crystals about Morgan vanished in a twinkling and she stepped silently forth, as splendid as an oasis at sunset.

"I thought she was beautiful frozen," murmured Angelica to Thunder, in awe, "but just look at her in motion. Just *look* at her. I wonder what she's going to say."

"Something profound, I imagine," whispered Thunder, "She's the greatest of sorceresses ever."

But it wasn't to be, at least, not on the surface. Because when Morgan noted them, all she did was stretch gracefully, yawn prettily, then peer down over glasses she wasn't wearing, like a librarian or schoolmistress alerted to tomfoolery, at the joyously spinning Shamus and Amena, still locked in a kiss; a kiss that'd progressed beyond public decorum and was frolicking openly about in the privacy of passion.

"Hey!" she suddenly shouted, making Thunder and Angelica jump despite themselves, while pulling Shamus and Amena back to the hearing part of normalcy at least, "When ye finish suckin' each other's glottis, we've got t' thaw the old fart out."

"Think ye so?" responded Merlin, stepping forth, as they all froze in shock and delight. "Think ye so? Goin' in be difficult; comin' out: a breeze—for the likes of me. Anybody got any wine?— the real stuff of course; rarely in me lives has anyone proffered homemade that didn't taste like they'd just pulled the pickles out."

The shock, of course, of so prosaic and accurate a comment, unused as they were to the great sorcerer's mind in motion, for so long, or at all, rendered them speechless as well as catatonic; an effect not lost to Merlin's amusement, considering his thousand-year rigidity had ended but moments before.

Chapter Nineteen

BACK TO THE PUB

$\mathcal{A}$s we know, an entrance of Shamus', even accompanied by Angelica and Thunder, was insufficiently powerful to release the denizens of his favourite pub when frozen in the spell of an Irish tenor executing a classic, but one would have thought the addition of Amena, Morgan, and Merlin should have tipped the balance in favour of motion and recognition; yet, as it turned out, they too, individually and collectively, lacked the power to jolt the sentimentality of the Celt from its heart's wallow.

"Lordy," sighed Shamus, with an affectionate chuckle, smiling at the little old fellow warbling beside his table next to the fire, "he's at it again. Not t' worry, 'twill soon be o'er. Let's seat ourselves." And with that, they occupied comfortable chairs at Shamus' table and amiably awaited the establishment's return to a less intangible sanity.

Chapter Twenty

A CLAP OF THE HANDS

"*H*ow did ye do it, Merlin?" enquired Shamus, between quaffs of ale.

"Do what?" replied Merlin innocently, bookending his remark with comparable quaffs of wine.

"Break the spell, of course," interjected Morgan, spearing an asparagus. "Holdin' out on me, weren't ye?"

"No, dear," responded Merlin, evasively, "Wouldn't think of it. 'Twas pointless t' mention an' it made ye all feel important; a useful cement, purpose be, for friendship an' focus."

"Cough it up," growled Brenna, with an affectionate scowl. "If it's annoyin' me, Morgan's dangerous near t' a boil."

"Very well," acquiesced Merlin, as all leaned forward intently, "'Twas merely a thought; movement an' utterance bein' impossible."

"S' simple?" gasped Shamus, astonished.

"Simple, think ye?" chuckled Merlin. "Try *not* thinkin' a necessary 'membrance, for a thousand year."

"This steak and kidney pie tastes even better than the other three I had before," enthused Thunder, savouring a bite. "Magic is great, but boy, I *love* corporality."

146

"That be the secret," agreed Merlin. "Much as I enjoy magic, I must confess, the smell of an herb garden, or the sight of a pond with cattails an' herons, kicks ass for me every time."

"I can't believe your choice an' abundance of words," reflected Morgan, puzzled. "Ye were ne'er s' crude or loquacious afore."

"'Tis 'cause we be all off t' New York an' Times Square," announced Merlin, "the crossroads of the Twentieth Century. An' if there's one thing Americans be, God bless 'em, 'tis *in—your—face!*" And with that, he clapped his hands once and vanished with the five forever, from the pub, leaving behind a melancholic sweetness in the air that anguished, yet enriched, the breast of all those lucky enough to be there.

Chapter Twenty-One

TIMES SQUARE

"*G*ood *Lord!*" intoned Merlin facetiously, gawking about and up, like a yokel. "Good *Lord!* Where be the trees?! An' what on *Earth* be those great, stinkin' metal abominations spewin' poison out their arses?!—Ye'd think, with wheels, they'd have hastened shameful out of sight long ago. An' where be the soil an' grass an' flowers an' frogs an' such? Where be Mother Nature's carpet? What be this hard stuff?" And with that, he stomped the sidewalk to test its strength and promptly plummeted out of sight with a rapidly-fading and surprised howl, when the concrete opened up under his foot, in a perfect circle, and he dropped twenty-six stories into the bowels of New York.

Thunder and Angelica, concerned, peered over the lip of the hole and down into its depths, then jerked back quickly, just in time to avoid collision with Merlin as he skyrocketed back up and rejoined them effortlessly. "Ye wouldn't believe it," he said, "There be humans down there—sandhogs they call themselves: men who moil in the depths in great gnawin' monsters, chewin' their way t' the country for water. I don't know where they get the guts; I'd be positively claustrophobic in seconds—was, in fact, come t' think of it. Nothin' like air. Even air that stinks like this.

Holy moly—look over there! Some fellow with a knife be threaten-in' an unarmed soul holdin' a sack—'tis dastardly!" And with that, he shook his fisted applewood staff at the scene and turned them both into flowering rosebushes, one white and the other red.

"That's better," he nodded with satisfaction, "A much-needed touch of beauty."

"I think you better turn the white one back into a person," advised Angelica, tugging at his sleeve, "He's probably got a family; I think it was a bag of groceries he was holding."

"He's better off," replied Merlin, reluctant to admit an error, "The fellow's *much* better off."

"Merlin," cautioned Morgan, in a tone of mild reproach, "If he's got a love, she won't thank ye for it."

"Quite right, me dear," conceded Merlin, "But I absolutely *insist* on leavin' the dastard a bush—a wee touch of justice in a place clearly in need of such." And with that, he gestured once casually and the poor white rosebush suddenly found itself turned back into a human clutching a bag of vegetables, looking down in catatonic astonishment at his beautiful and harmless former assailant.

"'Tis amazin' how oft moderns seem t' freeze when I'm about," reflected Merlin aloud. "'Tis clear t' me Science be still bullyin' Magic—even Religion, it seems, has flown."

"Lots of people are religious today," protested Angelica, "It's actually kind of everywhere."

"Say ye so?" enquired Merlin, looking about, "Then, where be the church?—all I see be eateries an' sleazy pawnshops. Still, mayhap ye're right: the beauty of woman be clearly worshipped hereabouts, that be encouragin' at least. It does me heart good t' see them so shameless celebrated in iridescence an' image."

"That's just neon gas in tubes, and cheap photographs," scoffed Angelica, slightly affronted, "All they're doing is advertising strip joints and porn shops. They should be closed down."

"Closed down?" puzzled Merlin, befuddled. "The only sign of sanity in this appallin' place?"

"I fear so," confessed Shamus sheepishly, casting a quick eye upon his Brenna. "They're not temples o' adoration; their sole function be t' arouse lust an' sell a surfeit o' grog."

"Enough!" growled Merlin. "We're out of here. Ye've work t' do in the world, ye an' Brenna, an' 'tis back t' the cave for Morgan an' I till there be clear signs of progress. Wake us in a thousand year."

And with that, he raised his great staff high and the heavens began to whirl.

"No!" shouted Thunder, "I have to go too! I have to!"

"I assumed as much," smiled Merlin affectionately, lowering his staff, "I included ye in the spell."

"Angelica!" anguished Thunder, turning to her, "Oh, *Angelica* ..."

"Go!" she insisted, heart bursting, "Go with him Thunder, it has to be!"

And with that, Merlin raised his great staff again, the heavens began to whirl, and the three vanished to the crystal cave, a spell, and a millennial sleep.

Chapter Twenty-Two

ANGELICA'S BUSH

"Anyone care fer some New York Fries afore we split?" enquired Shamus, to animate his friends. "Angelica? ... Brenna? ... No? ... OK, let's go back t' yer place, Angelica, we spent s' much time in real time this trip they undoubted called th' cops; we've got some talkin' t' do." And with that, he made the sign and the spell and the three materialized in Angelica's kitchen, just as her folks sat down for their first anxious cup of tea after hours of frantic and bootless racing about.

"Don't freak!" calmed Angelica, spreading her arms out wide and patting the air soothingly, "This is Shamus and his fiancée Amena the Honest, and they're sorcerers, and Thunder and I just had a great adventure with them and Morgan le Fay and Merlin and Arthur—whom I'm going to marry in a thousand years."

The Pearsons, shocked as they were so often of late, briefly flirted with telling themselves she'd been curled up asleep in an overlooked nook in the basement during their police-assisted search, but the presence of the dazzling Brenna, and the return of their imposing relative Shamus, made such refuge impossible.

"They're real, aren't they?" responded Angelica's father, with a surprising and pleasing complicity, turning to his wife, "They actually *are* real, honey; and we'll *never* be the same again."

"You're right," agreed Angelica's mother, slapped in the face, as he'd been, by fact. "You're right. It's *all* been real and we'll *never* be the same. ... Where's Thunder?"

And with that, Angelica burst into tears, ran out into the backyard, and threw herself beneath her favourite bush, seeking a solace she knew could never be, but she was wrong. Very wrong. Because, as she let her hand flop helplessly onto the grass, palmup in lonely surrender, the world's teeniest leprechaun popped into it, looking directly at her with earnest, unafraid eyes.

"'Tis not th' world's teeniest leprechaun ye see," he said. "I actually be a *giant*."

BOOK FOUR

A LIGHT IN THE DELL

Chapter One

MEXICO

*W*hen Angelica walked back into the kitchen at the end of her last adventure, her parents, enlightened by experience and flanked by a sorcerer and sorceress, had no difficulty in noticing the little leprechaun grinning at them from Angelica's overall pocket, nor did they fail to see the pot of gold in her right hand: a pot of gold overflowing with glittering doubloons, pieces of eight, Celtic and Roman coinage, nuggets, and other exquisite objects beyond immediate classification, all shining like children of the sun.

"We're rich," said Angelica with a brave smile, "And I've got a new friend. Meet Abel, everybody; he's a genuine, one-hundred-percent leprechaun prince, and he's come to bless our dull lives with a cause."

"A cause?" enquired her father.

"Yes, Shawn," replied Angelica, calling her dad by his given name for the first time ever, "A dell is in danger of 'development'. All the wee folk are in peril. We have to go to Mexico."

Chapter Two

ABEL'S ENTRANCE

As one might expect, Petie and Boris and Winston, having waited at Winston's all morning and most of the afternoon for Angelica and Thunder to show up to celebrate his first birthday, experienced dual emotions when they finally saw them approaching—namely, the release of relief and the knot of resentment. Relief because their tardy friends were safe and sound, and resentment because they'd been put on hold for so long without so much as a call, they'd actually got to the point where they were worried sick.

"No excuse for it," harrumphed Winston to Boris, under his breath. "Why, back in Old Blighty they'd have long since received a taste of the birch or the cane for it—and rightly so."

"True," agreed Boris, who'd suffered even more than Winston in his concerns about their tardiness, what with his well-oiled, hair-trigger imagination having long ago kicked into overdrive, "True. But if this were Russia, God bless it, they'd have hung by the heels in the public square by noon at the latest, awaiting full turnout and a taste of the knout. Not many ever came back for a second dose, I'll tell you that."

"That's nothing," offered Petie, "In Mexico they'd be dragged on a rope by horses, right into a cactus."

"Effective, is it?" asked Winston, with respect.

"Effective?" replied Petie, a touch of the scoff in his tone (always a mistake around Winston), "Effective? Why, it makes the Brits and the Rooskies look like the amateurs they are."

Now, under normal circumstances, whenever the three of them found themselves on risky ground as a result of a heartfelt flag waving (despite the fact not one had ever even been to his 'native' land) witty repartees or even a good-natured tussle was their traditional form of extrication, but this time they were all hot, hungry, frustrated, and relieved (a potent stew indeed), so, without further warning or ado, they suddenly jumped on each other and began an escalating mayhem; one no sane person would dare try to break up because of spittle, claws, flashing canines, and brains more or less completely on hold. Fortunately for the three however, a single growl from Thunder, a very formidable growl indeed considering it was his first adult one, froze them in their tracks long enough for sanity to surface.

"What were you sillies fighting about?" said Angelica, plunking herself down on the grass beside them with a grin, "It's Thunder's birthday, don't forget. We'd have been here sooner to celebrate with you, but we just had the grandest adventure you could imagine, with Shamus... you remember Shamus don't you, my uncle from Ireland—my sorcery uncle? Well, his girlfriend, Brenna—Amena the Honest—is handmaiden to Morgan le Fay, who is the soul mate of the great Merlin himself and... wait a minute! Thunder isn't supposed to be here! He's back in the crystal cave with Merlin and Morgan and he's frozen for another thousand years!"

And with that, Thunder looked at her with eyes full of tender acceptance and courage; eyes that said "see you later and I love you", and he vanished—to the astonishment of Petie, Boris and Winston, who, in their whole lives, had never experienced such a thing. Who had, if the truth be told, not actually believed a jot of what Angelica'd recounted them about sorcery and her adventures. That being the case, given the chance, they would, of course, have immediately embraced denial as the logical method for dealing with the fact of Thunder's disappearance before them, but Abel, grinning from ear to ear, popped up from the secrecy of Angelica's overall pocket, snatched his hat off and waved it about, saying, "'Tis muttonheeds ye be. Muttonheeds, an' no mistake." And with that, he leapt from her pocket and landed on Petie's back, Indian style, seized him by the ears, raked his flanks with imaginary spurs and *"Yeee-hawed!"* the little Chihuahua into a flat-out dodging run all over the yard, in a failed attempt to dislodge his wee tormenter.

"'Tis better than a donkey ye'll be fer me when we get t' Mexico," chuckled Abel to his frantic mount, "Just me size an' speed. Oh, th' fun we'll have."

"Mexico?" gasped Petie, skidding to a halt. "I'm going to Mexico?"

"Lucky blighter," asided Winston to Boris, "The lucky little blighter's going to Mexico."

"Yes," agreed Boris, looking way off and soulful, "But it isn't Russia he's going to. No, it isn't Russia."

"'*Six of one, half-dozen of another*', it's all the same to me if he goes to Mexico or to Russia," retorted Winston.

"And why is that?" enquired Boris, slightly miffed.

"Because neither is England, of course," replied Winston, with a wicked smile. "Neither is that blessed isle."

Chapter Three

THE INVITATION

"*I* should have hugged him," sighed Angelica sadly. "I should have hugged Thunder when I had the chance."

"'Twould have done ye n' good," offered Shamus, suddenly appearing beside her on the grass, with Brenna at his side, "'Twould have done ye n' good, yer arms would o' passed through him like mist. Be thankful he's chosen t' keep in touch from time t' time; I went a thousand year 'thout s' much as a how d'y'do from this cruel maid here by me side."

"Hey now," responded Brenna, with a grin, giving him a friendly dig in the ribs with her elbow, "Ye'd a lesson t' learn unassisted an' it took ye most o' that time t' learn it, bein' male an' all. Angelica, on t'other hand, isn't saddled with any self-indulgent impurities *an'* she's female, praise th' Lord."

"True," agreed Shamus, giving Brenna a hug and a kiss on the cheek. "I can't deny th' facts. 'Tis a wondrous sorceress she'll be, no doubt 'bout it."

"Am I *really* going to Mexico?" piped up Petie.

"Yes indeed," confirmed Abel, hopping off his back. "An' so are Boris an' Winston, if they've a mind; although, in actual fact, they aren't really required on th' expedition."

"Not required?" snorted Winston sarcastically, experiencing a not uncommon emotional blend of relief and resentment. "You mean, I don't have to go thousands of miles away from my just-right home here and fry my butt off in some godforsaken desert somewhere? Geee, that's too baaad."

"Well, personally, I'd *love* to go," mocked Boris, caught up in the same sarcasm as his friend. "Yes indeed, I'm really weary of my nice cool doghouse and big yard. And I'm *so* tired of my sturgeon and caviar and samovar from the czars. Please let me come. Oh, pleeeeze let me come; I'd adore ambling about under the blazing sun in hundred-degree heat, wearing my nice long coat. And just the thought of scorpions and lizards and banditos fills me with bliss."

"It isn't like that!" protested Petie defensively. "That's only in stupid Hollywood movies. Mexico's actually..."

"Ye wouldn't be goin' as dogs," interrupted Brenna, "Only Petie will. Ye an' Winston can go as humans. Shapechangin' spells be me specialty."

"Who? Me? A human? Bumbling about on my hind legs in the dark?" scoffed Boris, offended. "Me? A Russian wolfhound? The regalest of all beasts? Never!"

"Nor I," concurred Winston gruffly. "Canada's the closest I can get to Britain, next to New Zealand or Bermuda, and Canada's where I'll stay."

"Yer missin' a grand adventure," encouraged Shamus, "A *grand* adventure; an' welcome ye'd be. *Very* welcome indeed."

"Thank you," replied Winston, mollified and flattered, "Thank you kindly, but I'd rather remain here and hold down the fort. The truth is, although *he'd* never admit it, Boris and I are too old for travel and adventure. Serenity, peace of mind, and the comforts of home are more to our liking. Care for some tea, it's all piping hot and ready here under the cozy?" And with that, the three dogs, three humans, and the teeny leprechaun sat down to enjoy Winston's specialty: a late-afternoon tea, complete with

"By Appointment to Her Majesty" biscuits and cakes from Marks & Spencer.

Chapter Four

THE DIAPHRAGM

"*W*here will we be staying?" asked Angelica's mother, as they stepped off the train, in the middle of nowhere, a vast, hot desert stretching out to infinity on all sides, "It's so empty here I don't even see a cactus."

"I don't know," responded Petie, staring in awe at the subtle beauty all about, "But how blue the sky is. And oh, just look at the delicate textures of the sand." And with that, as the train chuffed off about its business, he expertly dug a little hole for himself and jumped inside to cool off, leaving just his cute little head with its big eyes and ears exposed. "It feels great! Dig a hole everybody and jump in—it's really great!"

"Well ...," hesitated Angelica, scuffing the sand with a dubious shoe, "I'm sure it is but I was kind of looking forward to a dip in the pool, with room service."

"Amen," agreed her parents in unison, far from certain the accommodations suggested by Petie would be to their liking.

"'*When in Rome…*'" quoted Shamus, screwing himself up to the armpits in the sand in a matter of seconds, "'*When in Rome...*'"

"'Tis a titch hot," encouraged Brenna, effortlessly twisting three adult-size holes in the sand with an utterance and sequential twirls of her finger in the air, before hopping into one herself. "Give it a go."

"It isn't so bad," confirmed Angelica's father, wriggling about contentedly, after jumping into the largest of the two remaining holes. "Quite comfortable, actually. Cool, even. Jump in, Evelyn." And with that, Angelica's mother, succumbing to the situation, removed her sandals and hopped in as well.

"'Tis some shade we'll be needin'," observed Shamus contentedly, after Evelyn had settled in, "afore our brains boil in our heads an' our eyeballs melt down our cheeks. Summon some fer us, Angelica, 'twill be yer first act o' conscious sorcery."

"But I don't know the sign or the sound for it," protested Angelica, "how can I do it?"

"Angelica, dear," offered Brenna, "Th' signs an' th' sounds o' sorcery be like prayer; they merely serve t' position ye t' an openness fer general request. 'Tis then th' filaments o' th' universe spill through an' fill it with what's supposed t' be there; a surprise t' us all, as oft as not. Give it a go."

"OK," replied Angelica, uncertain but willing, sinking to a seated position beside them.

And with that, they were suddenly protected by a very pleasant shade.

"'Tis undignified but serviceable," opined Shamus, looking up at a large, rotating pink diaphragm floating in the air above them. A diaphragm in which little, white, painted ballerinas and poodles pirouetted about, to the sounds of *Beautiful Dreamer*. (p.236)

Chapter Five

McGARNICLE

*W*hen the timeless charm of *Beautiful Dreamer* ended its music box tinkle the diaphragm stopped rotating, the poodles and ballerinas vanished, and they all found themselves looking up at a visage pressing itself into its now golden-rimmed opaqueness; a visage that popped through, revealing a little, tanned, white-whiskered face grinning down at them.

"McGarnicle!" gasped Shamus in delight, "McGarnicle, ye old wart hog!"

"Shamus!!" roared the face, in a surprising baritone, considering its size, "'Tis a small an' shrinkin' world we live in an' that's a fact!"

"Come and join us," offered Angelica politely, "I'll dig you a hole."

"'Tis kindness itself ye be," said McGarnicle, shifting his grin to her, "but I think perhaps 'twould be better if ye all joined me." And with that, the diaphragm settled on them so thoroughly they found themselves seated upon it rather than under it.

"Who are you?" asked Angelica's mother, intrigued and pleased.

"Why, McGarnicle's th' name, young lady, McGarnicle, th' oldest an' wisest leprechaun that e'er there be; father t' that wee grinnin' imp in yer daughter's pocket, an' leader, I'm sorry t' say, o' all that remains o' our brotherhood. But that's fer later, right now, I suggest we retire t' me place o' refreshment." And with that, the diaphragm, bearing the company, rose effortlessly, high above the desert, and shot south at a speed beyond measure.

Chapter Six

HAMMERHEADS

*T*he flight itself, proved a memory of a lifetime for all. Even McGarnicle would never forget it, due to his role as proud host to the travellers.

"Ye'd think," he said, peering down over the edge of the diaphragm at the vistas below, "someone born an' raised in Faerie an' Ireland would find th' sparser beauty o' Mexico a titch austere an' 'twould be so if what ye see beneath an' afore us proffered all there be, howe'er wondrous, but th' fact o' th' matter be there's no more delightful valleys anywhere in th' world as many in this fair land, an' no more fecund sea." And with that, the diaphragm tilted forty-five degrees and plummeted into the ocean, off the coast of Baja.

"Aaaaaaaaagh!" screamed Shawn and Evelyn and Petie. "Aaaaaaaaagh!"

"Shush," cautioned McGarnicle, "Ye'll frighten th' fishies."

"Frighten the fishies?" gasped Angelica, staring in awe at the vast school of hammerheads wheeling gracefully all about them, "Why, they're sharks! And they're *huge!*"

"Indeed they be," agreed McGarnicle, diving onto one of their heads, "Pick ye a mount each ever'one, they'll swim us t' me valley." And with that, he was gone, vanishing into the milling throng and beyond, with an effortless flick of his great mount's tail.

Chapter Seven

THE HOLE

"The diaphragm's melting," noted Angelica, to no one in particular.

"I'm frightened," added her mother nervously.

"No need t' be," soothed Shamus, "Ever'body's doin' a splendid job o' breathin' underwater, considerin' we've no gills t' speak of."

"That's true, Evelyn," encouraged Shawn, "Hop a shark; I'm right behind you."

And with that, each slid onto a mount and caught up with McGarnicle, just as he and his hammerhead vanished into a huge, vertical, aqua-green hole at the ocean's edge, in a cliff the middle of nowhere.

Chapter Eight

THE TUNNEL

*T*unnels, normally, however functional, tend to make a person feel enclosed, claustrophobic even, and as such, are things one is generally grateful to get through, but not McGarnicle's tunnel; for it was wondrously cored into exquisite, self-illuminating green marble by some unknown and ancient means, then polished by tidal fluctuations over millennia to a subtle perfection that soothed the soul beyond measure as one flowed down its ever-receding, harmonious continuity. With nothing to focus on, no protuberance or hollow in its face, no obvious variances of texture and colour, it seemed to banish past and future in the mind, bathing all who travelled it in the healing balm of nowness. A nowness without thought or emotion. A nowness ripe with the rejuvenating power of being—a rare and fortuitous intimacy for any and all who enter either end and come out the other, refreshed, and spared the speaking of it—for no words exist to sully it with simile.

Thus it was that even McGarnicle, experiencing the tunnel, as always, as if for the very first time, burst through its end, surfacing into a little sun-drenched lagoon fringed by succulent palms with a surprised and joyous shout; as did the rest, in delighted sequention.

Breaststroking their way to land, their mounts spiralling gracefully away, they then rolled ashore in a happy tangle of beatitude and contentment.

Chapter Nine

McGARNICLE'S RETREAT

"*W*ell now," said McGarnicle, looking about at his beached, languid friends, "Hungry, thirsty, or no, this be one o' those rare occasions when a libation an' snack hits th' spot nonetheless. 'Tis prawns an' cerveza time fer those old enough t' enjoy 'em, an' lemonade with peanut butter an' jelly sandwiches fer them with less jaded palates; so let's up an' at it, all—succulence awaits." And with that, they rose and ambled down an orchid-draped cathedral of trees into a delightful little sun-dappled village positively swarming with leprechauns of all ages and sizes.

"No doubt 'bout it, McGarnicle," opined Shamus, smacking his lips while peeling another large barbecued prawn, dipping it into lightly-garlicked melted butter, and popping it into his mouth, "No doubt 'bout it, no prawns on Earth be as tasty as these."

"Quite true," agreed McGarnicle, elbows on the table. "An' th' cerveza? What say ye 'bout th' cerveza?"

"Well," replied Shamus, taking a quaff, "I never thought I'd live t' say it but Mexican beer's now me favourite."

"I'm delighted t' hear ye say so," chuckled McGarnicle, slapping the table, as pleased as a host can be. "An' th' accommodations?"

"Beauty an' Comfort incarnate," spoke up Brenna, "How could anything surpass th' delight o' hammocks, a coolin' breeze, an' pleasant vistas? Th' birds an' th' flowers all about as well, I do confess, be balm t' an already contented spirit."

"She's right," enthused Shawn, "I've never known travel to be so refreshing an experience. Usually it just exhausts the wife and I; its pleasure being mostly in the retelling. But not this time. No sir. Not by a long shot."

"Enjoy it while ye can," cautioned McGarnicle, "'Tis but th' start o' an adventure that may prove perilous."

"Perilous?" echoed Angelica's parents, in unison, "Perilous?"

"I fear so," replied McGarnicle, "Th' last entrance o' Faerie inta th' world be at risk. If we fail t' secure it, Faerie an' Earth'll separate forevermore."

"Is that so bad?" asked Petie, "I mean, what will happen?"

"Faerie'll fade entire, 'thout contact with its material world," replied McGarnicle seriously. "An' th' Earth'll then quickly solidify inta a cold, dead place bereft o' change."

"That's dreadful!" gasped Angelica, shocked.

"More dreadful than ye realize," added Brenna, "fer Arthur would then die, as would ye—o' a broken heart."

"That cannot happen," insisted Angelica, rising calmly. "What great evil must we face?"

"Th' evil o' a misplaced light," responded McGarnicle. "Innocent technology in th' form o' an ever-risin', television communication tower; one t' be topped by a single, dazzlin' light."

"Only a light?" laughed Angelica, relieved. "No monsters and stuff?"

"Ye do not understand," explained Shamus, "faerie folk cannot bear an electric light at night. S' much as one, steals th' heavens from them—obliterates th' stars. This tower, blazin' its great blind eye inta th' only remainin' Earthly entrance to an' from both worlds'd spell doom t' us all. 'Twill be yer task t' terminate that tower 'thout makin' it a media event, fer a public focus on our trouble'd create s' many more th' secret o' Elfindale'd be trammeled beyond repair by speculators, th' curious, an' th' misguided."

"Elfindale?" wondered Petie, aloud.

"Aye," replied Brenna, "Home t' all about ye now, an' thousands more."

"So why are you here, McGarnicle?" enquired Angelica. "I mean, if Elfindale is in danger why aren't you there, wherever it is?"

"We be here 'cause this valley's been our home away from home fer so long, it be home too," replied McGarnicle; "Right, Abel?—right. An' besides, only a modern human can down a modern human construct, I'm sorry t' say; 'tis th' way o' it. Ye must do it, Angelica. Ye, an' ye alone."

"Why me?!" gasped Angelica, shocked, "It's too important for me to do by myself! I'll need help!"

"Panic's not much o' a beginnin'," warned Shamus, with a cruel smile, "Think maybe we should get 'nother little girl t' train who's up t' th' task? Someone worthy o' savin' an' marryin' Arthur? I bet I could find one. I bet..."

"Not a chance!" burst out Angelica, with a vigor that surprised even her. "I'll do it and I'll do it alone, if push comes to shove."

"'Twill," said Brenna, with a grin, "It always does. But till then, we be yer allies an' assistants. What do we do fer starters?"

"Well, for one thing," decided Angelica, firmly taking charge, "my parents will have to stay here, and for another..."

"Stay here?" interrupted her father, "Stay here? Why?"

"Because," replied Angelica, "I'm going to have to think and act fast occasionally and I can't help but feel like just a little girl around you most of the time, and besides, I've got the very strong impression both of you want to tarry in this valley and eat prawns and relax; have a holiday rather than an adventure, am I right?"

"Well," admitted her mother, shifting uncomfortably, "It really is *so* beautiful here and we haven't had a *real* holiday together since our honeymoon, and... but look, how can we desert you in your hour of..."

"Nonsense," soothed Angelica, with growing confidence, "I'll function much better if I know you're safe and having fun."

"What about me?" piped up Petie, "I really love it here; do I have to go too? I don't think I'd like Ireland very much."

"Ireland?" puzzled Angelica, "Is that where Elfindale is?"

"O' course," confirmed Shamus, "In County Cork; just a wee hop 'n a jump from me favourite pub."

"I see," reflected Angelica, "Well, I can't say why but I've got to get on the Jay Leno show first; anybody want to come with me?"

"I will," said Abel, "I don't feel quite right lately unless I'm in yer pocket." And with that, he sprang into his special spot and tipped his hat at the rest, with a grin.

"Anybody else?" enquired Angelica.

"Ye already know th' answer t' that," responded Brenna. "McGarnicle belongs here an' in Ireland an' so do Shamus an' I. By th' way, why th' Jay Leno show?"

"I've got to create a media frenzy," replied Angelica, an idea taking shape in her mind; "Then force the world to take down that tower, without knowing why. How long have I got?"

"She's near-built," said McGarnicle, "Th' light comes on to-morra."

"It's impossible," sighed Angelica sadly, with a noticeable slump, "I need at least three days to get famous. It's the only way I can stop the tower forever."

"No problem," offered Shamus, with a grin, "I'll blarney me way inside an' monkey wrench their intent here an' there. Ye'll have yer three days an' another t' boot, or I'm merely a lepre-chaun."

"Merely a leprechaun?" snorted McGarnicle with a good-na-tured grin, as he leapt on Shamus, quick as lightning, before bring-ing him crashing to the ground, by an expert ear twist. "Merely a leprechaun? Why, 'tis a sad soul I'd be if I was e'er t' degenerate t' th' lumberin' level o' a sorcerer. Try a spell on me now, I dare ye, an' ye'll spend th' rest o' yer days 'thout a lug."

"Alright, alright," chuckled Shamus, entertained by the amusement of all about, "There's nothin' wrong with bein' a lep-rechaun, if that be yer fate."

"Not enough!!" roared McGarnicle, twisting harder, "Not enough!! Th' truth, lad!! Out with it!!"

"I give! I give!" squealed Shamus, in genuine pain now, "I admit it! I admit it! Leprechauns be lucky, an' equal t' th' likes o' me!"

"That's better," laughed McGarnicle, releasing his twist on Shamus's ear.

"Big deal," grumbled Shamus, rising and dusting off his rai-ments, "Ever'one with half a brain knows ever'thin's equal t' ever'thin' else."

"Is it really?" asked Angelica's father.

"In th' eyes o' God, yes," replied Shamus. "Besides, think ye anyone here more beautiful than a bluebell? More graceful than a fish? Wiser than th' wind? Why..."

"I've got to leave now," interrupted Angelica politely, "Night is coming on and Abel and I have to be 'found' wandering in the desert. Which way do I go?"

"It doesn't really matter," advised Brenna philosophically, "Lost be lost."

Chapter Ten

THE DESERT RAT

"*G*et a move on, ye great brayin' jackass. Get a move on, I say. No? Stubbornness again, be it, Charlie? Full-moon madness? Perhaps a boot in th' rump'll waken ye t' me will." And with that, Cactus Jack O'Reilly, the poorest, least efficient prospector in the history of panning for gold, attempted to swing his long, aging limbs off the back of an old mountainous jackass; a jackass who, at the moment, possessed the lion's share of their mutual intellect and will, seeing as how it could see and smell better than Jack at night, and what it saw and smelled directly before them was a little girl sleeping in their path. A tinge of arthritis and a touch of bursitis however, kept Jack in the saddle long enough for him to spot the child and fail in his folly; for folly it was to kick Charlie when Charlie knew himself in the right, ever since, as a young jackass, he'd learned the absurdity of excessive respect for man when Jack led him off a cliff once, and had, consequently, long ago learned the effect of a well-placed kick to the vicinity of Jack's privates, should Jack attempt to exercise an excessive stubbornness while in the wrong. Spared an unforgettable blow to his unmentionables, Cactus Jack, however, was not spared the indignity of a sudden buck that rendered him airborne, before

175

tumbling him down a shaled slope, right into a pile of resting rattlesnakes.

Well, as you can imagine, it wasn't long before Jack scrambled back up the slope and made his "how'd ya do's" to a sleepy Angelica and a very, very alert little leprechaun indeed; a leprechaun he snatched out of Angelica's pocket with a roar of triumph, certain as he was, his ship had finally come in.

Chapter Eleven

FOOL'S GOLD

"'Tis yer gold I'll be havin'!" cackled Jack, capering about like a colt, blinded by his joy to the folly of it. "Wimmen! Booze! An' a place by th' fire in an Irish pub!"

"Right," snorted Charlie to himself, watching his aging human make a clown of himself. "Dance about. That's it, dance about on your old limbs and we'll see how sprightly you are come sunrise. I'll be travois-dragging your sorry butt for days while your foolish knees throb like tom-toms is what I'll be doing, and it serves you right."

"Excuse me, sir," said Angelica, standing up, "but I don't think you should be squeezing my leprechaun like that."

"So, 'tis true!!" bellowed Jack, right into Abel's face, "Ye really *be* a leprechaun!!"

"Yes, I *be!*" bellowed Abel back as best he could, "An' no gold will ye get from me from now till th' clap o' doom!"

"Give it up," insisted Cactus Jack with a chuckle, squeezing even harder, "Give up yer gold, I say, an' no tricks; I'm Irish, ye know."

"Irish?" chuckled Abel seductively, "Ye're Irish? Well, so be I; put me down an' let's have us a drink an' a chat 'bout th' Old Sod."

"Gladly," enthused Cactus Jack, placing Abel on a large, flat rock and striding to his saddlebags for a bottle, "Th' pleasure o' conversin' with a fellow Irish citizen, howe'er small, be a treat beyond price fer a homesick old devil such as I. Almost seventy, I be, did ye know that? Sixteen when I left t' seek me fortune an' I've ne'er been back. But now I've caught ye... Aaaah! I put ye down! I let ye go! Me bones'll bleach this desert after all; I'll ne'er get home now. Ne'er get home a'tall. I'm a fool. That's all there be t' it. I'm a dad, blamed, fool."

And with that, Cactus Jack sat down opposite Abel, took a slug of whiskey from the bottle, and placed it before the teeny leprechaun, too saddened by the realization he'd been tricked, to recognize his failure as a host.

"I can't drink with ye from th' bottle, sir," apologized Abel, "'tis twice as tall as me. Could I have a drop 'r two in th' cap?"

"Sartenly," replied Cactus Jack, pouring the wee fellow a three-drop, generous libation, "Sartenly. Next t' goin' back t' Erin a wealthy man, sharin' a bottle with a fellow Irishman be me greatest pleasure. Care t' hear me sing? I know a ballad 'r two."

"*Irish Rose*", sighed Abel nostalgically, "Can ye sing *Me Wild Irish Rose*?"

"Can 'n will," promised Jack. "Lean back, close yer eyes, an' I'll tenor ye inta bliss."

"Done," succumbed Abel, seduced into repose by logic and desire: logic because Angelica had all of his gold, and desire because, like every Celt that ever there was, he was a sucker for an Irish tenor.

"Gotcha!" shouted Jack with delight, slapping his hat down over a surprised, and now furious, Abel. "Gotcha! 'Tis clever, I be, an' no mistake. Few e'er outwitted a released leprechaun.

Few, if any, I've heard. 'Twill make th' gold an' the tellin' o' it all th' sweeter."

"What gold?" interjected Angelica, slapping his wrists and lifting his hat off Abel. "I've got all his gold, had it for days; he's none to give you."

"Oh, lordy, lordy, lordy," sobbed Jack, reaching blindly but expertly for the bottle, "I've no luck. Ne'er had any; ne'er will have any. So be it; 'tis th' fate o' a fool, an' deserved so. I can't complain, an' wouldn't, if it didn't feel s' good." And with that, he took another long pull on his bottle, before bending forward and amiably pouring another three drops into the cap, for Abel, who promptly forgot he was angry and took a sip.

"I don't have any treasure left t' give ye, 'tis true, but there's none better at sniffin' it out than we little folk, as our pots o' gold declare, so I can find ye more than enough fer a comfortable retirement back home, an' I will if ye see t' it Angelica's 'found' in a whirlwind o' media frenzy. *National Enquirer*, an' all that. 'Little girl rescued by grizzled old Irish prospector, minutes from death in th' desert'—get th' drift?"

"Done!" agreed Cactus Jack, slapping the rock with glee, then reaching for his bottle. "Done an' double done. 'Twas lucky indeed I found ye this night. An' that's me name from now on. Lucky Cactus Jack."

"Not as lucky as you might think," snorted Charlie to himself, casting Jack a baleful eye. "I'll teach you to claim a find that wasn't yours, but mine. I'll flatten your nads the moment you're in hoofing range—drink up."

"What are nads?" thought Angelica to Charlie, and then aloud to Cactus Jack.

"Why, they occupy th' nether portions o' a man's reproductive system," replied Jack, "Not a subject a young lady such as yerself should encounter 'r dwell on if ye do. I suggest ye drop th' issue till it arises at a future date, in health class."

"Very well," acquiesced Angelica, "But I suggest you protect yours; Charlie's planning on flattening them."

"How do ye know?" asked Cactus Jack, eyeballing Charlie with trepidation, "He's ne'er done it 'thout cause afore."

"He says he found us, not you, and you're claiming all the credit. Personally, I suspect he's afraid you're going to abandon him after you get some gold, and I think you should tell him that you love him and he's going to Ireland with you too."

"All o' that?" laughed Cactus Jack. "Ye heard an' understood all o' that from a big, dumb jackass?"

"Careful," cautioned Angelica, taking time out from her astonishment at realizing she now spoke the language of an animal other than dog, "Careful. He comprehends everything you say—and possibly, even think."

Chapter Twelve

FAME

*W*hen Cactus Jack appeared a half-day later in La Paz, near the tip of the Baja Peninsula, he had no difficulty in completing his part of the bargain. Picturesque in his own right, laden with saddlebags of Spanish coins Abel'd sniffed out, and accompanied by a little Canadian girl he'd 'found' in the desert, the local, then the national, then the international press went berserk. Being burdened, or blessed, depending on your viewpoint, with a healthy dose of the blarney, he immediately stole the limelight from Angelica by weaving a tall tale, stretching the truth beyond recognition. That being the case, Angelica had no choice, due to the restraints of time, but to proclaim she'd been 'visited' by a spirit in the desert, who'd not only told her all would be well but had given her the gift of willing any door open she chose, locked or otherwise, and she promptly proved it over and over again—on film. Needless to say, this immediately resulted in a tidal wave of representatives from Geraldo, Oprah, Letterman, Leno, and so on, waving contracts and thrusting pens in her face. Accepting Leno and bidding a fond farewell to Jack, who was busily booking passage to Ireland for himself and Charlie, Angelica then flew first-class to L.A. and appeared on Jay's show that very night.

After dutifully opening and closing doors all over the stage just by looking at them, she then, in the midst of tumultuous applause, suddenly and dramatically pulled a large, hollow, filigreed golden ball out of her bag and held it up for inspection. Within moments, a bidding frenzy for it broke out worldwide and before the show was ten minutes old she'd sold the object, by telephone, to the man from Missouri, for ten million dollars; a sum vastly in excess of its carat value but a bargain as a conversation piece *par excellence*, considering it was clearly a one-of-a-kind masterwork of unknown origin virtually thousands of years old. With the eyes of the world on his show, Jay, having bumped his first guest, decided to cancel the other two, as well as all commercial breaks, continuing with Angelica; an idea which proved more than fruitful, causing as it did, an absolute sensation, because when he asked Angelica where she'd found the object, she admitted she hadn't, her leprechaun had. The roar of laughter that went up from the audience unnerved Jay, but only momentarily, because, shortly after it started, Abel popped up from the cozy recesses of her overall pocket, doffed his hat at Jay and the crowd and shouted: "Muckleheeds, ye be! Muckleheeds, th' lot o' ye!"

Well, as you can imagine, hearing a pin drop would have been easy had anyone dropped one but instead, all sat rigid with wonder, and then a disgraceful spectacle ensued; everyone rushed the stage: guests from the wings, crew, and, *en masse*, the audience, each intent on seizing the little leprechaun, to squeeze a fortune from him.

It was at that moment, a moment fraught with peril, Merlin suddenly appeared standing beside Angelica, raised his great applewood staff, muttered a spell, and transformed every member of the stampeding hoard into a tree, sparing only Jay because only Jay, impeccable host that he was, never even thought to pounce on his hapless, wee, unexpected guest.

Chapter Thirteen

BACK TO NORMAL

$\mathcal{W}$ith a hand gesture and utterance, Angelica promptly closed and sealed every entrance and exit of the studio, then patted the guest couch beside her, inviting Merlin to sit.

"You stole my Thunder and now you're stealing my thunder," she said with a laugh. "Meet Merlin, Jay."

"Merlin?" gasped Jay, mouth agape and eyes bulging, "*The* Merlin?"

"The selfsame one," grinned Angelica, "but don't try to shake his mitt, he isn't really here and all those trees aren't really trees, they just think they are." And with that, she made a pass with her hand and everyone turned back into a human, frozen in awe at the sight of Merlin.

"Return t' yer seats," advised Merlin calmly, "An' keep those cameras rollin'; *we'll* show the Networks the meanin' of ... 'ratings'."

Complicity, of course, was a foregone conclusion.

Chapter Fourteen

BYE, FOR NOW

"*W*hy did you choose me instead of Letterman?" enquired Jay, of Merlin, flattered.

"We wanted Arsenio," replied Merlin, with a wink to Angelica, "He gorks with such amiable awe in the presence of triflin' luminaries we were curious t' see if his eyeballs would actually 'scape their sockets in me presence, but alas, he's no longer on the tube, so we settled for ye."

"Oh," responded Jay, hurt, "I thought maybe you liked my show."

"There be worse things on the air," conceded Merlin, "Like all those damned infomercial channels cloggin' the ethers. 'Twas bad enough when they bought time on existin' networks but when they branched out an' started buildin' their own communication towers an' such..."

"I'll take it from here," hinted Angelica nervously, "It's time you hit the road; you're starting to fade."

"I am?" said Merlin, looking down at his increasingly transparent form, "Well, bless me, so I am. Now why be that, I wonder?"

"Perhaps it's because you only returned to stasis a few days ago and your batteries aren't quite up to snuff," suggested Angelica.

"What about Thunder?" puzzled Merlin, "He was under even less than I an' *he* had no difficulty in visitin' ye."

"True," replied Angelica indelicately, "but he's a lot younger than you."

"Hey, now!" protested Merlin, hurt, "Are ye sayin' I'm gettin' old?"

"Oh, no," hastened Angelica diplomatically, "but Thunder didn't do any spells, as mist. It must be very debilitating, to drain even you."

"True," agreed Merlin, mollified, "Yes, 'tis undoubted true; I ne'er did it afore so 'tis doubtless the case. Well, good-bye an' good luck."

And with that, he vanished.

Chapter Fifteen

POKER

I haven't got time to argue with you," warned Angelica, looking right into the eye of the world, "There's fifteen towers in the following countries and the following locations that have to be removed completely in the next twenty-four hours and if they aren't, I'll turn every man, woman and child on the globe into a tree and that's the end of it."

And with that, she rose, clapped her hands once, and vanished to County Cork in Ireland, leaving in her place a scrolled map pinpointing fourteen red-herring towers and the real magilla: a map immediately raced to an emergency meeting of the United Nations, which sprang into action by capitulating on the spot, with no dissenting vote – for the first time in its history.

Chapter Sixteen

A SAD MOMENT

*W*hen Angelica and Abel arrived in Ireland a nanosecond after vanishing from Leno's show, they appeared at a scene of grief. Grief because an uncontrollably-sobbing Shamus was there, on his knees under the stars, keening over the still-smouldering ruins of his favourite pub; despite the presence of Brenna.

"'Twas here in all its glory but days ago," sobbed Shamus. "We all sat at me table an' Merlin an' I quaffed a brew, 'member, Angelica? Thunder ate his beefsteak an' kidney pie; Brenna, asparagus; an' ye yer crêpes – an' now 'tis gone. All gone." And with that, he began his sobbing anew, refreshed by the greater anguish of spoken remembrance.

"Was anyone hurt?" enquired Abel innocently.

"Hurt?!" moaned Shamus. "Hurt?! O' course someone was hurt! *Ever'one* was hurt!"

"He means," said Angelica, tapping a toe with surprising annoyance, "Was anyone *physically* injured?"

"No," offered Brenna, bearing the brunt of a baleful glare from Shamus directed at them all, "No one; an' if this big boob'd release his throttlehold on grief an' stop graspin' at th' joys o' th' past we could all slide o'er t' Elfindale an' ensconce ourselves in a *real* pub."

"Real pub, y'say?" sobbed Shamus, still on his knees, "Real pub? Why, there's naught there, nor e'er has been, but denizens o' Faerie an' leprechauns. Not a blessed human in th' lot."

"Well, there be now, ye big lug. We've a new proprietor— Cactus Jack; as big a blowhard as yerself, by any standard."

"Cactus Jack?!" exclaimed Shamus, brightening, "Cactus Jack O'Reilly?!"

"Yes," confirmed Brenna, patting him on his pate, "Now, get up; if there's anythin' more pitiful than a grown man on his knees snivellin' o'er a pile o' ale-soaked memories I've yet t' see it—nor care t'."

"Right," said Shamus, leaping to his feet and brushing off his dazzling raiments, "'Tis an entrance I'll be givin' th' lad he'll not forget; worthy o' a round 'r two o' freebies, I warrant."

And with that, effecting a collectively-executed finger-dance and spell, Shamus, Brenna, Angelica and Abel vanished to Elfindale.

Chapter Seventeen

ELFINDALE

*I*f Angelica thought McGarnicle's valley in Mexico was splendid and hard to beat she had to admit verdant Elfindale clearly shared the prize, or even seized it by a hair. Describing its rocks and rills and trees and mosses and flowers, all blended by the effortless hand of Nature over millennia, then husbanded delicately by generations of leprechauns, would merely do insult to perfection. Suffice it to say, Elfindale, under the sun or the stars, and in every season, was nothing more than Beauty and Balance incarnate.

Charlie, of course, being a jackass, knew better than to waste his time in the tavern, and was, consequently, contentedly cropping grass outside the front door when the four suddenly appeared, and amiably settled into a nice long chat with Angelica and Brenna while Shamus made his grand entrance into the establishment, sporting Abel perched thirstily on his shoulder.

"Well, well, well," said Cactus Jack, polishing a glass behind the counter, "'Tis wee Abel, an' a fellow leprechaun; what'll it be, Abel?"

"I'm *not* a leprechaun!" protested Shamus, "I'm a sorcerer! Look at me raiments an' staff!"

"Make up yer mind, Shamus," chortled Cactus Jack, with a wink to all about, "Make up yer mind. When last we spoke fifty-odd year ago ye swore up an' down ye were a leprechaun an' now ye think yerself a sorcerer. Will I live long enough t' hear ye claim t' be somethin' else, at full bellow?"

"I'm warnin' ye, Jack," threatened Shamus, raising his staff, "'Tis a hoppy toad ye'll be in seconds if this continues."

"Say ye so?" replied Cactus Jack amiably, "Then who would serve ye drinks at yer very own table there by th' fire? Come, lad, sit down. 'Tis loved an' missed ye've been; 'twas merely th' pleasin' return o' an old friend I tweaked ye with. Full-welcome be ye, an' that's a fact."

"Well," grumbled Shamus, mollified by amiability and flattered he'd a permanent table reserved by the hearth, "Just one ale I'll be havin'. One at a time, that be."

And with that, he sat down with a grin, rubbed his hands into the fire, and looked contentedly about, until his eyes came to rest on a familiar little fellow seated at the other table of honour beside the hearth and across from his own; who rose and, to Abel's delight, burst into a joyful rendition of *My Wild Irish Rose.* (p.237)

"Lord," chuckled Shamus, shaking his head, "Th' more things change, th' more they stay th' same. Well, s' be it. Contented I am; just 'bout ever'thin's back in place." And with that, he looked up just in time, as Cactus Jack plunked a flagon of Mexican ale down before him, to see the retired pubmaster of his former favourite haunt enter, accompanied by his beaming wife bearing a huge platter of tasty pork chops.

Chapter Eighteen

THE TOWER

"*I*s that the tower?" asked Angelica, of Brenna, their backs to the blind side of the pub, "Is it that wee little thing off in the distance?"

"Yes," replied Brenna, "That be it, an' 'tis all it takes. Praise be, she's comin' down."

"Now all I have to do is buy up all the land as far as I can see," thought Angelica, "Buy it all, then keep it pristine forever. It'll be a cinch."

"Yes it will," agreed Thunder, appearing by her side, "Yes it will; and the years will fly too, until you and Shamus and Brenna and Merlin and Morgan and Arthur and Abel and I are united, in the flesh."

"Won't I age by then?" enquired Angelica, pleased as punch to see her beloved Thunder again, but practical, as always.

"Only until you're twenty-five," answered Thunder, "And at the pace you decide."

"Why twenty-five?" pressed Angelica, "Is that the age Arthur will be in a thousand years?"

"Bingo," affirmed Thunder. "You can even go and kiss his side every now and again if you choose, this being the entrance to Faerie and all. But be warned, just one more smooch and your heart will bond you fast to Elfindale, until his return. Elfindale and Faerie. Everywhere else will pale for you. Pale into insignificance."

"What about my parents?" hurried Angelica, as Thunder began to fade.

"They've already decided," said Thunder, embracing invisibility as he continued, "They're going to stay in Mexico and live out their days in McGarnicle's valley; when they aren't visiting you here."

"Will I see you again soon?" called out Angelica, anxiously looking about. "Will I, Thunder?"

"Try to stop me," was his reply, as his voice began to fade, like delicate lace. "Just try to stop me."

BOOK FIVE

RAWHIDE

Chapter One

THE BLOODHOUND

*W*hile the rest of the world stared in befuddled awe at the goings-on on the Jay Leno show, Captain James P. McQuarter of New Scotland Yard (Ret'd) slapped the worn armrests of his favourite stuffed chair and sprang to his feet with a shout, to the delight of his beloved wife Winifred, who'd observed his gentle slide towards lassitude during the first twelve months of his pensioned years with increasing concern.

Her husband had been an excellent detective because he was born with a fortuitous balance of perspicacity and tenacity, and because he was blessed with such a cheerful little round physiognomy and demeanour no one initially took him seriously as a very formidable servant of the law indeed.

If he was handicapped at all, at least in the 'case' before him, it was because, after a lifetime of dealing with 'facts', he'd not only never experienced any magic, he didn't believe it even existed, assuming all its manifestations to be nothing more than the chimera of hallucination, hypnosis, or outright fraud.

Nonetheless, in spite of his failings in that area, or possibly because of them, for the keepers of the secret of Elfindale, fate could not have chosen a more formidable opponent.

To understand the *why* of this, one must go back to his nativity and we will, as soon as he gets off the phone that just rang. A phone plugging him into a four-way conversation with the presidents of the United States and Mexico, and his good friend—the Prime Minister of Great Britain.

Chapter Two

THE BEGINNING

At his birth, suspended by the heels and slapped on the rump, little James P. McQuarter, although a traditionalist at heart, failed to offer up the expected squawk, for he was trying to puzzle out why everyone was upside down except himself. He was trying to make sense of it because it unnerved him to be different, and thus, it was with a considerable degree of satisfaction he soon realized it was actually *he* who was upside down, and that the condition was temporary.

Nestled snugly up to his mother's bosom moments later, as a reward, he thought, for having just solved the puzzle of an inverted universe, he decided then and there problem solving was the way to go, and he never looked back.

Chapter Three

PRESCHOOL

*H*appily for the infant James, his mother was amiable, intelligent and full of a lifetime's laughter, as was his father; a rare and fortuitous combination of parenting skills indeed. Consequently, neither found the habits of their quaint, plump little offspring a cause for concern, so they cheerfully ignored the advice of self-appointed, or actual, experts in child psychology and let him pursue his unique interests from day one. Paramount among these was his extraordinary habit of minutely inspecting, on his hands and knees, every rivulet of water that stained the driveway after his father washed the family car, including all their tributaries, however insignificant. He also, like Einstein, didn't speak until he was three; not because he lacked the ability to do so, but because he was born intuitively aware that repeating information is a sacrifice, since nothing new is learned, whereas listening and watching makes a lie of secrecy, enfeebles dissimulation. Literacy, of course, was an early must for him as well, because it proved a gold mine of the condensed knowledge of others' experience: knowledge which, despite his eight years, had garnered him an understanding of humanity that rivaled many a respected graybeard's.

All of this and more, naturally, was a delight to his youthful parents, who wisely insisted on loving each other as much as they loved their only son; so it came as a shock to them all, when, at age twelve, the law *insisted* they send the lad to school. A British school. A school where fascism reigned supreme.

Chapter Four

SCHOOL DAYS

*A*ssigned as a "fag" to a brutal, aristocratic, "senior", James was ordered by the wretched little tyrant, on the evening of his very first day, to "assume the position", for having failed to properly prepare his master's bedtime toast. James however, not only neglected to assume the required position, due to the injustice of it all (the toast being perfect), he seized the cane from the smirking brute and promptly thrashed the daylights out of the chap, to the delight of his fellow juniors and the secret bemusement of the other seniors and staff; all of whom had long since found the wretched little blueblood he'd bested, a royal pain in the ass. Some censure for his act may have followed nonetheless, what with "tradition being tradition", but in his case it didn't because before the headmaster could make a ruling on the incident James took part in his very first rugby game and proved a natural. The plumpness of his infancy having leisurely replaced itself with muscle, he was, quite simply, built like the proverbial tank: a tank possessing that rare combination of wind, speed and power playing fields demand from the best of the best. Dangerous as a badger in the scrum, he was even more formidable at running the ball and capturing it from others; oddly enough however, but not to himself, he was a team player *par excellence* rather than the high-scoring grandstander he could so easily have been, preferring as he did, to make full use of all the powers at hand. Add a wicked sense of humour to his extraordinary sporting and scholastic skills and the package proved unbeatable. He was, consequently, loved by all (other than the rat he'd bested, who'd 'changed schools' forthwith) and fit quite contentedly into a system that had broken many a boy less sensitive than himself.

All this, of course, was nothing more than fine tuning. An inadvertent training of the lad for the vocation he was born to, but as yet, unaware of. A training which lasted six years, graduating a confident, amiable youth with formidable skills of body and mind. A natural detective.

Chapter Five

OXFORD

*A*lthough Cambridge wrestled Oxford doggedly in a herculean effort to get its mitts on James, he decided to attend his father's old university nonetheless, simply because he knew it would please him. Surprisingly, he eschewed taking part in the savage sport that'd made his reputation (because he intended to have a pleasant long life and his mother had convinced him no athletes in history could lay claim to such after brutalizing their bodies with youthful excess). Disliking the rapier thrusts of repartee endemic in debate he neglected to join any formal ones, despite entreaty; and he avoided chess and bridge like the plague as well, finding their rituals and chance unsuited to his temperament. He also discovered a heartfelt aversion for all the sciences involving animal sacrifice: as well as poetry and drama clubs, wenching, pub-crawling, fashion, and so on and so on; his only loves being reading, punting, gourmet food, cross-country running, and a quiet but amiable observation of his fellow man. An observation that made him a master of subterfuge and body language—all grist for the detective mill.

Chapter Six

THE RESCUE

*G*raduating at twenty-two with a PhD in Modern History, James suddenly found himself standing at the crossroads of life in the full bloom of a premature adulthood, uncertain of which path to take, but fate, as always in the case of extraordinary souls, took a hand; he saved the life of the future Prime Minister of England.

He did this by joining Her Majesty's armed forces at the height of the "Suez Crisis" in '56, just in time to be dumped into a hole in the desert, which was promptly raked by machine gun fire that clipped an important artery in the neck of another young recruit, who'd been assigned the hole but two scant hours before. Spouting a fountain of red up into the bluest of skies, the pale, brave chap seized James by the lapels with surprising strength and ordered him to tell his mother he'd died well. James, of course, merely applied the proper pressure to an obscure spot he'd read about, carried the lad to safety in a hail of bullets, then remained by his side to cheer the fellow and assure him when he surfaced from the anesthetic that he'd not only survived the incident, he now possessed the red badge of courage enabling him to rise as high as the Prime Ministership if he chose, which the dazed but appreciative fellow promptly, and successfully, set about doing, never forgetting the amiable little bulldog who'd saved his life and cheered him through his convalescence.

Chapter Seven

SCOTLAND YARD

$\mathcal{N}$o one should underestimate the importance of having friends in high places because a nod from one in the presence of the appropriate company can open doors with ease: doors which otherwise simply do not exist, or cannot be located, without divine intervention. The wounded youth he'd saved proved to be the son of a very influential man, who recognized James' vocation during a long and pleasant summer when the young fellow was their much-appreciated houseguest at his country estate. During those halcyon months James discovered a lifelong love of fishing and sunsets, that sustained him during his dangerous days of wading about in the sewer of the all-too-prevalent dark side of humanity. A cheerful, optimistic demeanour was the result, regardless of circumstance, and James, consequently, found himself popular amongst the denizens of the underworld *and* his fellow detectives: the former because he was a fearless "straight shooter", who saw the good side in even the most self-despising, or arrogant psychopath; and the latter because the company of a balanced, witty and intelligent optimist is much prized during the inevitable tedious hours of watching and waiting.

Throughout his long and successful career he picked up a tip or two here and there, from both sides of the law, and succeeded in investing sums of hard-earned cash in various stocks and on the nose of more than one surprising winner at the dogs or ponies. As a result, by the time of his retirement, he'd succeeded where most policemen fail; he was both healthy and very well-off indeed—the ideal candidate for an extremely delicate and important task. Namely, the surreptitious tracking of Merlin, Angelica, and Abel.

Chapter Eight

THE DREAM

*W*hile James was busily preparing for his most secret of assignments, Angelica, a week into her new life in Elfindale, had a dream: a dream which caused considerable consternation to all, because she dreamed the countenance of what she mistakenly took to be the world's biggest leprechaun—a leprechaun unknown to anyone—a leprechaun that never existed—a leprechaun whose visage was a dead ringer for James P. McQuarter.

All this was disconcerting enough in its own right but a night later she dreamt the same face, only this time she saw its body; and it was the body of a bloodhound—a bloodhound in motion—a bloodhound, clearly, hot on the trail.

Chapter Nine

QUESTIONS, QUESTIONS, QUESTIONS

*W*ith all the resources of three governments at his disposal James never doubted he could get to the bottom of the mystery as quickly and as discreetly as he chose. Due to a plethora of eager television viewers, he knew who Angelica and her parents were and where they used to live in Canada. He also knew they'd gone to Mexico in the company of a Chihuahua named Petie and an as-yet-unnamed young 'sorcery' couple, had left the train in the desert in the middle of nowhere, and had promptly vanished. All of that was clear enough, even understandable; but how had the little girl shown up a couple of days later in La Paz, some five-hundred-odd miles away, in the company of a well-known local character and his jackass?—who'd seemingly abandoned her, sailed for Ireland, and promptly vanished; a major feat in itself. And where were the child's parents? Where was the young sorcery couple? What had happened to the Chihuahua? How on earth had Angelica unlocked all those doors without touching them, located a priceless gold ball, and vanished before billions, on the Jay Leno show, after auctioning off said ball for a fortune?

How could anyone her age create such a powerful illusion so as to 'manifest' a leprechaun and Merlin; who 'transformed' a crowd into a grove of trees, thereby panicking the U.N. itself into a pre-mature, and humiliating, capitulation? And why, for heaven's sake, did she insist, with all of her extraordinary powers, on the removal of those fifteen television communication-towers world-wide; towers of no real importance to the security of their nations or the Earth? None of it made sense, not really, which deeply, and deliciously, gnawed at James's sense of sanity and proportion.

A lesser man would have flown to Canada, and then to Mexico, and then L.A., to snuffle out clues, but James wasn't that kind of bloodhound. He knew, instinctively and logically, there was no point in wandering about a Canadian suburb, or the backwaters of Mexico, or the concrete of La La Land. No, all that, he saw, would be a waste of time. Understood, in short, he'd only one clue; one trail to follow. Namely, to hunt down Cactus Jack O'Reilly and his jackass Charlie, somewhere in Ireland—af-ter things cooled a bit.

"I always wanted to go to Peru," enthused James to his wife, adjusting a recently-purchased, and oversized, pith helmet, "I think I'll start there."

"Suit yourself," replied Winifred, folding and packing his shorts in a valise, "As long as you're not in a hurry I'm sure that's the way to go."

"Not in a hurry?" repeated James, evasively.

"Well," smiled Winifred, "fifteen countries and fifteen towers, right?"

"Right," confirmed James.

"How many of them also have a missing Irishman and a jack-ass, other than the one in Ireland?"

"None," admitted James sheepishly.

"You knew that, didn't you, dear?" continued Winifred.

"Yes," answered James, "I confess, I did. But I always wanted to go to Peru. Are my fishing rods packed?"

"Is the pope Polish?" queried Winifred, with a smile.

"Last time I looked he was," responded James with a chuckle. "Yessir, the last time I looked he was indeed."

Chapter Ten

A POIGNANT MOMENT

On the very day James flew off to Peru in pursuit of his 'objective', Angelica had a revelation during her only visit to Avalon since moving to Elfindale, after kissing Arthur's wound and seeing him respond with a spasm of pain, recognition and longing: for she saw clearly that the worm in the apple of Camelot stemmed from a tragic error of timing and perception; because Arthur and Guinevere had wed mistaking mutual respect for love, just prior to the arrival of Guinevere's soul mate, Lancelot, and none of the three could find a way out of their dilemma, representing, as they did, to the nation, the personification of law and virtue. Others, in short, could divorce, but Arthur and Guinevere could not. Nor could they create an 'arrangement' because, as Queen, Guinevere was responsible for continuing Arthur's line, kingship at that time, and frequently thereafter, being mistaken for blood. Theirs, therefore, was an impossible situation which led, inevitably, to tragedy, to dissolution, to Arthur's wound and long and painful rejuvenation: a rejuvenation still in progress; one that would not be complete until Angelica and Arthur, as true soul mates, wed a thousand years hence. This revelation proved so painful to her she never again returned to his bier, preferring to wait for him, as Arthur must wait for her, until that glorious day.

Chapter Eleven

A DARKENING TAN

$\mathcal{P}$eru proved everything James hoped it would be: as did Australia, Sri Lanka, Jamaica, and the Virgin Islands. Madagascar, the Maldives, Tonga, Indonesia, and South Africa were delightful as well, groaning as they did, like the previous five, with an extraordinary variety of exotic fish and beautiful sunsets. The locals everywhere, of course, were as friendly as they were unhelpful, so he happily made no progress in solving the mystery, as was his intent. Ireland, after all, he knew, would be his battlefield, his Waterloo (from a British perspective, naturally) and he was in no hurry to get there, despite several calls from the PM: calls increasingly tinged with suspicion, due to the paucity of his reports; and his innocent tendency to send his old buddy daily photos of his fishing successes, complete with a darkening tan.

Chapter Twelve

CONFIDENCE AND CONCERN

*W*hile James was contentedly dragging his delighted heels abroad, gearing up for the 'contest to come', Angelica too was girding her loins for battle. A battle she had to win. A battle, despite her confidence, wiser heads now knew was far from a foregone conclusion, thanks to Shamus' enquiries.

"His buddies at Scotland Yard call him 'Rawhide', Angelica," cautioned Shamus, quaffing an ale by the fire.

"And why is that?" chuckled Angelica, "He looks more like a leprechaun than the Marlboro Man."

"That, I think, be th' point," replied Shamus, "'Tis an affectionate sobriquet. Unfortunately, 'tis also a description o' his nature; he simply doesn't know th' meanin' o' quit. Considers a dead end a step closer t' th' truth. An obstruction, nothin' more'n a treat. Yer work, I fear, be clearly cut out fer ye."

"Ya?" challenged Angelica, making a pass and turning Shamus's ale pot inside out, to the distress of his raiments, "Let him try, I've never reversed a butt before and I wonder what it'll look like; think his pants'll fall down?"

"What if he be an honest man?" posed Shamus, "Yer spells'd have no effect then."

"An honest man?" laughed Angelica, "He's fishing his ass off all over the world at public expense and he knows damned well Ireland's the arena. I'll turn him into a *toad*."

Chapter Thirteen

ZEROING IN

*A*fter stretching out his last four countries to wring every conceivable drop of enjoyment from them, James amiably set sail for Ireland and his appointment with destiny, arriving in Dublin harbour after a fortnight's pleasant sail on a catamaran purchased in Tahiti. Although sixty-five years of age, he debarked fit, contented, and confident as innocence, so certain he was of success.

"I'll wrap this case up right smart then write my memoirs," he thought to himself, "Publish a bestseller, and sail round and round the world with Winifred, if I can just lever her out of London. Life's too short to hole up in only one spot."

Like most speculative forays into the future however, neither his short-term plans nor his longer ones were grounded on precognition, since neither bore anticipated fruit. Why?—Because his chances of prying Winifred away from her beloved cottage and garden unassisted, to wander aimlessly about, were zero right from the start; and because finding Cactus Jack and Charlie proved no easy task, despite the fact James headed straight for the former site of the tower in County Cork and proceeded to spiral out from it with an assured, meticulous precision. Why again? Because the closer he got to Elfindale the more ephemeral

everything became, increasingly-wrapped as he was by a decep-
tive ambience generated by the place itself, abetted by the willing
skills of Angelica.

Chapter Fourteen

PHASES ONE AND TWO

*A*ll sorcery isn't spells; some of it, the best, many would say, involves healing and weather control. Had Angelica fully understood difficulties were mere sauce to Rawhide's doggedness she would have refrained from deluging him with torrential rains during his first three days of tramping out his spiral, and jumped straight to phase two: sun, and more sun, with lovely wind-puffed clouds and glorious sunsets. When she saw however, discomfort wouldn't deter him, she did just that and he immediately fell, as everyone does, in love with Ireland at its best. Balmed by glorious skies, and verdant rolling hills tastefully glorified by myriads of variegated flowers and berries, he began to contemplate the possibility of buying a bit of what he'd tramped.

"Superb," he thought, sitting by a rill and eating a sandwich, "Subtle, too. I wonder if this wee rivulet enters a stream, and I wonder if that stream has any trout? Trolling is great, deep-sea, surf casting; it's all great and I love it so, but for perfection, for absolute perfection of harmony, grace, and skill, fly casting takes the prize, hands down. I'd stay here, I would, if trout were plentiful ... Yessir, I'd summer here with Winifred and winter in London— the best of all possible worlds."

And with that, he rose, stretched luxuriously, and began his spiral anew, never noticing that Abel, nestled in a hollow by his fly-rod and pack, had heard every word.

Chapter Fifteen

SHAMUS GETS THE GO-AHEAD

"Th' sun isn't workin'," reported Abel to Angelica, in the pub, "He isn't lazin' about soakin' up th' scenery. In fact, he's pickin' up th' pace."

"How can that be?" puzzled Angelica, "Who could tramp out a spiral hour after hour in such beauty? How can he possibly concentrate like that? He should be meandering all over the place looking for trout streams—didn't you say he was a fishing nut?"

"That he be," assured Abel, "He's as gone on fishin' as ye be on Arthur."

"Fear," spoke up Shamus, rising majestically, "Let me give him a dose o' good, old-fashioned fear; that'll send th' little quahog scurryin' back from whence."

"Well," hesitated Angelica, "I really don't like scaring people, it isn't a very nice thing to do. What if he's got a bad heart?"

"Bad heart?" scoffed Shamus, "That little badger? He'll outlive us all. He's got t' cease forthwith, I tell ye. 'Tis drastic measures time. At present, he'll be 'pon us in days. Give me a free hand, an' we'll see him n' more."

"Won't he tell ever'one what he saw?" queried Brenna, forking in the last of a slab of blueberry pie, with relishment. "Won't he bring all th' forces o' modern madness down on us?"

"Not a chance," laughed Cactus Jack, from behind the bar, "There ain't a gumshoe livin' 'r dead'll admit bein' on th' receivin' end o' magic."

"And why be that?" replied Brenna.

"Let's put it this way," answered Shamus, "Ever hear o' a pilot *insistin'* he saw a UFO? Course not, 'lessen he wants t' fly a desk fer th' rest o' his career, or get stuffed inta a booby-hatch. Ye see, th' official line be, 'They do not exist.'"

"Don't exist?" giggled Brenna, "Don't exist? Do ye mean t' tell me modern officials *insist* there be no such thing as a UFO? Why, 'tis too funny fer words," and with that, she collapsed on the floor and rolled about, laughing to beat the band.

"Are you sure it'll work?" enquired Angelica, of Shamus, unconvinced, "Do you really think you can scare him off?"

"Course I can," confirmed Shamus confidently, "He'll be poopin' himself minutes after ye give me th' go-ahead."

Chapter Sixteen

PHASE THREE

$\mathcal{R}$awhide wasn't a drinking man, had never taken it beyond the "medicinal" stage or a "wee drop" at Christmas, so he couldn't blame John Barleycorn for what happened to him, nor could he blame swamp gas, because there weren't any swamps about. He'd been sleeping well and eating well and getting all kinds of the right exercise lately and had never in his life been subject to strange dreams, waking visions, or hallucinations. Further, he hadn't met a fellow human since he'd begun his spiral and was thus able to eliminate hypnosis or drugs as a possible source for the dragon that flew at him from out of the sun, picked him up by the scruff, and deposited him back at the starting point of his three-day endeavor, thereby eliminating all the progress he'd made to date, because he was so disoriented he didn't trust the acuity of his curtailed sweep.

Sitting down and pouring himself a capful of 'medicinal' brandy, he knocked it back with an alacrity that would cringe a connoisseur, then calmly watched the dragon fly leisurely back into the sun, and vanish.

"Well now," he said to himself, "Well now, well now, well now, ain't that one for the mystery file."

And with that, he did the only thing he could do; he got up, pulled a revolver out of his pack, and began his spiral again, in the opposite direction, just in case he'd missed something.

Chapter Seventeen

❧

PHASE THREE—IN SPADES

"What's that on his hip?" asked Angelica, flanked by Cactus Jack and Shamus, as all three, flat on their stomachs, peeked over a hillock and down at Rawhide.

"'Tis a .38," replied Cactus Jack calmly, "An' loaded too, I warrant."

"Can a dragon from Faerie take a bullet between the eyes?" wondered Angelica.

"No more than ye nor I, nor any other creature," answered Shamus, "'Tis a pity too; I'd planned on a posse o' satyrs tossin' him about in a blanket, afore some saucy nymphs stripped him naked an' switched his bum all th' way back t' Dublin—what an effective an' droll sight it would've been. Could ye see any man puttin' *that* in a report t' his betters?—not likely."

"Why didn't you *start* with that?" enquired Angelica, giggling in spite of herself.

"How was I t' know th' Brits'd taken t' packin' heat?" protested Shamus defensively, "I thought all they ever carried be a truncheon."

"Well, 'tis too late now," opined Cactus Jack philosophically, "Th' question be: What's next?"

"A spell," insisted Shamus, "I'll scare th' bejesus out o' him with all th' uglies I can muster."

And with that, he rose, held aloft his great snake staff, from whence poured roll after roll of darkening, sulphureous-green cloud, which obliterated the sunny skies as he screamed a sickening tirade of unrepeatable queasiness until, in a flash, startling even himself, his snakes disentangled and slithered at great speed down the slope towards Rawhide; a host of banshees, giant worms, and the living dead of grotesque creatures that never existed springing up behind and following at close quarter.

"Lordy," groaned Angelica, her stomach, already soured by the sound of his spell, threatening to upchuck every morsel she'd ever ingested, at the sight of the unholy host, "Lordy, if that doesn't do it we're in deep you-know-what."

But it didn't, of course, because, as we already know, courage was Rawhide's middle name. Thus, in spite of the fact his weapon was useless and the only conceivable escape was flight, Rawhide stood his ground and more, disappearing, as he did, in a tidal wave of shrieking, writhing, 'living' stink.

Chapter Eighteen

PHASE FOUR

"Th'bravery o' th' man," gasped Cactus Jack, releasing the pinch he'd placed on his nostrils, as the spell, having lived its terrible life, melted away, leaving Rawhide standing alone in the sunny field again, "Oh, th' bravery o' th' man. He'll not be stopped, Angelica. Th' secret o' Elfindale'll be his in a matter o' days."

"Shapechange," said Shamus, shaking his head in awe, "A shapechange be all we have left. "'Twill not be a toad, I'll tell ye that, Angelica. Fer s' noble a heart, only a falcon will do."

"No," insisted Angelica, putting a staying hand on Shamus' rising palm, "If he disappears, all the powers of modern human enquiry *will* descend on us, and everything shall be lost."

And with that, she rose, and walked down the hillock towards Rawhide, who promptly levelled his weapon at her.

Chapter Nineteen

HIGH NOON

"*W*ho *are* you?" demanded Rawhide, steady as a rock, "And *don't* come any closer."

"I'm from the Pleiades," replied Angelica adultly, "We've been here on Earth for centuries, on and off, awaiting the maturation of humanity."

"Nice try," scoffed Rawhide, releasing the safety on his weapon, "Try again."

"I'm just a little girl from Canada," suggested Angelica, "with a great imagination. Even other people get to see what I think, sometimes. Would you like to see what it's like to be a hawk for a bit?"

"I've got a better idea," countered Rawhide, "How would you like to see what it's like to be a dead duck—permanently?" And with that, he cocked his trigger.

"I know where there's a stream with trout in it you can't even imagine," offered Angelica, "trout that fight, and taste, even better than they look."

"So you know my weakness," responded Rawhide calmly, the barrel of his .38 never wavering for an instant from the little girl's midsection, "Unfortunately for you, it's 'real' trout I like fishing for, in 'real' streams; now turn around and cross your wrists behind your back, I'm taking you in."

"You can't," resisted Angelica firmly, "If I leave Elfindale or Faerie, I'll fade away and miss marrying Arthur like I'm supposed to. Even worse, both worlds will probably die if you bring the Feds in on this, what with them being so ham-fisted and all. No, you have to join us now, protect us, there isn't any alternative."

"Move an inch and I'll gun you down," warned Rawhide grimly, "The only thing I believe about you is that you are dangerous and something's got to be done about it. Now, turn around and cross your hands behind your back or I'll do what I never thought possible; I'll shoot a pretty little girl."

"Pretty?" queried Angelica, with a dazzling smile, "Do you really think I'm pretty? I must be growing up. How old do I look to you?"

"Twelve, maybe thirteen," replied Rawhide, in spite of himself.

"Well, I just turned ten yesterday; right, boys?"

"Right," chorused a host of leprechauns, who'd stolen silently up on Rawhide and fanned out in a semi-circle just behind his peripherals.

"'Tis a fact," added Shamus, appearing beside Angelica, and behind Rawhide, who'd spun around to encompass the impossible—a field of leprechauns.

"'Tis true," confirmed Brenna, appearing beside her beloved Shamus, and staring Rawhide right in the eye, since he'd spun back to front again, "She's only ten; I can vouch fer it."

"Speakin' of which," said Merlin, appearing suddenly in their midst, flanked by Morgan and Thunder, "We forgot t' wish ye happy birthday yesterday, Angelica, what with the goin's on an' all. So, happy birthday, darlin'; only nine hundred an' ninety t' go an' ye'll be Queen t' the Once an' Future King."

"This is madness," gasped Rawhide, so shaken he unconsciously holstered his weapon, "Madness. I've got to consult a physician."

"No need," soothed Morgan, "'Tis merely a hop, step, 'n a jump t' Elfindale, an' one of Cactus Jack's healin' toddies."

And with that, she, Merlin, and Thunder (who exchanged a love look with Angelica far better than words) vanished again to the crystal cave.

Chapter Twenty

OUT LIKE A LIGHT

Uncommonly brave that he was, after reaching out and touching Angelica and Shamus and Brenna, Rawhide was still able to hold his ground, so certain he was they were merely illusionists, however extraordinary, but when teeny Abel hopped up in his palm and he actually *felt* the little fellow, he did something he'd never done before—he fainted dead away.

Chapter Twenty-One

CONVINCING WINIFRED

"It's true, darling, I swear to God it's true. You and I now own a thousand acres in County Cork in Ireland, thanks to a pile of leprechaun gold, but we can't tell anybody why because if we do the world will end; Merlin and Morgan le Fay kind of live at one end of it, only their kind of 'frozen' in a crystal cave, with a great talking dog named Thunder; and King Arthur kind of lives there, only in another dimension, in Avalon, and he's going to marry a little sorceress named Angelica who lives there—in a thousand years; and, let's see, oh yes, Elfindale is full of a zillion leprechauns, friendly ones; and there's a great pub there run by that old prospector I went looking for—Cactus Jack O'Reilly, you remember him, and his jackass Charlie is there too; and, oh yes, the whole place is positively riddled with the greatest of trout streams ever."

"I see," said Winifred, looking her happy husband right in the eye. "Well, I believe the trout streams, at least."

"I forgot to tell you about McGarnicle's valley in Mexico, he's the king of the leprechauns, and his son is called Abel—he's the one who convinced me I wasn't nuts and it's all real. So we have to go to Elfindale to live, it's *way* better than London, you've got to believe me."

"I do, do I?" doubted Winifred, glancing out her window at her prize roses and tapping a toe. "Well, I don't and that's that. We'll say no more."

I thought you'd be stubborn about it," chuckled Rawhide enigmatically, handing her a little biscuit tin, "so I brought you proof."

"Proof, did you?" replied Winifred, with a tolerant smile, pleased as she was by her husband's new-found zest for life, but disturbed by his obvious derangement: a derangement she was sure a week or so of 'good-old English tea' and bangers would moderate to acceptable levels. "Proof? Well, let's face it, proof, from time to time, is a very useful thing." And with that, she unscrewed the little tin's littler lid.

"Hi!" grinned Abel, popping out through the top while doffing his hat, "Ye must be th' missus. Abel's th' name. Got any cookies?"

—The End—

MUSIC APPENDIX

A

O CANADA! Calixa Lavallée (1842 - 1891)

O Canada! Our home and native land!
True patriot love in all thy sons command.
With glowing hearts we see thee rise,
The True North strong and free!
From far and wide, O Canada,
we stand on guard for thee.
God keep our land glorious and free!
O Canada, we stand on guard for thee.
O Canada, we stand on guard for thee.

B

RULE, BRITANNIA! James Thomson (1700 - 1748)

When Britain first, at Heaven's command
Arose from out the azure main;
This was the charter of the land,
And guardian angels sung this strain:

"Rule, Britannia! rule the waves:
Britons never will be slaves."

The nations, not so blessed as thee,
Must, in their turns, to tyrants fall;
While thou shalt flourish great and free,
The dread and envy of them all.

"Rule, Britannia! rule the waves:
Britons never will be slaves."

Still more majestic thou shalt rise,
More dreadful, from each foreign stroke;
As the loud blast that tears the skies,
Serves but to root thy native oak.

"Rule, Britannia! rule the waves:
Britons never will be slaves."

Thee haughty tyrants ne'er shall tame:
All their attempts to bend thee down,
Will but arouse thy generous flame;
But work their woe, and thy reknown.

"Rule, Brittannia! rule the waves:
Britons never will be slaves."

The Muses, still with freedom found,
Shall to thy happy coast repair;
Blest Isle! With matchless beauty crown'd,
And manly hearts to guard the fair.

"Rule, Britannia! rule the waves:
Britons never will be slaves!"

C

THE LAST FAREWELL Ron A. Webster/Roger Whittaker

There's a ship lies rig and ready, in the harbour,
Tomorrow for old England, she sails,
Far away from your land of endless sunshine,
To my land full of rainy skies and gales,
And I shall be aboard that ship tomorrow,
Though my heart is full of tears at this farewell,
For you are beautiful: And I have loved you dearly,
More dearly than the spoken word can tell.
For you are beautiful: And I have loved you dearly,
More dearly than the spoken word can tell.
I hear there's a wicked war ablazing,
And the taste of war I know so very well,
Even now, I see the foreign flag a-raise,
Their guns on fire as we sail into hell,
I have no fear of death, it brings no sorrow,
But how bitter will be this last farewell,
For you are beautiful: And I have loved you dearly,
More dearly than the spoken word can tell.
For you are beautiful: And I have loved you dearly,
More dearly than the spoken word can tell.
Though death and darkness gather all about me,
And my ship be torn apart upon the sea,
I shall smell again the fragrance of these islands,
In the heaving waves that brought me once to thee,
And should I return safe home again to England,
I shall watch the English mist roll through the dell,
For you are beautiful: And I have loved you dearly,
More dearly than the spoken word can tell.
For you are beautiful: And I have loved you dearly,
More dearly than the spoken word can tell.

D
DANNY BOY Frederick Edward Weatherly (1848 - 1928)

Oh Danny boy, the pipes, the pipes are calling,
From glen to glen and down the mountain side,
The summer's gone and all the flowers are dying,
'Tis you, 'tis you must go and I must bide.
But come you back when Summer's in the meadow,
Or when the valley's hushed and white with snow,
'Tis I'll be there in sunshine or in shadow,
Oh Danny boy, oh Danny boy, I love you so.
And if you come when all the flowers are dying,
And I am dead, as dead I well may be,
You'll come and find the place where I am lying,
And kneel and say an 'Ave' there for me.
And I shall hear, tho' soft you tread above me,
And all my dreams will warm and sweeter be,
If you will not fail to tell me that you love me,
Then I simply sleep in peace, until you come to me.

E
MOTHER MACHREE Chauncey Olcott (1860 – 1932)

There's a spot in me heart which no col-leen may own,
There's a depth in me soul nev-er sound-ed or known;
There's a place in my mem-'ry, my life, that you fill,
No other can take it, no one ev-er will.
Sure, I love the dear sil-ver that shines in your hair,
And the brow that's all fur-rowed And wrin-kled with
care.
I kiss the dear fin-gers, so toil-worn for me,
Oh, God bless you and keep you, Moth-er Ma-chree!

Ev-'ry sor-row or care in the dear days gone by,
Was made bright by the light of the smile in your eye;
Like a can-dle that's set in a win-dow at night,
Your fond love has cheered me, and guided me right.
Sure, I love the dear sil-ver that shines in your hair,
And the brow that's all fur-rowed And wrin-kled with
care.
I kiss the dear fin-gers, so toil-worn for me,
Oh, God bless you and keep you, Moth-er Ma-chree!

F

BEAUTIFUL DREAMER Stephen Foster (1826 - 1864)

Beautiful dreamer, wake unto me,
Starlight and dewdrops are waiting for thee;
Sounds of the rude world, heard in the day,
Lull'd by the moonlight have all pass'd away!
Beautiful dreamer, queen of my song,
List while I woo thee with soft melody;
Gone are the cares of life's busy throng,
Beautiful Dreamer, awake unto me!
Beautiful dreamer, awake unto me!

Beautiful dreamer, out on the sea
Mermaids are chanting the wild lorelie;
Over the streamlet vapours are borne,
Waiting to fade at the bright coming morn.
Beautiful dreamer, beam on my heart,
E'en as the morn on the streamlet and sea;
Then will all clouds of sorrow depart,
Beautiful dreamer, awake unto me!
Beautiful dreamer, awake unto me!

G

MY WILD IRISH ROSE Chauncey Olcott (1860 – 1932)

If you lis-ten, I'll sing you
a sweet lit-tle song
Of a flow-er that's
now drooped and dead,
Ye-t dear-er to me, yes,
than all of its mates,
Th-o' each holds a-loft its proud head.

'Twas gi-ven to me by a girl that I know;
Since we've met, faith,
I've know no re-pose,
She is dear-er by far
than the world's bright-est star,
And I call her my wild I-rish Rose.

My wild I-rish Rose,
The sweet-est flow'r that grows,
You may search ev-'ry where,
but none can com-pare
With my wild I-rish Rose.
My wild I-rish Rose!
The dear-est flow'r that grows,
And someday for my sake,
she may let me take
the bloom from my wild- I-rish Rose.

They may sing of their roses
which, by oth-er names,
Would smell ju-st as sweet-ly,
they say, But I know that my

Ro-se would nev-er con-sent
To have that sweet name ta-ken a-way.

Her glan-ces are shy
when-e're I pa-ss by
Th-e bow-er where my true love grows,
And my one wish has been
that some day I may win
Th-e heart of my wild I-rish rose.

My wild I-rish Rose,
The sweet-est flow'r that grows,
You may search ev-'ry where,
But none can compare
With my wild I-rish Rose.

My wild I-rish Rose,
The dear-est flow'r that grows,
And some day for my sake,
she may let me take
the bloom from my wild I-rish Rose.

ELFINDALE TOO

to
sahuaros

"Vigilance be the price of Freedom."
(Merlin—whispered in the ear of John Philpot Curran—1790)

PART ONE

CALM BEFORE THE STORM

Chapter One

NEXUS & PLEXUS

"*L*ong afore languageless-man hunkered fearful in a tree on fireless-night, Faerie an' Earth were one. Long afore th' great lizards dominioned th' world, then vanished in a cosmic cataclysm, Faerie an' Earth were one. Long afore th' universe itself began its present great burst inta bein', Faerie an' Earth were one—fer long afore th' afore-o'-all-afores, Faerie an' Earth were one; an' long after th' after-o'-all afters, Faerie an' Earth will be one. How can that be?—Well, 'tis simplicity itself," chuckled McGarnicle, leaning contentedly back against his stump by the fire, outside Cactus Jack's pub in Elfindale, "simplicity itself. 'Tis clear as th' stars 'bove us now. Ye see, 'tis me opinion." And with that, he puffed on his pipe, rose, tapped it on the heel of his boot, and hopped with such speed and skill high above Cactus Jack's roof, disappearing down the chimney, it astonished the young leprechauns seated about the fire, despite the fact they'd seen him do it frequently, for as long as they could remember. The brightest of them surmised he did it to let everyone know he was, and would clearly remain for some time to come, the king of the leprechauns but the truth is, that was merely a corollary; the actual reason he did it was he really enjoyed startling the bejesus out of his old sorcerer pal Shamus O'Shaughnessy, by suddenly leaping, as if in a magical shower of sparks, out of the fire and onto Shamus' permanently-reserved table by the hearth. Enjoyed startling Shamus' six-foot-five-inch, majestically-robed, bald physiognomy into an embarrassing, terror-induced, involuntary levitation and shout; the best of which were usually accompanied by an unexpected gaseous expulsion, commonly referred to as: a fart.

Chapter Two

THE SUBSTITUTION

"'Tis pleased I be t' hear yer bowels an' voice in such fine form," laughed McGarnicle, slapping the tabletop with delight as Shamus came crashing back down, and through, his chair; breaking it, as usual, into a zillion splinters, before his great bulk rolled to a stop in an ungainly but amusing sprawl on the hearthstones.

"'Sblood!" shouted Shamus, his hands simultaneously sprinkle-dancing a spell into the ethers, as he delicately husbanded a million golden droplets of his favorite ale back into his tumbling tankard, before it settled contentedly into his hand. "'Sblood! Me ale! Me precious Mexican ale! 'Tis th' last one till month's end! Th' *last* o' th' *last* o' th' *last*, I've Jack's word on it! Nothin' left after this but ever'thin' else! Ye've a wicked soul, McGarnicle! A wicked, wicked soul!" And with that, he rose effortlessly, taking a powerful swipe at his little tormentor: a swipe of such force and speed no average mortal would spot the shadow of its execution: a swipe McGarnicle easily hopped over before relaxing comfortably into his accustomed place across from Shamus, observing, with a grin, his pal settling with a grunt into his chair—a chair which reassembled itself for him and slid under his descending bottom just in time, so used to the necessary spell had its fragments become.

"Pardon me surliness, McGarnicle," sighed Shamus, "but th' thought o' no more cerveza fer a week has cut inta me humour sorely."

"'Tis why I sit afore ye, Shamus," chuckled McGarnicle, "I've a keg 'r two in me cellar; a present ferried by Angelica's parents, fresh from Mexico but an hour ago. Since I be in large part responsible fer yer foolish but understandable preference fer cerveza 'bove all else, eschewin' as ye do, th' even higher delights o' abstinence, I feel some small responsibility fer yer emotional well-bein', so..."

"Yer after somethin', ain't ye?—ye crafty little wretch," surmised Shamus, rising majestically, quaffing the last of his ale, then placing his hands on the table and lowering his massive head down and down till it was face to face with that of the leprechaun king. "Spit it out. It's got t' be big if yer willin' t' share yer last two kegs."

"Yes ... well ..." bluffed McGarnicle, grinning with a ferociously dishonest affability, "there be somethin' I desire of ye but 'tis a trifle. Ye'll feel debted t' me after I ask, e'en 'thout th' ale."

"Do it involve dismemberment?!!" roared Shamus suspiciously, rising back to his full majestic height and glowering down at McGarnicle, "If it do, 'twill be both kegs ye'll be coughin' up, not just one, I warn ye now!"

"No," promised McGarnicle, standing erect on his chair, "nothin' s' simple. I want ye t' take o'er teachin' me evenin' class o' leprechaun tykes fer a month. Give me a bit o' a breather."

"What?!" snorted Shamus, as McGarnicle leapt onto his shoulder and they headed for the door, "Teach yer kiddies?! That be *all*, ye say?!"

"Three kegs o' cerveza; I think I might have just one more saved," encouraged McGarnicle seductively, "Three whole kegs o' cool, glistenin' Mexican beer; th' last o' th' last o' th' last in Elfindale, till month's end."

"Four," insisted Shamus, with conviction, "Four, an' ye've got yerself a deal. Crammin' restless minds be no task fer th' faint-hearted; I'll need me sustenance."

"Four it be," agreed McGarnicle, slapping Shamus' back. "'Tis fair; 'twill gives us that many each till month's end. More than enough t' see me through, what with th' other ten I hold in re-serve."

"'Tis no accident ye be king o' th' leprechauns," laughed Shamus, "I know ye well an' I believed ye'd no more'n half a dozen."

"To lie, an' almost lie, be more than a gift o' leadership," chuck-led McGarnicle as they entered his home, "'tis a prerequisite."

Chapter Three

THE BIRDBATH

*I*n all of Elfindale there was no place excelling the beauty of Winifred's garden. Tempted as she'd been to uproot her roses in London, wrest bulbs from the ground and sever cuttings from vines, she'd decided, once committed on moving to Ireland, to leave them all contentedly behind and start from scratch. This decision, an act of great courage and humility, considering her age, resulted in the granting of a mixed boon by the Fates: a boon whose blossoming was her ability to see, from time to time, in her rose-entwined stone birdbath, past events, and the essence of those happening, and to come—cloaked, as *they* always are, in relative possibility. This gift, combined with her truly extraordinary and innovative cookie baking skills, made Winifred both respected and beloved throughout Elfindale, without thought to her other considerable merits. Had she chosen, for example, she could have earned a respectable living in the world as a poker player, so easily could she fleece even the great Merlin himself with her cheery, sensible, smiling face; only McGarnicle, and occasionally Abel, being deceitful enough to give her a run for the money. That being the case, she'd quickly taken over the banking of Elfindale in its dealings with the world and thus successfully provided a useful, harmless 'front'—to the relief of all. Further, her knowledge of herbs, particularly soothing herbs, made Winifred a natural healer for the ill and the lovelorn, who came to her often to be therapized by her teas and garden. And if that wasn't enough, her sense of humour was much cherished by every age, being as it was, a perfect blend of English restraint and Italian voluptuousness; all of which Winifred needed as she stood, transfixed, by her birdbath that very afternoon, staring in awe down into its depths.

Chapter Four

ARIEL'S RETURN

*I*n the three years Rawhide and Winifred had resided in Elfindale so far, Rawhide spent most of his waking hours fishing for trout in every cranny of that well-stocked paradise and, in doing so, became somewhat of an eccentric; one who nodded affably at all who chanced upon him then ambled further upstream, silently fishing. Consequently, since everything was going so well few thought he'd ever have much more to do or say, he basically faded into the background. Like Churchill before Munich, it was generally assumed he was over the hump and comfortably ensconced in a well-deserved retirement, even dotage, however charmingly executed. Winifred, it must be said, albeit reluctantly, came to feel the same way about him; which explains her ongoing, astonished stare down into her birdbath, because there he stood, talking affably and on equal terms with a great warrior she'd often seen in its depths—a female warrior—a warrior crowned in dazzling, filigreed, Celtic gold and garbed in a splendid, purple-trimmed, white-silk tunic; punctuating her animated conversation with lightning thrusts of a wicked, bejeweled sword which danced in her palm like thought itself.

Chapter Five

MISCHIEF

"*W*hatever are they talking about?" mused Winifred aloud to herself, peering closer, but to no avail, as a wayward feather fell on her watery mirror, banishing its depths with surface agitation. "How can I help if I cannot see?"

"Help who?" enquired Angelica curiously, stepping through the hedge of Winifred's garden, like a cat.

"Bless me," gasped Winifred, startled, backing up a few steps. "Bless me, child but you *are* the silent one. Graceful you've grown—no sign of baby fat; quite like I wanted to be in my youth. And tall too; taller than me by a good six inches. Yes, you're quite the grown-up now; guess I can't even tempt you with one of my world-famous chocolate-chip cookies—they're fresh from the oven. Still warm. Personally, I like them best that way, however tasty they are cool. Something about heated choc- olate melting in your mouth, blending with the moistness of warm dough."

"I'd *love* one," said Angelica, eyeballing a muslin-draped plate beside Winifred's Brown Betty, her taste buds, at least, complete- ly seduced, "but that won't get you off the hook; I can see you're stalling, trying to hide something potentially unpleasant from me and I'll not have it. *'Forewarned is forearmed'*; fill me in."

"Very well," succumbed Winifred, passing Angelica a steaming chocolate-chip cookie while simultaneously pouring cups of amber tea, "I think Rawhide is smitten by another woman. A little creature, but a woman nonetheless and a formidable one. I may have to take up trout fishing to win him back."

"Who is she?" asked Angelica, doubtful but intrigued, leaning forward with a grin, pleased Winifred could have so romantic a thought about her little, round, balding mate. "Does she live in Elfindale?"

"I've never seen her hereabouts; only in my birdbath," replied Winifred, "She's about my age but oh my—is she a feisty one. I've seen her at the head of a host of flying dragons wheeling about in the sky, doing battle with loathsome things. I've seen her plummet from great heights, just for fun, into the sea, shrieking with laughter. I've seen her feast like Beowulf in his prime and I've seen her dance like the devil himself. I've..."

"Like the devil himself?" interrupted Angelica curiously. "How does the devil dance?"

"Buck-naked, darling," reddened Winifred, discretely patting Angelica's rounding knee, "Buck-naked, and without shame; I'd prefer we alter the drift of this conversation."

"Is she evil?" enquired Angelica, disturbed. "Are we in danger?"

"Sadly, no," sighed Winifred, shaking her head, "I could do battle with evil but I'm afraid she's goodness and courage personified—that's the impression I get."

"Good lord," thought Angelica aloud, "Could it be Ariel? It sounds like Ariel to me."

"Ariel?" echoed Winifred, astonished and pleased, "Ariel? McGarnicle's wife? The queen of the leprechauns?—Why, she vanished from the world three hundred years ago."

"True," agreed Angelica, "but this is Elfindale, Faerie is all about, and leprechauns have no known life span: only accident, battle, or the willing exit of an extreme old age leads to their ascension—and *nobody* clings so tenaciously to incarnate life as they do. Was she dressed in Celtic gold and a purple-trimmed white tunic, with a fiery bejeweled sword?"

"She was indeed," replied Winifred.

"And was she talking his ear off while animatedly jabbing that sword effortlessly about?"

"Yes," replied Winifred again, even more hopefully.

"Then it *was* Ariel!" cried Angelica in delight, clapping her hands as if she were five, "McGarnicle will be *so* pleased!"

"I've heard they're soul mates, she and McGarnicle," hinted Winifred, freeing Hope while simultaneously screwing the lid back down on Jealousy.

"Yes," affirmed Angelica, from the contentment of experience, "they are. Like Arthur and I, Merlin and Morgan, Brenna and Shamus, my parents, and so many more hereabouts, they have eyes only for each other."

"Then I've nothing to fear," said Winifred, "Nothing to fear from her, at least."

"Nor anyone else," encouraged Angelica, from the heart. "If ever I saw two soul mates in the flesh it's you and Rawhide."

"But he's always fishing," complained Winifred, passing Angelica another cookie.

"And you're always in your garden here," countered Angelica, with a chuckle and bite of still-warm cookie, "When you're not in your kitchen, that is."

"Bless me, it's true," mused Winifred reflectively, "I guess I'm just as busy as he. And he *is* home every night for supper and sleep and breakfast and such. Besides, I don't love him any the less for his absence."

"Bingo!" confirmed Angelica, "And it's exactly the same for him."

"I feel ever so much better about Rawhide now," continued Winifred, looking about nervously, "but I'm afraid my paranoia has just been replaced by a general sense of foreboding."

And with that, Elfindale plunged into darkness.

PART TWO

THE GATHERING STORM

Chapter Six

INSTANT RESPONSE

*W*hen Elfindale plunged into darkness it didn't cause the stir one might expect. The reason for this is simple; its duration was less than a second, a heartbeat, a blink. Further, since there was no electricity in Elfindale, no clocks or machinery of any kind were affected. All that happened was, Elfindale curtsied briefly to the god of darkness then continued on its merry, sunlit way. Any who noticed, paused for a moment, cocked their head reflectively, then went on about their business. Only Rawhide; Ariel; McGarnicle; Abel; and dimly, Winifred, understood something was amiss. And Merlin, of course: who surfaced alertly from his meditations in the crystal cave, whistled Thunder to consciousness, and stepped forth.

WAR & WEDLOCK

$\mathcal{M}$erlin alone understood most of what was to follow, realizing, as he did, no one in the flesh, as is so often the case, had bothered to consider that the dark side of Faerie would inevitably be drawn to the plum of Elfindale. Would lust to own its rills and dells lock, stock, and barrel. Would be willing to risk death for so tempting a prize. No one, that is, except McGarnicle—and Ariel, who'd been fighting to keep them at bay for the last three centuries of Earthen time, in Faerie, thousands and thousands and thousands of years, on that side. To be told, however, his spouse was back and hanging out in the deeper recesses of Elfindale with Rawhide was a mixed blessing indeed for McGarnicle, despite how much he'd missed her; for no longer would he rule Elfindale and his Mexican valley alone. No longer could he come and go as he pleased. Further, his ale consumption would be drastically curtailed, his diet and garb radically changed, and his sleeping habits as well. Yes, his better half was back—all that was wanting was the entrance she was undoubtedly preparing. An entrance involving a cerveza-reserve-draining ball, at the very least.

Chapter Eight

A QUADRANT EACH

*A*ngelica possessed all of the power of Morgan as a teen but none of the mischief. Having 'united' with her soul mate Arthur, at ten, she somehow matured in the next three years into quite a unique creature entirely. For one thing, she'd developed the most extraordinary patience by husbanding herself for the long haul of next-to-a-thousand years that stretched before her in Earthen time, till the full healing of the Once and Future King's wound in Faerie. This patience had corollary assets as well, for part of doing time quickly is effortless grace: a grace which fit her like a skin as she flowed like a panther about the realm, disappearing for long periods of time from the sight of leprechauns, humans, and faerie folk alike.

During these sojourns, and because of them, she took great joy in her animal existence; which bode well for her nuptial night with Arthur, sporting, as she did, with all the creatures that flew, swam, slithered, or syncopated about Elfindale's rivers, dells, fells, lakes, and forests. Only McGarnicle, Abel, and Rawhide had a comparably detailed map in their mind's eye of everyone's beloved haven. And only Merlin had any idea of how desperately their special skills would be needed.

Chapter Nine

A JEALOUSY SPASM

"You're late for dinner!" snapped Winifred, with uncharacteristic suspicion, at her startled spouse.

"Look, I got a dozen trout," offered Rawhide, backing up with a sheepish grin as he held out his catch, "We've a guest for supper and she says she's got a lust for real trout more than anything."

"Is she good-looking?" grilled Winifred, tapping a toe.

"Not my field; judge for yourself," replied Rawhide wisely, as Ariel swept briskly under his arm, hauled down Winifred's head with both hands, and planted several enthusiastic kisses on her startled and helpless cheeks.

"Whatever yer havin's fine with me," proposed Ariel, with a great beaming smile on her little round face, "I'll just fry up th' trout after dessert."

"What a wonderful creature you are," stammered Winifred, completely charmed, "Are we going to be close friends?"

"So dang close," assured Ariel, sliding an arm around her host's waist, "people won't see daylight twixt us."

"Actually we were having deviled eggs," blushed Winifred, pleased: "deviled eggs, crustless cucumber sandwiches, and chocolate-dipped strawberries."

"Sounds yummy t' me," enthused Ariel, hopping up on a chair at the table, "Toss in a bunch o' homefried spuds an' them trout an' we'll have us th' makin's o' a first-class repast."

"Done," laughed Winifred, "Now that I've met you I'm as happy and as hungry as the day the War ended."

And indeed she was: so happy and so hungry she didn't notice the quick glance her husband and Ariel exchanged—a glance fraught with significance. A glance of those in the know.

Chapter Ten

A HISTORIC MOMENT

*H*owever much Angelica missed Thunder in the flesh, her lone-liness was generally assuaged by her steadfast companion, Abel, but Abel, for purposes of his own or on a secret mission for his father, had been away from Elfindale for a week, his longest absence in the three years they'd known each other. Consequently, assisted by the unkindness of a harvest moon so rare it was blue, Angelica sought out a favoured night-time ledge overlooking the forest, far from the bustle of her loved ones, and gazed at the haunting moon, which bathed her, and everything about, with that rarest of patinas—the very essence of poignant melancholia.

About to remove her overalls and sink, naked, into her soli-tude, Angelica's hands were arrested at the first fastening by a *snap!* in the forest; a snap experience told her was made by a large creature in its prime and in a hurry, careless of disturbance. Only fear or joy would motivate such a slip and her stomach and nos-trils eliminated the former. Clearly, she mused, great joy was ap-proaching her, at speed. And it was; for seconds later Thunder bounded out onto the ledge and stood panting at her, in all his magnificence.

"I'd give anything to be able to hug you now," sighed Angelica, rising wistfully, despite her pleasure at his presence.

"And why is that?" enquired Thunder teasingly, with a sound thump of his tail.

"Because nothing under the sun has ever felt quite so good, as if you didn't know," replied Angelica.

"Not even scritching your ear, like this?" suggested Thunder, loudly and rapidly scratching his ear, with a hind leg, "Not even that?"

"Ohmygod!" squealed Angelica, "I *heard* you in the forest and I *heard* your tail thump and I *heard* your ear-scritching!"

"Well, duh!" chuckled Thunder, crossing his eyes mockingly.

"You're in the flesh! You're in the flesh!" shouted Angelica, pouncing on him like a cat and squeezing him till he groaned, "You're in the flesh!"

"I fear he has t' be t' function entire, in Elfindale an' Faerie, as he an' ye'll shortly be doin'," explained Merlin, stepping out of the forest and onto the ledge.

"We will? Why?" asked Angelica, too happy at Thunder's corporeality to realize only great peril would have governed Merlin's decision to bring him fully back into both worlds.

"Because," replied Merlin, squatting beside her, "all in Faerie be in the astral—ghostlike—not quite real, includin' its denizens. Even married t' Earth as it be for moments, it bears with it somethin' of the ephemeral."

"I thought that was good," said Angelica, her arms still hammer locked around Thunder.

"From the way you're squeezin' me mutt there, I'm compelled t' say, like meself an' ever'one else, the tangibility of Earth holds formidable appeal t' ye as well. Imagine what it be like for the darker souls of Faerie, Laocooned as they be by prejudices, fears, an' rapacious appetites, t' dine, even fight, in, an' on, mere mist. No, Angelica, they want Elfindale now an' they want it bad. I'm sorry t' say, young as ye be, ye'll have t' gird for battle."

And with that, he placed a sword in her hand, complete with scabbard, and vanished.

Chapter Eleven

THE FAINT

$\mathcal{N}$either Winifred nor Rawhide had the power to travel to Faerie, so their contribution would, perforce, take place in Elfindale and the world, should the invading host succeed in bullying its way past the defenses of Faerie; all of which were weakened considerably by the necessity of reinforcing Avalon, to guard the irreplaceable, healing Arthur. Consequently, Merlin had determined the only way to protect him without the use of legions armed to the teeth was to place a very devil by his side; a whirlwind of maternal competence and rage—namely, the love of the youthening king's life, Angelica, backed up by his beloved Thunder—thereby freeing the forces of Avalon to assist in the containment of the invading hoard to an evacuated corridor leading from dark Faerie to Elfindale's 'gate'.

All this, Angelica fully understood intuitively, as the sword and scabbard placed in her hands by Merlin transformed her, in a twinkling, from girl to woman. From cat to she bear. From 'sorceress' to *sorceress*.

Rising calmly, she fastened the weapon about her hips effortlessly, as if long familiar with its usage, as indeed she was; for as she unsheathed the blade and held it aloft it whispered its name to her: a name unutterable to anyone other than herself: a name which brought back in a flash to her, full remembrance of all her previous lives, right down to her Earthly beginnings in the primordial sea, and before—long, long before in galaxies that flowered, flourished, and returned to the great mix again and again and again.

Needless to say, this tidal wave of information, previously barely hinted at, promptly overwhelmed her sensibilities and sent her to the mat in an ungainly, unconscious lump, despite the fact, mere seconds before, she'd been standing proudly upstretched, her sword dancing among the very stars themselves.

Chapter Twelve

THE DEAL

*T*he reason Abel was in Mexico rather than in Angelica's pocket in Elfindale was both top-secret and simplicity itself: a troll had been discovered in McGarnicle's valley; a ferocious troll, despite its diminutive size. Rounded up by Petie and imprisoned in a roomy cage by the leprechaun elders in charge in McGarnicle's absence, it fell to Abel as the best linguist in leprechaundom to somehow decipher its grunts and snarls; somehow piece together fragments of communication, to ascertain the why and the how of its presence. It took some time but he finally realized ninety percent of its language was a stream of invectives of questionable taste. This lessened the field considerably for him and over the next few days he put together that it was five years old and that it wanted its mommy. Succumbing to its demand for a specific treat before it showed him the spot it fell through from Faerie, he gave the young troll a huge, loathsome wormsicle and manfully did his duty as ambassador by refraining from upchucking or looking away, while it enthusiastically slobbered it down; empathizing all the while with England's own sweet queen, Elizabeth, who more than once has 'appreciatively' dined on dubious substances pre-masticated by toothless crones.

Chapter Thirteen

MERLIN'S GLADE

*T*he moment Merlin received Abel's report he summoned Morgan from the crystal cave and Angelica from her reverie in a hammock, scratching Thunder's ears. In her dream Angelica'd been dancing a waltz with Arthur, under the stars, on a candle-lit balcony. In hers, Morgan had been surrounded by thousands of big, yapping mice, or little dogs; she couldn't be sure which. In either case, neither stopped for coffee as they hurried down disparate paths to rendezvous at Merlin's fire, and both had their mettle tested in doing so, for each was challenged on the way: Morgan by a giant, and Angelica by a bear.

Morgan, despite her recent awakening, dispatched hers calmly with a lightning bolt of energy through the genitals and continued on her way, but for Angelica, a virgin in battle, the bear was a totally different reality. As it rushed her with a roar, she only had time to shout out an adrenaline-pumping: "This is it!" before drawing her sword, for the second time, and plunging it into the great beast's heart.

When one dispatches evil an unpleasant odor is part of the deal but for both ladies, surprisingly, their assailants, 'slain', turned to golden flowers, and then air, perfuming all about with the delicacy of wood violets.

"*Merlin*," muttered Morgan suspiciously to Angelica, as their paths melted together, "'Twas just a wake-up call. How do ye feel? Exhilarated?"

"Well," replied Angelica, sheathing her sword with a grin, "I do confess I got a buzz nailing the bull's-eye without hesitation. That bear was toast, real or not."

"Welcome t' the world of action," chuckled Morgan affectionately, putting an arm around Angelica's shoulder, "The next time ye unsheathe that thing ye'll be stabbin' butts by the hundreds, I can see it now."

And with that, they stepped into Merlin's glade.

Chapter Fourteen

THE SEEING

*A*t the very moment Merlin was telling Morgan she was off to Mexico forthwith to do battle, with Petie and all the Chihuahuas he could round up serving as her legions; at the very moment he was simultaneously instructing Angelica on the need to make haste, and all her own decisions, in the defense of Arthur in Avalon; Winifred found herself staring down into her birdbath at a kaleidoscope of creatures and events. First she saw innumerable flexibly-plump, fluorescent, pink or blue, worm-like tubular rods writhing seductively together in a huge, evil ball; before the mass blew up and each shot away from the other, fleeing the coupling in unseemly haste. Then she saw seven rather attractive lizards, each reposing on a leaf, over a peaceful pond in the moonlight. Then she saw a great host of beautiful trolls and other creatures of grace and skill charge into an army of grotesque trolls and repulsive giants heading towards a larger number of their odious kind pressing to enter a vortex of fluorescent, spinning worms. Then she saw a very strange creature made out of what appeared to be icicles step out of a one-seater flying saucer and disappear into Merlin's cave. Then she saw Angelica and Thunder standing on-shore in Faerie, staring across at Avalon. Then, god help her, she

271

got a taste of what being separated from Rawhide for a thousand years would feel like—she looked into the heart of Angelica.

Chapter Fifteen

COURAGE

*A*ngelica knew she couldn't bear to view Arthur again, even if it might be for the very last time, and Thunder knew it would cause her an anguish, however nobly she bore it, if he were to pop over for a smooch and a snurf, so he refrained from taking the opportunity and silently gazed upon the resting place of Arthur, in the distance. Avalon, of course, was too lovely for words but that was neither here nor there, for Angelica could not sink into nostalgia, had to maximize her will and her rage in order to put the ultimate mile-deep and impossibly-high barrier of impenetrable thorns around all that healing isle; and she succeeded, as Merlin knew she would, spurned on in her sorcery, as she was, by the vulnerability of her legendary mate. Then, being who she was, she promptly capped it off by turning Avalon into a 'lake', from above; rendering it invisible in the sea, from that quarter.

Stunned, Winifred turned aside from her birdbath, sparing herself the anguish of experiencing Angelica's expression as she, having entombed her other half, and seeking a greater usefulness, walked away.

Chapter Sixteen

SUBSTITUTE TEACHING

*W*inifred didn't know what to make of the perplexing image of the spacecraft and the alien, and the alien's unopposed entrance into Merlin's cave, a feat in itself, but it startled her into action so she went inside to bake a bunch of cookies, since cookie baking invariably soothed her, as well as everyone else, and by the time she'd made a couple of batches the ambrosia from her kitchen had pretty much permeated the nostrils of all in walking distance, attracting a considerable throng—to Shamus' consternation—because the earliest to show up, and thus abandon him, had been his very first class of leprechaun tykes. Good at stirring things up, as a teacher he'd quickly discovered the opposite was needed because his exuberant charges were perpetually exploding in all directions, like popcorn shaken over dancing flames. He'd tried a calming spell on them thereafter and they hadn't even yawned. Then he tried feeding them into a stupor but that'd merely warmed them up for Winifred's cookies, which they'd beelined for, the moment they caught a waft, outracing even McGarnicle to the first batch.

Repairing to the pub for an ale, to think things over, Shamus didn't bat so much as an eye when McGarnicle shortly burst out of the fire and landed on his table, with a roar.

"Thought yer nerves'd be shot fer sure," laughed McGarnicle. "Opined me tykes'd wind ye up like a rubber band then spit ye out like yesterday's gum. Thought, in short, twixt us, we could spur ye t' a personal flyin'-fart record but there ye sit, rooted t' yer chair."

"Don't mean t' hurt yer feelin's," sighed Shamus, "'tis just yer poppin' in all sudden-like, howe'er surprisin', can't hold a candle t' them tykes failin' miserable at roll call an' whate'er follows. Take what's left o' yer beer back, McGarnicle, I beg ye. Take it back an' we'll call it quits; I'd rather be off t' th' wars."

"Sorry," chuckled McGarnicle, with a touch of compassion behind his twinkle, "So would I."

PART THREE

THE STORM

Chapter Seventeen

NO BRIDGE BETWEEN

*U*nicorns pawed the ground gently and looked down their horns in silent wisdom at the assemblage. Having earlier reported to Ariel on the advance of the armies of the dark side, they stirred in pleasure when great fires were lit to warm and illuminate the gathering host, just before the leprechauns from McGarnicle's valley, in their thousands, every man, woman and child, appeared at a stroke as Merlin rose and bade them welcome. All were dressed in their best, bearing swords appropriate to their stature; delicate swords, for speed and vigilance would win the day, not brute strength. Nonetheless, because this was a party, a ball in fact, honouring Ariel's return, weapons were an affectation, a fashion statement as it were, rather than a necessity. Should anyone doubt this, all they need do was look at Merlin strolling amiably about alternating humorous anecdotes with quaffs of ale. So great a personage as himself, surely, all thought, would not offend Time and Energy by abusing them with unseemly paranoia nor waste them with baseless bravado. No indeed. His cheery demeanour, obviously, was an honest one. The calming effect this had on all about must be experienced to be understood fully, but that left its effect no less visible to the unicorns observing the happy throng.

278

A throng focused for the most part on Ariel, whom clearly had been missed by all the leprechauns over three hundred years of age—the majority of those yet live on Earth.

Ambling their way down to the celebrants, then nuzzling their way amiably up to Ariel, the unicorns added to the contentment of all by emanating confidence and beatitude, in the presence of their diminutive commander in chief; before, protocol fulfilled by prancing a circle around her, they wheeled about in unison and went for a moonlit run, filling their souls with the realness of Elfindale, stocking up memories for their imminent return to Faerie.

Back at the party of course, things began to heat up, as ale and wine flowed in balanced necessity, easing inhibitions while old friendships renewed, old flirtations flowered. Gossip, too, naturally, became increasingly rife, as speculation provided its usual enjoyment.

It was rumoured McGarnicle's valley, always on the borderline, had finally flowered into a full-scale gateway to Faerie, with all the inherent dangers that implied in these risky times; and that Morgan, Petie, and a zillion Chihuahuas from all over Mexico would be its sole defenders. It was also rumoured the denizens of the attacking host from the dark side of Faerie, when they bunch up at the gateways to Elfindale and McGarnicle's valley, blocked by Merlin and Morgan, didn't know they would lose their identity by being caught up in the brutal mindlessness of the collective howling mob they'd constitute and would, thereupon, uncontrollably morph into plump, six-foot-long, primal, fluorescent 'worms'; worms that, individually, should they succeed in bursting past the legendary sorcerers, would flee each other and everyone hunting them, seeking sufficient solitude to re-form into their natural selves, be it troll, giant, or whatever. Re-form, to escape the helpless bondage of tubular florescence and regain their former formidable powers and appetites.

It was further rumoured Merlin had already placed Rawhide, Abel, McGarnicle, and Angelica in sole charge of a quadrant each of all the lands of Elfindale; to lead the meticulous sweep of every rill and dell, every hole and ledge, every crack, where a fluorescent worm could hide until it transformed into full-blown bad news.

And all of the whisperings were accurate, since all had been circulated by Merlin himself, because he wanted everyone to know at least that much of the truth and he knew there is no more expedient way of making something general knowledge than by presenting it as rumour. No surer way of bestowing the mantle of fact. The problem was of course, Angelica was in Faerie and there was no earthly way she could get back once she'd inflicted an all-too-necessary phase-two assault on the fortunes of Faerie's darker host, which was rapidly, within the hour in fact, going to attack Merlin and Morgan head-on in a sudden 'surprise assault', the knowledge of which was so clearly known to the great sorcerer and his mate it was laughable, thanks to the intercession of the normally neutral unicorns. The problem of Angelica however, remained. How was she to get through to lead her quadrant? She was irreplaceable; had to get back. But how? Not even Merlin knew, and it troubled him just a bit, because, without Angelica, horror would be visited upon Elfindale. And fear; a permanent fear—for no child would ever again feel sufficiently safe there or in McGarnicle's valley—a monstrous thought. A humiliation too appalling for the old warrior to bear. No, Angelica had to get back, and so did Thunder to protect her, but the how of it eluded even the great Merlin himself. No one watching as he danced a final reel with Ariel would have believed from his countenance and bearing however, he was pondering his weakness and Elfindale's peril; aware as he was, that for total victory, he needed Angelica in two places, one after the other, with no bridge between.

Chapter Eighteen

THE OPENING GAMBIT

$\mathcal{A}$ssuming a weakness in their foe that didn't exist; and damaged by their nature, ego incarnate, the denizens of the black hoard were handicapped, as villainy usually is, on more than one front; not the least of which was attempting a two-pronged attack on the world, rather than an all-out assault on either quarter. This decision was made because dark Faerie was blinded by the patent 'absurdity' of Abel returning the infant troll to its mother on the other side, thereby revealing McGarnicle's valley as an awakening portal—to its peril. Only weakness; only a sappy sentimentality of the most inexcusable kind could bring forth such lunacy, they reasoned. Victory, over so foolish a foe, would be facile.

Since it was also reasoned Merlin would prove the most formidable opponent, only a third of dark Faerie's forces assailed Morgan—a terrible drain and a mortal mistake—for, as tricky as Merlin, and as powerful in her own right, she had no great difficulty in holding the bulk of them back until the press of their malignancy squeezed each individually-surprised horror into its primal, fluorescent-rod stage, all of whom wriggled like the devil to bully their way beyond her spell-induced forcefield and flee into the tangible pleasures of Mexico; but those that did soon found themselves envying those turned back, and even the dead, for Petie and his legions made painful work of the mere thousands who got past Morgan's inhalations (sorcery being at its most vulnerable then), pouncing on them with all the speed and savagery of their kind when aroused—ripping holes in the great worms' sides with their needle-sharp little teeth, deflating them into sad, little, floppy, lifeless sacks. Not one, of all that broke through, achieved a transformation. Not one got to devour a single Chihuahua. Victory, for Morgan and Petie and his fellows, was complete in half an hour; after which, as before, peace descended on the valley.

Chapter Nineteen

PETIE PARTIES

*H*ad she the power to assist Merlin further, Morgan would have left Petie and his brethren to celebrate alone and made speed back to his side but the truth is, despite the seeming ease of her victory, it'd taken the lion's share of her energy to hold up her end, so she bowed to the inevitable, abandoned hope of spelling herself to Elfindale forthwith, and settled in to feast with Petie and the boys on prawns and cerveza.

A hundred thousand happy, increasingly-inebriated little Chihuahuas celebrating their first collective victory in the history of their species however, proved formidably ebullient and thus succeeded where the invading host had failed; they soon exhausted Morgan—into lassitude, contentment, sleep.

Chapter Twenty

SLUMBERING

*T*hings for Morgan had gone as well as anything could go, a clean sweep in fact, because the 'surprise attack' had been no surprise at all and because Petie and his legions easily outclassed in speed and dexterity the fluorescent rods that'd slipped past her forcefield. Further, the attack had come in daylight, when the power of the dark side is at its nadir; a necessity however, from their point of view, because it was reasoned essential the assaults be as simultaneous as possible and that the greatest number and force hit Ireland at midnight, when the invaders were at their strongest and Elfindale its weakest. The real reason their forces weren't evenly dispersed however was, since ego and self-aggrandizement rule the underworld, the fiercest of the dark side's denizens, rather than defeating a 'mere woman', all wanted the honour of taking Merlin head-on; each seeking the glory coming to the one who brought him down. Invading generalship, consequently, at the Morgan front, as well as numbers, proved sorely lacking. Many other factors were involved in the ease of her victory as well: terrain, for one, since McGarnicle's valley was only verdant about the village and the bay, all the rest being desert— beautiful but Spartan, and largely bereft of places to hide.

"All in all," mused Morgan, succumbing further to the sand-man, "when ye get right down to it, me part of the job was a cakewalk, a holiday, a present from me beloved Merlin, the old rascal."

And with that, she stretched luxuriously in her hammocked rest, tuned into her hubby, and drifted contentedly deeper off to sleep with a chuckle: a chuckle which mystified those all about her because it contained more than humour; it contained absolute confidence in the outcome of the tableau she was watching still.

Chapter Twenty-One

TORNADO

$\mathcal{M}$eanwhile, "back at the ranch" as they say, all hell was breaking loose. At the peak of the assault, Merlin was standing on Angelica's ridge, arms and staff outstretched in the moonlight, facing a howling maelstrom of fluorescent pink and blue worms funneling up into the sky. This 'tornado' had him so buffeted his robe was in rags, snapping and flapping like whips at a circus, and his long gray hair accompanied it to a T.

The tornado however, menacing though it be, was of Merlin's making. His way of containing the onslaught at its height. His way of keeping as many tubes as possible in a vortex till they exhausted themselves and withdrew or perished. As it was, many still managed to explode out of the howling maelstrom with his every inhalation and disperse themselves in all directions; seeking to fill Elfindale while intuitively distancing themselves as far from each other as possible, to shorten precious minutes of gestation time. Should enough survive, spread out in such a fashion, to become themselves again, no power in Elfindale could stand against them and all would be lost.

Fortunately for Elfindale, Faerie, and the world however, those numbers that escaped the twister were proving to be manageable, in every quadrant except Angelica's. Acutely aware this was his only weakness, a part of Merlin's very busy consciousness prayed full-time that the young warrior-sorceress and Thunder could finish their tasks on the other side and somehow find a way back, to lead the rooting out of her quadrant before the helpless horrors hatched, and soon; for, powerful though he was, Merlin's energies were beginning to flag, the tornado was slowing down, and more and more rods were flying away from the vortex and vanishing into the Elfindale night, racing for their lives, and succeeding in ever-increasing numbers in eluding the tiring elderly leprechauns, who'd been battling at top speed for over an hour.

Of all the leprechauns, to his great pride, it turned out to be Shamus' tykes that proved the most inexhaustible, and inventive; for it was they who, in their exuberance and dexterity, first took to riding some of the worms, using them to run down others for dispatch; a practice soon commonplace among the younger and more adaptable leprechauns; a practice which, along with Angelica's efforts, turned the tide of success in Merlin's favour, for the young were able to hunt on and on, long after the bulk of the leprechaun people had gone home for supper and sleep, their contribution having been made, to the best of their abilities.

Abel and McGarnicle, of course, remained inexhaustible and wallowed in the hunt in each of their quadrants like princes of India, devising ever-more complicated leaps and tumbles in the air before dispatching another shining worm, with a wicked backhand, poniard thrust, or even, daringly, a throw. Since the actual death of a rod involved no more than its piercing, after which all its innards poured out the hole, like a cascade of faerie dust; followed by the comic wheeze it made in doing so, and the even *more* comic collapse of each vigorous, wriggling tube into a limp sack, empathy wasn't a factor to either father or son, for the demise of a foe positively invited laughter, despite the fact it heralded the end of a life, demon-driven or no.

Yessir, like it or not, to Abel and McGarnicle it was a fun time, with no end in sight; for only with the dawn of the following night would the surviving, transformed invaders step forth in all their dread, with blades and axes and clubs designed to bring death and dismemberment to the innocent and the kindly and the helpless—the flip side of tonight's joyful hunt.

Being male, of course, neither McGarnicle nor Abel were going to let that future possibility spoil their present fun; rather, they'd use it as an impetus to be thorough, as well as merry.

Rawhide, in his quadrant, consigning leprechauns to little-known areas, found he rather enjoyed the hunt too. Found second-guessing fluorescent malignants hiding underwater, in hollow trees, behind rocks and in caves and such, was so akin to trout fishing he actually began using his fly-rod as a weapon—a far more effective one than any other devised that night; for with it he could snag underwater worms, worms wriggling by on land, even flying worms—snag them, then, with a delicate little "pop!" bite a hole in each the size of a pinhead. A pinhead which bulged them, inviting an explosion like a chrysanthemum firework—an explosion of far greater beauty than the mere wheeze and dribble of a sword-dispatched foe. Thus it was, hundreds met their lonely death at his calm hand that night—an inspiration and a beacon to all—for his were the most numerous, continual, and beautiful, of kills. Those requiring the least effort—the greatest skill.

Chapter Twenty-Two

MORE COOKIES

*A*bout an hour preceding the present state of affairs, just before the invasion began, Winifred, at the very last moment (due to her oft-voiced fear and dislike of travel—especially travel involving flight), had been introduced in her garden to Emile by Brenna, an old friend of his; a friend who'd summoned him from afar, at Morgan's request, via a sympathetic vibration from the earth-dragon's teeth in Merlin's cave, in order to introduce the alien to Winifred by someone they commonly held a friend. This was such an old-fashioned, 'British' thing to do Winifred was immediately charmed by him. So charmed, she readily accepted the graceful, crystal creature was an ally from space, and the plate-size saucer floating above his right shoulder would indeed expand to fit her perfectly, should she decide to sit in it for a bit, which he promptly invited her to do, with an expectant smile; a smile he knew, being British, she would be unable to refuse, phobia or no, because it simply wasn't polite.

Thus it was, he smoothly deceived her into the spaceship, after expanding it like a taffy-pull, prior to offering her a hand as she innocently walked up invisible steps and settled into the craft's comfortable interior.

"All its coordinates are preset," instructed Emile, smiling down at her in his fashion; causing him, because he was basically an honest soul, to turn pink with a universal blush. "All will be well. Just push that button there once you get well-noticed over wherever it takes you."

"Are you nuts?!" shouted Winifred, rising from the seduction if not from the seat, since he'd already snugly cinched her in, "Are you nuts?! Lemme out of here! Help! Brenna!—How *could* you?!"

"Shut up an' listen!" snapped Brenna, smacking the vehicle's skin for effect, "We don't want anybody gettin' shot down an' ye look like th' proverbial little old lady from Pasadena—get it? Ever'body's cookie-bakin' grandma—who'd shoot ye? Ye're th' safest we've got, next t' a child, an' we don't want t' risk one."

"OK, OK, I'll go," surrendered Winifred, shamed by the child image, "I'll go... Hey! ... Go where?! And why?!"

"There's going to be a storm," tinkled Emile, pointing a beautifully-articulated, albeit multi-jointed, limb at the moonlit sky, "A forcefield storm; an electrical storm here in Elfindale, generated by Merlin's vortex: one of such magnitude meteorologists will note and investigate. We can't have the eye of the world here at the most peaceful of times, much less when hell's a'poppin'."

"What's all that got to do with me?" persisted Winifred, rendered less acute than usual by the sneaking suspicion she was about to take a ride regardless of protest, fear, or even reason itself.

"'Tis quite simple," encouraged Brenna, patting her reassuringly on the shoulder before pushing a button, which zanged a clear, uncompromising canopy over the startled Winifred, "Where'er it stops just push that big red button afore ye, 'twill tell ever'body below where ye're goin' next, then take ye there in one-t'-three seconds; sorry fer th' speed, 'tis painless but ye won't get t' see much. Th' whole world has t' be starin' at ye, or where ye're goin' next, in amazement—fer a while at least, 'cause far as th' Earth be concerned, Ireland must cease t' exist. Ye're our only cover. Fortunately, ye're also our best." And with that, she slapped the craft's bubble once and Winifred, mouth agape, instantly began the first leg of what proved to not only be a successful mission, but a pleasant one as well; for Brenna and Emile had included in her itinerary of astonishing the great cities of the world, and thus the bulk of humanity, tranquil, minute-long pit stops at places of surpassing beauty. Places like Victoria Falls; Ayers Rock; the Grand Canyon; an underwater, Red Sea choral reef; and the little cottage of her birth.

Upon her return a few hours later, all she had to say was it was the best experience of her life because it was the only piece missing; she would never again repeat it; and what she really wanted now was bake up a tidal wave of chocolate-chip cookies, which she proceeded to do, to the delight of an Elfindale saved by her efforts from the scrutiny of the world but still battling for its life—with the worst to come.

Chapter Twenty-Three

AS THE WORM STIRS

*D*eep in the moist bowels of Angelica's quadrant, DNA ticked its inevitable tick as one of a thousand-odd, mud-slicked, fluorescent rods altered its shape slightly, bending and rounding gently in the middle; for a troll was beginning the earliest stage of its regeneration. Helpless as yet, and for some time to come, it was the first of all the assaulters of Elfindale to do so, the one with, therefore, the best chance of survival. There were still hundreds about Elfindale being hunted down and hundreds more spewing off Merlin's weakening vortex but only Angelica's quadrant lacked the generalship to root the bulk of them out before they became successfully entrenched and hard to find, and there was nothing to be done about it until, somehow, the tornado either increased containment by speeding up, or shook loose the last of its worms, because, as it stood, there was no way back for Angelica, no reserves, and every other quadrant was fighting its heart out to just break even. Once again, as before, when she had to stare down Rawhide and save Elfindale, it was all up to Angelica: Angelica and Thunder; since they, and they alone, were in a position on the other side to rally Merlin's strength by most effectively decreasing the number of malignants still pressing forward to join the fray. Frustrated, hot, thirsty, angry, and fed-up to the tusks with two hours of roaring without yet seeing any of the action, mocked at a tempting but dangerous distance by enemy forces from Avalon and elsewhere, the remaining portion of the dark army from Faerie was now ripe for phase two of Angelica's battle plan, the one laughingly foreseen by Morgan; for the moment had come to unsheathe her formidable blade a third time.

Chapter Twenty-Four

LIKE A ZIPLOC BAG

*D*arting in and about the rear of the black, heaving hoard pressing forward proved facile for Angelica, disguised as a young male troll; simplicity itself, as she stabbed hairy, misshapen posterior after hairy misshapen posterior, while Thunder inflicted the same pain and worse all about her, raking haunches mercilessly, as the hungry saber-tooth she'd made him. In the confusion, then mayhem, of the all-out fighting that ensued, as one outraged and insulted monster after another savagely attacked other bewildered suffering innocents, blaming them for wounds received, Angelica and Thunder worked their way deeper to the front, spreading the ever-increasing cancer of discord in a previously united host until as many were battling each other, successfully and to death, as were pressing forward into the vortex Merlin'd made of the once so peaceful entrance to and from Faerie and Earth. Unfortunately for Angelica and Thunder however, though a stroke of good luck in the long run, they suddenly found themselves caught up in the madness of the fury of all about and they too, like the rest, found their souls so utterly awash in a condensed, collective evil that they quite lost consciousness of them, as well as their physical shapes and identities, compressing into helpless, fluorescent worms: worms whose only instinct was to enter the vortex and hope for the best on the other side; a best leading to transmogrification and victory—or death.

Fortunately for Angelica and Thunder, when they were sucked into Merlin's whirlwind after being hurried forward into it by the press of other eager luminescents, Merlin's powers were so confidently on the increase, thanks to the utter mayhem they'd instigated on the other side, he paused to give himself his first deeply satisfying breath in an hour, and, consequently, Angelica and Thunder were able to burst through with an unusually large number of combatants, just prior to Merlin's mighty exhalation—which blasted the tornado into oblivion, terminated all those sucked into it, and sealed the gateway shut like a ziploc bag.

Chapter Twenty-Five

THROUGH

Catching the defenders off guard like they'd done, governed by the laws of randomness or destiny, Angelica and Thunder and their brethren shot in large numbers between the hacking leprechauns, who, spurred on or no by the explosion of Merlin's vortex and the consequent deaths of so many fluorescent tubes in it, lacked the energy or numbers to get them all before a goodly portion managed to make the cover of the wood, heading for the untrammeled perimeters and byways of Elfindale at its least known.

Chapter Twenty-Six

HIDING OUT

*B*eing a flying luminescent rod was an adventure to Thunder, who'd already regained consciousness of his identity; and an eye-opener to Angelica, who hadn't. All she knew was, she was awash in radiant beingness. Lacking muscles, bones, joints, or a brain, yet smoothly mobile, in a pain-free state, she felt herself an immortal. Paradoxically however, she also felt, at some level, that "not being", a "bad thing", would result if she didn't hole up and hide, as soon as possible—so she did—assisted, for some reason, by another rod bumping against her repeatedly, steering her into the towering shaft of a large, truncated, hollow beech prepared some years before by a bolt of lightening. Thunder knew the spot well, for it was one of his favorite meditations to curl up inside the great trunk and nap in its soothing mossy comfort while the sun or the moon illuminated it high above. This tree also happened to be in Angelica's quadrant, a serendipitous occurrence or not, I leave it to you. What I can say is, like all the other fluorescent worms fleeing for their very lives from Merlin's power and the stabbing teeth of the little leprechauns' blades, neither Angelica nor Thunder had any conscious knowledge to begin

with that they, in their blind dash for life, had chosen her quadrant as refuge.

Chapter Twenty-Seven

"IT AIN'T OVER TILL IT'S OVER"

With Angelica and Thunder definitely missing and possibly even dead, Elfindale found itself robbed of the opportunity to get careless with celebration, and all who could focused instead on doing one, final, predawn sweep of Angelica's quadrant before wearily returning home for refreshment and rest; the other three having been so thoroughly cleaned out Merlin contented himself with McGarnicle, Abel, and Rawhide as their sole defenders, with owl spies assisting as eyes and ears. Consequently, only Brenna, Shamus and his tykes, and Merlin (who'd gone off to sleep for a bit) remained within Angelica's quadrant's borders as the sun turned breakfast to brunch. And that is as it should be; for only they, of all his available fighters, possessed the stamina for what was to come.

Chapter Twenty-Eight

"QUE SERA, SERA"

$\mathcal{M}$erlin, lying on his back under an oak, enjoying the midday sunlight dappling warmly through the leaves and his joints, smiled up expectantly at a unicorn which stepped silently forth from a degree-of-no-magnitude, only to be quietly told Angelica was nowhere in Faerie, and Avalon was still a lake from above and thorn-encircled below; a situation all would prefer she remedied as soon as possible, for larders were running short and commerce had ground to a halt on that happy isle. None wished her to inconvenience herself, fully-appreciative as they were of the significant role she'd played for the common weal, but since the enemy had not only left the borders of sunny Faerie, they'd quite withdrawn to their own dark interior, surely it was time to get on with the peace.

"So they're out there," mused Merlin to himself, as the unicorn politely withdrew, "Out there, on *this* side; which means they're either dead sacks or holed up somewhere till tonight's metamorphosis. There's nothing I can do if death be already their fate, but since I'd root them out for sure if they be with us still, I'd best withdraw an' wish them luck, while the best of their friends try t' hunt them down. What an irony. Ah well, 'tis in God's hands;

there's naught else I can do." And with that, embracing the wisdom of *"que sera, sera"*, he entered into a daylong, rejuvenating slumber, abandoning Thunder, Angelica, and all the rest, to their fate.

Chapter Twenty-Nine

CHANGING SPOTS

*T*hroughout the general sweep of Angelica's quadrant by the leprechaun hosts, she and Thunder rested on undisturbed, snuggled by the mossy contentment of their great, hollow tree; he now fully-aware of what'd happened to them; and she, in an amiable, unknowing, plumply-contented state. Had either been one of the other tubes that survived the sweep however, their experience would have been radically different. For one thing, the rest were all in pain; pain induced by the bilious rage perpetually boiled throughout their vitals in whatever form they took, voluntary or otherwise. Further, and sufficient in its own right, their metamorphosis had advanced far enough already they were making an appalling discovery. A discovery which, fortuitously, rendered Angelica's intimate knowledge of her quadrant irrelevant. Namely, the nooks and crannies and holes in the ground which hid the great majority of them were becoming too tight; becoming a potential horrific death, rather than a refuge. A six-foot fluorescent worm might compress and snuggle its way, like an octopus, into the most surprising of openings but the same creature, forming into a troll or giant, made of great slabs of bone and muscle and sinew, would find itself dying horribly at the very moment of its rebirth. Crushed to jelly by the merciless mor-phology of mitosis and granite. That, of course, as Merlin soon realized, was where Rawhide, McGarnicle, Abel, Brenna, and Shamus and his tykes would be all-important, because, shortly, and in fact, already, hundreds of the surviving luminescents, al-most all of whom were in Angelica's quadrant, began frantically worming their way to the surface, desperately seeking room to grow. Already partially metamorphosed, they were however, and would remain, mutually indistinguishable for some hours to come, until late afternoon in fact. This was unfortunate for Angelica and Thunder because they too would be indistinguish-able from the rest and it was too much to hope, just because Thunder'd flagrantly hid them in a very obvious spot (what with the fervency of the night's hunt and the morning's mass sweep-ings by armed and excited leprechauns, it being not such a bad choice), that the afternoon hours and the more rational perspec-tive of the available hunting cream of Elfindale (namely Brenna, and Shamus and his tykes) were unlikely to overlook the obvi-ous. Thus it was, Thunder determined they should move; and quickly. Unfortunately, the "where" eluded him completely.

Chapter Thirty

GETTING ORGANIZED

*I*t took an hour or so for everybody to wise up but eventually it became clear to all, for reasons of his own (since no one, rightly, could imagine him in any difficulty), Merlin wasn't going to return. That being the case, Brenna took the high ground, Shamus the mid-ground, and the tykes the low ground, and all set out cautiously, unnerved by the ever-growing groans and occasional half-formed bellows of agony which so incongruously arose from nascent troll and giant throats, in the near and far of this part of verdant Elfindale.

Chapter Thirty-One

SEEKING WHOLE SURVIVORS

The first three hours were a turkey shoot. Desperate, luminous tubes wriggling to whatever surface lay above them, either punctured themselves in their haste or fell leisurely prey to the now-experienced, and refreshed, hunters. In fact, all went so smoothly it seemed more like a game than reality but as suppertime approached and the day turned to evening the real horror of war surfaced, for it was then the first troll to begin metamorphosing found itself bellowing out its last, crushed between two partially-buried slabs of rock. Favoured by chance for survival, it'd not managed to make it all the way to the surface, due to the extreme depth of its original safety, and was dying, it thought, alone; its pelvis and spine noisily crushing themselves to splinters, as they grew. Alerted by its pain however, Abel poked his head into the crevasse and stared at one of his mortally wounded adversaries. Unpleasant and dangerous though it was, this creature had a wife and offspring, friends, neighbours—in short—a life, and now, more than anything, it just wanted to go home, but it wasn't to be; for Abel, after seeing all this in its eyes, dispatched the half-crushed troll with compassionate disgust and withdrew, seeking whole survivors.

Chapter Thirty-Two

ALOFT

*I*t's hard not to root for the losers in a rout, Sapiens' sentience being what it is, and that may have saved Angelica and Thunder. Not knowing which way to go when fleeing their nest, Thunder, with a now-consciously-aware Angelica-tube, shot straight up the hollow tree and burst far out the top; leaving their fate, for the nonce, to the winds. In doing so, they were easily seen by all of course, floating about like balloons, but because Thunder chose to keep them aloft and in full view, rather than seeking out another seclusion, they were held as less of a threat (the invisible and the unknown being ever more frightening) and left, consequently, and for the moment, alone.

"They'll be th' last t' die," thought most, "Th' last afore th' feastin' an' th' braggin'."

"We'll be the last to die," surmised Thunder, from his vantage point aloft, observing the all-too-successful hunt below with newly-grown eyes, "and soon, by the looks of things—only a handful of us left—with nowhere to go. Where's Merlin, Angelica, for heaven's sake?!" And then he spotted him, resting in a meadow.

"He's down there! I can see him!" shouted Thunder to her, "Neither of us can fly much longer before we change all the way!"

And with that, as the sun began to set, he and Angelica shot in streams of luminescence down to the sleeping Merlin and lay, full-length, iridescent and transforming, on either side of him.

Chapter Thirty-Three

THE FINAL PUSH

$\mathcal{A}$s twilight turned to night, Shamus wisely determined his leprechaun tykes, with fewer and fewer tubes to hunt and increasingly unnerved by the agonizing bellows of trapped trolls and giants, should retire from the field and be escorted back to their homes by Brenna. Then, staff at-the-ready, he grimly bellowed out a prearranged invitation to Abel, McGarnicle and Rawhide (now armed with his .38) to assist in his quest to dispatch the tortured remnants of the invaders in Angelica's quadrant, by covering a quarter of it each; before joining forces in a final sweep of Elfindale as a whole.

PART FOUR

APRÈS STORM

Chapter Thirty-Four

BEEFSTEAK & KIDNEY PIES

*A*wakening from a pleasant nap with Angelica snuggled up to him on one side and Thunder snuggled up to him on the other was a rare treat for Merlin, so used was he, when not in Morgan's presence, to the loneliness that awe bestows. Affection, consequently, flowed copiously from his heart in generous proportion. Balmed by its pleasure, Angelica and Thunder stirred in their rest and awoke, the one to a hug and the other to an ear scritch.

"Hey!" protested Angelica, "I'd rather have a hug! I can reach my own ear!"

"Sorry," apologized Merlin absent-mindedly, "I kind of love ye both the same. By the way, since it turned out ye be not needed here, ye've got t' get your butt back t' Avalon forthwith, disperse that barrier, an' open up the skies; even the pollen drifts right out t' sea."

"Done," agreed Angelica, vanishing with a grin as Morgan, materializing from the ethers with an even bigger grin, skillfully occupied the young sorceress's vacated spot.

"It seems t' me ye've earned a couple of Cactus Jack's beefsteak an' kidney pies by now," said Merlin, looking kindly down at his beloved dog, after contentedly embracing Morgan with a welcome-back hug and smile.

"How come we're not at the pub yet, then?" enquired Thunder, sniffing gravy.

"Hold on t' yer hat," replied Merlin, "if ye'll pardon the expression."

And with that, they were.

Chapter Thirty-Five

SO NEAR AND YET SO FAR

For Angelica, alone in the moonlit night, restoring Avalon to normalcy was facile; mere sorcery. But turning her back on her beloved Arthur, separated from him though she be by sea, shore, and mount, was no easy matter, despite, and possibly because of, the fact that love, renown, and revelry awaited her in an Elfindale agleam with victory fires and fellowship. The great king, slowly healing on a marble bier in a blue-lit palace on a blue-lit island in a blue-lit sea would have to remain behind, present only in the hearts which loved him, however numerous. No victory waltz would be hers with him that night. No swirling, entwined, happily about on a balcony, with a fireplace and a big soft bed nearby. No, she would celebrate, as perforce she must, alone, surrounded by friends; while Arthur, unaware of the details, but balmed by the fact of her victorious defense of him, slept blissfully on and on and on.

Chapter Thirty-Six

WINNERS & LOSERS

Angelica's entrance at Jack's pub, bursting in with a roar as she did, McGarnicle-style, from the fire, rendering Shamus *and* McGarnicle airborne with startled shouts and respectable farts, not only made everyone laugh, it squeezed the hearts of all those old enough to understand she did so to mask her loneliness. To the others, the younger ones, her entrance was pure delight—frosting on the cake. As for Angelica herself, being a realist, she knew better than to wallow excessively in the stress of the unchangeable, and thus was soon able to join fully in the victory celebration.

How they carried on! The singing and the dancing and the feasting lasted throughout the night: a night in which Shamus' boasting about the exploits of his now-permanent class of leprechaun tykes delighted all. A night in which Ariel announced she was: "Retirin' t' Faerie t' laze about an' keep an eye on th' dark side." A night in which McGarnicle decided to join her; passing the crown to Abel, Elfindale and the valley's new king. A night in which Morgan and Merlin withdrew to the cave, leaving Angelica and Thunder to make their farewells, before Thunder joined them in the great dreaming. A night in which Shamus and

Brenna conceived the first of a dozen children, so enamored had Shamus become of little ones. A night in which, retiring early, Winifred and Rawhide slept like babes, happily, in each other's arms.

In short, a night in which all of Elfindale, Avalon, and the good side of Faerie rejoiced, while the dark side licked its resentful wounds and avowed to avenge its dead.

Chapter Thirty-Seven

ALONE AGAIN

"*I* feel there's more to life now than just waiting," said Angelica to Thunder, about to spell him back into place beside Merlin and Morgan, "Something for me to *do* in the world."

"There is," assured Thunder, "First, you can give me a final hug; second, you can spell me under; and third, you can spend the next thousand years enjoying yourself as best you can, while maintaining a warrior's vigilance, for the good of all. None died this time because dark Faerie was overconfident and uninformed; unlike Merlin, who struck early and well and true—And now must you."

"I will," promised Angelica, turning briefly aside, to husband the necessary resolve for spelling her beloved friend under, "I will. I've no choice."

And with that, she turned back to Thunder, gave him a final rib-cracking hug, signed and uttered the spell, turned again, and stepped out into the dawn.

—The End—

ELFINDALE FAREWELL

to
numen

"An amateur plagiarizes, a professional steals."
(Morgan—whispered in the ear of Stravinsky—1882)

PART ONE

PRE-PARTY
(9:50 PM—7:30 PM)

Chapter One

THE LESSON

"*W*hen Nothin' existed, afore it became All it had t' become One. This be th' Miracle: th' Primal Miracle. After that, anythin' was possible an' ever'thin' inevitable."

"Maybe so, Uncle Shamus," piped up Sparky, the bounciest of his leprechaun tykes, "but can ye do this?" And with that, the little fellow suddenly pulled his hat down over not only his ears, but his entire body as well, except for his feet, and proceeded to waddle hilariously about, to the amusement of all around the fire outside Cactus Jack's establishment, including the giant sorcerer himself.

"'Tis time t' be serious, sprout," chuckled Shamus down at his secret favourite, "fer as ye know, 'tis Angelica's quarter-century tomorra an' Elfindale entire will be celebratin'."

"How 'bout puttin' us tykes in a cake an' we'll 'splode out ever' which way all o'er th' pub tomorra night?" suggested Sparky, with his already famous ear to ear grin.

"'Tis undignified an' messy," replied Shamus, "In other words, perfect. I'll leave it t' ye an' Winifred t' make it so. Now off t' bed, rapscallions, 'tis nigh ten."

Chapter Two

BURGERLAND

*W*hen the great earth-dragon gave up its teeth to its old friend Merlin's necessity and formed the bulk of Prospero's Island it did so without regret or inconvenience, for dragons live until they die, having no specific life span. Time, therefore, being inconsequential, it merely contented itself for a pleasant nap, allowing the flora and fauna of centuries to gradually populate its generous back.

Flourishing in a natural state, untrammeled or inconvenienced by man (other than the occasional lost Spaniard), Prospero's Island eventually boasted a treasury of amenities much-prized by humanity: a humanity only a legendary, dragon-induced shipwreck would bring to stay, triggering the creation of a great epic, Shakespeare's, *The Tempest*; for ringing its beauties lay and grew the most treacherous ship-eating reefs in the world, buffeted by what seemed ever-eager allies to those jaws of death, terrible and unexpected seas and winds. And it was during one of those fearsome hurricanes man first came ashore to colonize when, in 1609, the *Sea Venture*, fresh from England and on its way to the American Colonies (peopled by whites dedicated to wresting all of Eden from its duped Indian inhabitants), foundered on Prospero's reefs. One, William Strachey, secretary-elect for Virginia and passenger on the hapless vessel, described the islands (soon to be called Bermuda) as follows:

> *"It was a place so terrible to all that ever touched on them—such tempests, thunders and other fearful objects are seen and heard about those fearful islands that they are called The Devills Islands, feared and avoided by all sea travellers above any place in the world."*

Fortunately for those who made it ashore on that extraordinary day however, within the gentle confines of the dragon's deadly skirt of coral, Beauty and Bounty proffered themselves shamelessly.

Imagine balmy temperatures year-round, the occasional cool day but an excuse for a pleasant evening fire and toddy. Imagine a place so close to perfection in its natural state only a subtle and dedicated horticulture suited the fecund surface of the sleeping dragon's marvelous form. Imagine over three hundred ensuing years of pastel cottages, quaint shops, and no industry; married to sun, sea, and sand: with pink beaches, turquoise waters, glorious skies, and tasty seafood of every conceivable variety. Then imagine present-day Islands: with no taxes, no slums, no overpopulation, no unemployment, no major crime problem.

And then imagine some bozo, despite being fed a clear message in 1995 when Bermudans voted against his proposal of independence from Great Britain, imagine that bozo then resigning as her Premier (yes, I said Premier, for he was the Islands' 'leader'), only to promptly sally forth, fervently scheming to bring 'burgerland' there. *'Burgerland'*. Its odious, bloated presence violating the splendour of those living jewels; harbinger of strip-mall mania, donut joints, and speedy 'just-about-anything'. "Sweet God Almighty!"

And with that, Merlin 'awoke' with a shudder in the crystal cave and decided it was time. Time to put Angelica and Thunder to work—far away from Ireland.

Chapter Three

THE DOORSTOP

or

WINIFRED'S GIFT

*I*n the twelve years that'd flown since the defense of McGarnicle's valley and Elfindale, almost half her life, Angelica had neither seen nor heard from Thunder, Morgan, or Merlin. Reports on, but no visits from, Ariel and McGarnicle in Faerie, were frequent but personally unsatisfactory. Winston and Boris, she was sure, were long dead, since they'd been elderly at the start of her adventures fifteen years before. And Abel, however lightly he bore the crown of leprechaun kingship, was far too busy with affairs of state to spend more than the occasional fleeting moment in her pocket. It must not be thought however, that she was either lonely or unfulfilled, for she'd grown to be a most singular creature indeed; which presents me with a problem because to attempt to do Angelica's portrait justice in print, on this the morn of her twenty-fifth birthday, would be both an exercise in futility as well as an unkindness to language. Her beauty, wit, talent, grace, and power simply defy description. The best that can be said of her is not a soul in all of Elfindale failed to find her friendship less than a jewel in their personal bag of treasure, real or metaphysical, and no one, no one in that happy land loved her more than Winifred; because Winifred, at seventy-two, considered Angelica, for all practical purposes, to be her daughter – the daughter she'd never had.

"Come in," she beckoned, seating herself, pleased as punch to see the delightful-one poke a smiling face through her diaphanous kitchen curtains, "Come in, my sweet darling, come in and sit yourself; I've prepared us a light brunch and your timing, as always, is perfect. And a good thing too; porridge can wait all day if it has to, even thrives on the delay, but, as you know, with eggs it's a different matter. Oh my, yes."

"No kidding," agreed Angelica, placing a hand on the windowsill and effortlessly vaulting into Winifred's inner sanctum and public oasis, "Anyone fortunate enough to be served a perfect boiled, fried, poached or whatever egg, should never visit upon it the discourtesy of tardiness."

And with that, she plunked into a chair opposite her host, sliced the top off a flawless two-and-a-half minute egg, sprinkled in some salt and pepper, then proceeded to violate its succulent interior with dip after dip of buttered toast fingers; all of which seemed to enjoy being masticated by her pearly whites before gratefully sliding down her appreciative, maidenly gullet.

"My," thought Winifred, watching the young lady effortlessly savage three before slowing down enough to properly savour a fourth, "My, my, my, if it was anyone else I'd caution they've a long day of feasting ahead."

"Don't worry," chuckled Angelica, reading her mind with disconcerting ease, "I can still chomp Shamus under the table despite his married girth and frequent fatherhood, and, next to me, he's the champ, now McGarnicle's so seldom about."

"I've a gift for you," smiled Winifred, reaching under the table. "It's too precious to wrap, but here it is nonetheless." And with that, she reverently passed Angelica a beautifully-embossed, leather-bound, hand-scripted-on-vellum, seventeenth-century volume of the complete works of Shakespeare; a one-of-a-kind treasure, collectors would, quite literally, kill for. A treasure written and signed by the great bard of Avon himself.

"I don't know what to say," gasped Angelica, stroking its textured cover appreciatively, "I really don't know what to say except 'Thanks' and, if you'll pardon the rudeness, 'Where on *Earth* did it come from?'"

"I got it from Shamus," answered Winifred, rising and dusting her hands with flour in preparation for her day-long baking of a zillion chocolate-chip cookies and Sparky's 'surprise' treat for Angelica, "in exchange for a giant-sized carrot cake; which he consumed on the spot, before my very eyes. Are you *sure* you can out-eat him?—I swear he *inhaled* that cake. Positively *inhaled* it."

"Maybe he *did* write *The Tempest*," mused Angelica aloud. "Maybe he really *did* know Shakespeare. Maybe they actually *had* a disagreement and a 'partin' o' th' ways', as he claims."

"Could well be so," chuckled Winifred, "He was using that precious volume as a doorstop."

Chapter Four

THE MUD SKIPPY COMETH

Deep in the subterranean bowels of a moist place in Faerie no one could find, a dirty little amphibian stirred in its rest (as if responding to an indecipherable call), popped open its extraordinarily-large-for-its-size, intelligent eyes; looked about, and said:

"'*You have often*
Begun to tell me what I am; but stopp'd
And left me to a bootless inquisition,
Concluding "Stay; not yet".'"

And then it rose, higher and higher in a slick, vertical mud pipe; a pipe that gradually cleared and cleansed as the little brown creature rose ever higher and higher, till it appeared with a *pop!*, all orange and yellow and sparkly, in the gentle, lower confines of Winifred's remarkable 'birdbath'.

"Who are you?" whispered Angelica, staring rudely down at it, eyes bulging out in an inadvertent mockery of the little fellow, "And what are you doing in Winifred's..."

"'*I am from the beginning and live without end.*'" quoted the mud skippy up at the handsomely bug-eyed young creature.

"Shakespeare?" guessed Angelica, hands on the cool rim of the birdbath, nose now inches above its marvelous surface.

"Ralph Waldo Emerson," corrected the little fellow, "Though I knew him intimately for a spell."

"Emerson?" responded Angelica, confused, "You knew Ralph Waldo Emerson?"

"No, silly," chuckled the mud skippy, "Emerson was far too solitary an' eccentric a chap t' *really* know; personally, that be. No, I meant Shakespeare."

"Shakespeare? You *knew* Shakespeare?" gasped Angelica. "Say, were he and Shamus buddies till Shamus wrote *The Tempest* and Shakespeare stole it?"

"Nonsense," replied the skippy with a snort, "Utter, utter nonsense. 'Tis common knowledge *I* wrote *The Tempest*, not this 'Shamus' ye speak of; I an' I alone."

And with that, he suddenly popped out of the water and landed on Angelica's shoulder squishily, having decided, for no particular reason he could consciously summon, to spend the day with her.

Chapter Five

YOUTHFUL OLD FRIENDS

*W*hen Boris and Winston were first approached by Abel, on the behest of Merlin, some four years after they'd lost Angelica and Thunder to Elfindale, convincing either to take part in a conspiracy enabling them to move to Prospero's Island proved no small task, for, in their great age, Nature had bestowed the urge to sleep their remaining days away regardless of request. Thus, having already outlived their allotted fourteen-odd years, even the promise of seeing Angelica and Thunder again was an insufficient lure to either, despite the great love and regard both bore for the young sorceress and Merlin's magnificent companion. Nor did the promise of rejuvenation hold allure, since neither, in their long lives, had felt the urge to reproduce, and both were pleasantly curious to see what lay behind the veil of 'Death'. So why did they do it? Why did they agree to exchange their tranquil backyards and just-right doghouses in Canada for an unknown, wind-swept dot in the Atlantic? Seduction, that's why. Seduction and Compassion: Compassion motivating Boris to attend his older and far-from-healthy bulldog friend Winston, and seduction because by the time Abel'd got done convincing Winston that Bermuda, England's oldest and most loyal colony, was now more English than England, there was no stopping him. Especially after Abel'd further promised him, when Her Royal Highness Queen Elizabeth II and Prince Philip made an official visit there in 1994, Winston would have tea with them and the Queen Mother; should she be well enough to travel.

That did it of course. The possibility of taking tea with his beloved Queen, and maybe even the Queen Mum herself, was more than the old royalist could resist. Happily, by the time Angelica's twenty-fifth rolled round, both animals, rejuvenated by Merlin for a grand purpose, had long since decided Bermuda outstripped even England and Mother Russia in perfection, and both, in their present vigour and circumstance, wholeheartedly agreed children were the way to go. Thus, married, repeatedly bred, fierce and content, it proved no small task for Abel to convince them once again to up stakes, even for just a trip, but he succeeded, after long parlance, in convincing them that, if they were to trust in his magic, there was no chance they would go shooting off into space a stream of uncollectible atoms, as they feared, rather than appearing, as they soon did, in Cactus Jack's pub in Elfindale, welcome additions to the many surprises being prepared for Angelica's party that night by those in charge of the evening's festivities.

Chapter Six

THE TRUCE

"*I* don't believe it," snorted Angelica at the mud skippy on her shoulder, "I simply don't believe you wrote *The Tempest*."

" '*What seeist thou else in the dark backward and abysm of time?*'" quoted the skippy.

"You're not Prospero and I'm not your daughter Miranda, and this isn't Act One of *The Tempest*," laughed Angelica. "What you are is a funny-looking little geek with big bulgy eyes and..."

"Kiss me," interrupted the mud skippy, puckering his lips, "Kiss me an' I'll turn into a prince."

"No thanks," shuddered Angelica, "I've already got a *king*; the lazy bum."

"Lazy?" enquired the skippy.

"Well, more sleepy than anything; he's been sawing wood for over a millennium now."

"Wow!" exclaimed the mud skippy respectfully, "An' I thought *I* knew how t' hibernate. Who be he, and where?"

"He's the Once and Future King," answered Angelica proudly, "Arthur himself, and he's my soul mate and he's resting in Avalon."

"Sure he be," mocked the mud skippy, "An' I'm Michael Jordan; wanna see me dribble?"

"You already are," replied Angelica, flicking him off her shoulder, with a thumb-and-finger snap, "And it's disgusting."

"No fair!" shouted the skippy up at her from the centre of one of Winifred's roses, "No fair! Be that any way t' treat he who penned *The Tempest*?! Be it, I say?!"

"If I dumped you out of that flower and stepped on you, barefoot as I am," threatened Angelica teasingly, shaking the stem and tumbling him to the grass, "would you bubble up between my toes all repulsive-like?"

"Try it!" challenged the mud skippy defiantly, "Just try it! Think ye he who whispered *The Tempest* in Shakespeare's ear be deficient in powers? Ye'll wed Arthur with flippers 'stead of pretty arches; *that* I promise, in the least."

"There's stranger things than this little creature," thought Angelica, squatting and looking at him with an odd blend of affection and fear, "Stranger things; there has to be."

"Damned right there be," he retorted, reading her mind. "I otta know, I'm lookin' at one."

"Funny," she said, "Very funny."

And with that, she put her hand down to it with a grin and the skippy hopped aboard, secure in their truce, at least.

THE TROUTMASTER

$\mathcal{R}$awhide, with his .38 on his hip (just in case), at seventy-seven, standing by one of his favourite streams, possessed a flexibility and strength that belied his unthreateningly round physiognomy. Nonetheless, this made him no less amusing to look at; an effect he did nothing to alter with the comfortable, fashionable folly of his fishing garb. Sporting hip waders, with striped T-shirt and old school cap (ideal for holding treasured trout flies), he was, despite his formidable intelligence, indistinguishable from Tweedledum or Tweedledee. As comfortable in his body as a foot in a revered slipper however (having long ago freed himself from the tyranny of self-image), he sank unobstructed into the harmonious adventure of all that lay about him at the moment, and what lay about him at the moment was Rawhide bliss.

No sound injured the sun-dappled perfection of his solitude, other than the delightful atonality of Nature's harp: the breezes dancing the leaves of tree and bush, the watercourse xylophoning its own sweet way, the splash of a teasing trout. No sight disturbed his eye that did not ring with the wondrous subtlety of the Creator's hand alone. No taste violated his lips other than the

335

burst of a perfect berry or the sweet, cool trickle of his beloved stream.

Seeing him standing contemplatively, before silently slipping into the pretty waters and slowly wending his way upcurrent, rod in hand, one could be excused for thinking the slightest obtrusion would foil the aim of a consummate angler's serious intent and it would be so, for Rawhide was about to undertake the next phase of his fishing career; a phase few even know exists, much less master. He was about to attempt to fill his creel with trout, without the assist of a hook. Was about to invite the fleetest and most beautiful of the piscine brethren to strike and hold fast to a pearl wedded to the thinnest of lines, to swim and fight and dance in painless delight, before accepting higher incarnation by dropping lifeless into his proffered basket.

Unbeknownst to himself, formerly one of the great disbelievers of all time, he'd just crossed the threshold to sorcery.

Chapter Eight

"THAT'S ALL I CAN STANDS: I CAN'T STANDS N' MORE!"

$\mathcal{M}$erlin and his friend the earth-dragon went back, as friends are wont to do, before even the concept of Earth, so he knew its temperament intimately. Thus, his present concern about the well-being of the flora, fauna and peoples dwelling on his old comrade was well-founded. Patient and loving though it was, its irritation with humanity had been growing for centuries. During the first six-hundred-odd years of its rest all went well, since no humans violated its generosity with so much as a footstep. Nor did it take offense, after the earliest hours of its colonization by man, because, being practical, it saw the necessity in a warlike, empire-building age, of the bristling fortifications they erected on its personage, contenting itself with the knowledge no ships were sunk by them, no innocent people or animals killed. It was less forgiving in its heart when it came to the importation of slaves beginning in 1616, to dive for pearls and harvest tobacco and sugarcane, but that too, it knew, was widespread in the world of the time, and hence, somewhat forgivable. No; what caused its first great heart's grief with the peoples of Prospero's Island came in 1775, because Cain slew Abel. Occurred because an innocent French prisoner was slaughtered on the altar of "necessity" when the Bermudans, threatened with starvation, slew the unfortunate wretch for haplessly happening upon local conspirators 'stealing' a hundred barrels of gunpowder to give to the American revolutionaries in exchange for lifting their blockade. War was war, but the killing of that poor fellow, alone, helpless, and far from home, wasn't fair play. Wasn't "British". The symbolism of them then brazenly burying his body in the foundation for the Unfinished Church, married to the calumny heaped on his memory thereafter (the Frenchie being a very handy scapegoat; accused of the theft itself for a hundred years), quite frankly stuck in the dragon's craw. Which caused it, finally, five years later, to give itself a good cleansing, summoning up, as it did, the Great Hurricane of 1780, driving selected ships ashore and flattening many unrepentant homes. Happily, in 1834, when the British, the first to do so, abolished slavery throughout the Empire, the dragon considered all the Bermudans' karmic folly to date wiped clean and the Islands were free to start afresh; never knowing how close they came to complete physical annihilation.

For the next twelve years all went smoothly and the dragon rested content, even sighing happily when, in 1846, the first lighthouse in the colony was built, to reduce the number of shipwrecks. Unfortunately, this karmically-happy time was to last only an additional fifteen years, for, in 1861, the Bermudans, sacrificing honour for profit, sympathized with the slave-holding South in the American Civil War, and grew fat by pipelining the Confederacy both munitions and supplies, in exchange for cotton bound for London; cotton picked by slaves. This caused the dragon to rumble discontentedly in its sleep, but it forgave them once again fifty-four years later when some of their gallant lads paid the ultimate price, fighting for the freedom of others at the Somme, Arras, and Ypres, in World War One.

It didn't mind, even enjoyed, the railway stitched up its spine in 1931 and regretted its sale to British Guyana in 1948. Further, when women landowners were finally given the vote in 1944 it benignly considered it a forward crawl, if not a step. All, in other words, was well. Then man, in his cyclical folly, took a giant leap forward in destroying harmony by, in 1946, permitting internal-combustion-driven automobiles on its disgusted person. Happily, there weren't so many of them, to begin with and for some time thereafter, that it felt compelled to cleanse itself with another devastating hurricane and it patiently awaited, vainly as it turned out, the enforcement of a cleaner mode of conveyance. Unfortunately however, twenty-five years later, Cain slew Abel once again when one, Erskine "Buck" Burrows, hanged for the deed in 1976, shot down Governor Sir Richard Sharples and his aid, for no fit reason. Because he was brought to justice and no real villainy occurred in the ensuing eleven years one would be justified in asking why the dragon still summoned an appalling hurricane, Emily, in 1987, which battered the bejesus out of Bermudans, injuring over seventy and causing millions in property-damage but the fact is, a fact revealed to puzzled humanity for the first time here, a native-born Bermudan cricketer, during a very critical match indeed, not only *cheated* in the finals of that fateful year, the bounder then failed to feel guilty and fess up. That, of course, was too much for the dragon, who, steeped in a British sense of fair play, on its back and in its historical friendship with Merlin, felt it had to make its disapproval known and promptly did so with Emily.

All of this Merlin knew and understood (having been in open telepathic communication with his old ally since their mutual 'internment'), so he was fully aware of its formidable self-control and compassion but things, nonetheless, are increasingly coming to a head, despite the fact all Bermuda's fortifications and navy yards and bases, both British and American, were permanently closed in 1995; and the fact Winston's beloved Queen did come to the Islands in 1994, and did have tea with the delighted old royalist.

Why then are things coming to a head? Why are all Bermudans, Boris and Winston included, in danger of oblivion, should the great resting beast suddenly rear up and roar out its protest, at the extreme limit of its patience?—Taste. Taste, pure and simple. For Merlin knows what the dragon, and so little of humanity, seems to know. He knows, when Evil wants to get a toehold on Paradise, it seduces with Mediocrity. Blinds the eye to the finer sensibilities. In short, it tries to erect a 'burgerland', or any one of its 'fast-anything' brethren; and that is what is happening: Mediocrity is scratching on the doors of Paradise.

It's always a straw which breaks the camel's back, never a boulder. Always one, last, tiny insult that compels a forbear-ant creature to snap, and the dragon's final straw has come. Overtouristed, with less-than-pristine sound and air, its patience has been increasingly tested for decades but now, at Millennium's cusp, full-blown mediocrity, instant 'culinary' gratification, with all its appalling decor and consequences, threatens the dignity of the dragon—an intolerable offense.

"Keep yer shirt on, old-timer," Merlin assured it, seated out-side his cave, "Today's Angelica's twenty-fifth; I'll send her t' ye tomorrow, an' me Thunder too."

"Not enough!!" roared the dragon, in Merlin's mind, as the great sorcerer patiently put the final polish to a jewel-encrusted crystal dagger for Angelica's birthday, "Not enough!! Ye'll have t' come as well!!"

"Do ye mean t' say," responded Merlin, astonished, "Ye ex-pect me t' up stakes an' move me cave from Elfindale t' Bermuda *forthwith?*"

"I do indeed," affirmed the monster, "I want me teeth back— yesterday—an' as well ye know, deprived of them, the insurance of Emile an' his brethren be lost t' ye; a risk I'll not permit."

"It really be peeved," thought Merlin to himself reflectively, "An' as I learned long ago, once it gets like this there's no turnin' it 'round. Looks like Morgan an' I be shiftin' our rest t' Bermuda tomorrow. Hope she doesn't get cranky—never met a female yet didn't lose it somewhat on movin' day."

Chapter Nine

THE DEBATE CONTINUES

"*Hope is the last to die,*'" whispered the mud skippy in Angelica's reluctant ear, as they peered through a bush at Rawhide failing in cast after cast to lure a willing trout into his creel. "'*Hope is the last to die.*'"

"Shakespeare?" queried Angelica, curious.

"Old Russian sayin'," chuckled the little fellow. "Funny thing, I'd heard ye were well-read."

"All I have to do is go *poof* and you'll be dodging minnows nipping your ass," threatened Angelica, "That's all it'd take— then you'd be too busy flopping about and begging, to shoot your mouth off."

"Try it," responded her little companion, "I'll block ye in midspell an' turn ye into somethin' even funnier-lookin' than ye already be."

"Ha!" snorted Angelica, "Everybody says I'm beautiful, even animals and plants. You're all alone in your opinion."

"Doesn't make me any the less right; the masses, in case ye haven't heard, be asses."

" 'If thou more murmur'st, I will rend an oak and peg thee in his knotty entrails, till thou hast howl'd away twelve winters.'" quoted Angelica.

"Act One, Scene Two, *The Tempest*," laughed the mud skippy, diving off her shoulder and heading upstream towards Rawhide's casting pearl.

"Big deal!" called out Angelica, "Big, fat, deal; it's a famous line!"

"Not t' me it isn't," shot back the little fellow, "comin' as it did from me very own quill s' long ago."

And with that, he submerged, preparing, with chuckles, a surprise for the little round angler.

Chapter Ten

THE M.C. WARMS UP

*T*welve years ago, when McGarnicle handed his Earthly crown over to Abel and joined his wife to live in Faerie, he hadn't been all that sure he'd like it there, his robustness being more attracted to the tangible pleasure of Earth, but to his surprise he quickly found himself missing neither pork chops nor Cuban cigars, and, after thousands of Faerie years, even his own worldly friends; whose memory of him, after a mere dozen Earthen years, remained very much alive indeed. Consequently, Merlin and the leprechaun's formidable wife Ariel determined he'd not only attend Angelica's twenty-fifth in Elfindale, he'd host the proceedings as well. Fortunately, spiffed-out in all his finery (frequentwear, now his other half'd got her fashioning hands on him), the old leprechaun looked in the pink, and knew it; so convincing him proved an easy task, vanity and leprechaundom being synonymous terms.

"Mirrors don't lie," he smiled at himself in its reflection, "Not 'less ye insist, an' I don't; 'twould be a waste o' breath, me splendour bein' self-evident."

"No doubt 'bout it," sighed Ariel affectionately, "ermine becomes ye as much as yer golden crown. Pleased be I t'day, an' ever'day, since I burned yer rags twelve year ago."

"Aye," growled McGarnicle, "But did ye have t' do it in-transit? I be still livin' down th' embarrassment o' me naked intr'duction t' Faerie as its leprechaun king."

"'Twas meant t' be," chuckled Ariel, "Yer punishment fer slidin' s' disgraceful inta stubble-cheeked bumhood th' moment I left ye unsupervised s' long ago. Well, that be then, full-splendid look ye this noon. Come, 'tis time we supped on nectar an' cheese, then 'tis off t' polish our double-helix throughout th' afternoon."

"Not Th' Comet!" gasped McGarnicle anxiously, "Not Th' Comet! Could we skip lunch?—eight hours be barely enough."

"For ye perhaps," laughed Ariel, "I can do it in me sleep."

Chapter Eleven

CAKE PROBLEMS

The fashioning of Sparky's cake wasn't going as well as Winifred assumed it would when she'd begun. Its taste, texture, and decoration proved facile, since she'd a genius in those departments, but figuring out a way to keep its shape was proving a tussle indeed; for Sparky and his buddies were suffering from a prolonged and unaccountable attack of the giggles, each round of which sent them popping off like a string of firecrackers, all about her kitchen.

She tried controlling them with scoldings, cookies, even entreaty, but all merely set them off again, into higher and higher realms of hilarity.

"That does it!" she snapped at last, eyeballing the clock, "I've no time for this! I'm telling Shamus! *He'll* know how to handle you!" And with that, she flounced out of her kitchen—to the sound of a dozen leprechaun tykes in danger of apoplexy, at the very ceiling of merriment itself.

Chapter Twelve

JACK'S LIFE DOES A ONE-EIGHTY

*I*n all his long years in Elfindale it'd never occurred to Charlie to enter Cactus Jack's pub, preferring as he did, the higher succulence of the grass about its perimeter and the dew that clung to it, over pork chops, beefsteak and kidney pie, and ale. In the early afternoon of Angelica's twenty-fifth, nonetheless, he felt it his duty to supervise his well-meaning but less-than-thorough old master's cleaning of everyone's favourite establishment. Jack however, having already outstripped himself in that department, was relaxing with a cerveza by the freshly-scrubbed hearth as Charlie entered, and beckoned him over with an affectionate insult.

"'Tis shocked I be t' see ye enter me poor hovel after all these lonely years..." began Jack.

"Stow it," interrupted Charlie, "I've an acre more to crop by seven tonight if we're to accommodate half the numbers I anticipate."

"An' do ye expect me t' assist in th' nibble?" chuckled Jack, slapping his knee.

"You could," replied Charlie dryly, "You're long enough in the tooth."

"'Tis true enough," sighed Jack philosophically, "I seem t' be agin' faster than th' rest o' ye, fer some reason. Ah well, 'tis me fate; ye'll not be hearin' me squawk."

"I've never known you not to," laughed Charlie, "but in this case a fool could see what you're about."

"An' that would be?" enquired Jack.

"You need a wife. You're lonely. If you want to get younger you've got to marry, and soon, or you'll be pushing up daisies, wed to the Infinite."

"Can't say which I'd prefer," mused Jack, quaffing his brew. "Now Shamus' all brooded an' ensconced, in matrimony; an' McGarnicle's gone, as 'twere, I confess I'm a titch lonely, filled as I be t' repletion by this darlin' pub fer th' last fifteen year: but I am powerful curious 'bout th' beyonds o' beyond, an'..."

"There's nobody for you here, you know that, don't you Jack?" continued Charlie, "They're all too short. Take my advice for once and move to Prospero's Island with Thunder and Angelica and Merlin and Morgan and I, the change will be good, give you a new lease on life; and besides, there's lots of rich women in Bermuda, ones appropriate for your height, and breedable: you're bound to find someone amenable, all someone of your temperament needs."

"'Tis true," laughed Jack, rising and slapping Shamus' table in delight, "I've loved a jackass fer nigh on thirty year, 'tis proof enough I've a ready an' affectionate nature ... Hey! Whadda ya mean movin' t' Prospero's Island?! Ye an' Thunder an' Merlin an'..."

"They're going to, for some reason, and I've got to," sighed Charlie, "I'm experiencing occasional debilitating inflammations no spells or potions can soothe, it's simply too damp here for my bones now. Bermuda, I'm assured, is old jackass heaven; I'll not be lacking companionship and conversation, other than your own, once you wed and catch up with Shamus, in the baby department."

"An' who would tend th' pub in me stead?" asked Jack, warming to the idea while looking about nostalgically, "Who would keep Shamus' an' th' wee warbler's whistles proper' wet in just proportion?—'tis n' easy task, ye know."

"No problem," replied Charlie affectionately, moved by Jack's confession he'd loved him all along, "However deep the friendship or outstanding the skill, we're all replaceable, employment-wise."

"True," agreed Jack, placing an arm about his old friend's neck, "true indeed. Need just will not tolerate Vacuum."

Chapter Thirteen

THE VALKYRIE

*S*hamus' wife was once a Valkyrie, a fierce Norse beauty who cheered and scorned ancient warriors into acts of transcendent bravery. Then she was a spirit for centuries, soaring about till her 'ever-expanding consciousness' threatened to enfold itself delusionally around all Creation, so she wisely advised herself to reincarnate as a humble, plump little monk, which she did, bestowing many healing herbs and heartfelt prayers on suffering humanity during Europe's early Dark Ages; perishing nobly of a plague while battling one of them in a hospice for the terminally infected.

It was no small wonder then, when she returned shortly after as Shamus' beloved Brenna, she came through lusting for love and laughter, so perfectly did she blend courage and compassion. Little did she know however, that children would be her forte: children and an unfailing instinct for what Shamus needed, as opposed to what he wanted. Cactus Jack, in other words, aughtn't have worried; it was time for Shamus, after centuries of frequenting alehouses, to finally run one.

"'Twill be me birthday present t' Angelica," laughed Brenna to Charlie and herself prior to his previous entry into Jack's pub,

"Full-pleased she'd be t' know ye an' Jack'll be her companions in Bermuda, an' happiness itself t' see her beloved Shamus fittin' employed. What a fine sendoff she'll be havin' t'night. As fine a birthday as e'er can be."

Chapter Fourteen

ABEL'S ENTRANCE

"*E*asy ... Easy ... *Now!*" prompted Rawhide to himself under his breath, snapping his rod tip up just as his pearl bobbed beneath the surface for the third time.

At the very moment the mud skippy'd been about to nab Rawhide's lure a little creature twice its size appeared from nowhere in a flash, seized the pearl in its teeth and tugged at it three times; all the while grinning affably at the skippy while doffing its hat, the only thing missing in the greeting being Abel's usual, "Top o' th' marnin' t' ye", because his mouth was otherwise employed. Unable to do anything but bug its startled eyes out even further, the skippy goggled in open-mouthed awe as the diminutive king of the leprechauns suddenly shot out of the water and disappeared into the sky, transformed by his mischief into a golden trout arching through the air in glittering splendour, before vanishing back into the stream a breathtaking distance away.

"Lord!" marveled Rawhide, "Lord!" And then he dug in delightedly for the fishing experience of a lifetime. *Mano a leprechauno*, he'd fight this magic trout with all of his skills and more till it, exhilarated and fulfilled, offered itself joyously up to his creel.

For an hour they danced, watched by Angelica on the shore and the mud skippy in the stream, where Abel'd first taken the bait.

Not being a fly fisherman of any reputation, I, as narrator, must demure from attempting in words to tread the path of that particular ecstasy. What I will say is, when the golden fish finally threw the pearl in mid-flight, then arched splendidly towards Rawhide's opened creel, all, observers and participants, were fully aware they'd just experienced a thrill rare in any incarnation. So rare, each knew the great fisherman would reopen his basket and proffer the god of fishes back its life and freedom, but when he raised the lid to lift it reverently forth, out popped Abel, doffing his hat.

"Top o' th' marnin' t' ye, Rawhide, Top o' th' marnin' t' ye."

"'Top' is right," laughed Angelica, "It's closer to three than noon."

"Angelica, me darlin'!" exclaimed Abel happily, "I thought 'twas ye flashin' about in me peripherals from time t' time." And with that, he hopped into her overalls pocket and blew her a cheery kiss.

"Look," said Angelica, "see those big goofy eyes approaching, attached to that fat little slug it calls a body?—he's a mud skippy. Hey, Skippy; what do you think of my little buddy here? Think *he'd* hang out with a loser?"

"'*I might call him a thing divine, for nothing natural I ever saw so noble,*'" quoted the skippy reverently, staring in wonder at his new hero.

"'*At the first sight he has changed eyes,*'" paraphrased Angelica, pleased to see her little tormentor taken down a size or two by awe, as Shamus had sometimes done to her in the early days.

"'*There's nothing ill can dwell in such a temple,*'" sighed the skippy, still staring at an increasingly nervous Abel.

"'*He'll receive comfort like cold porridge' from me,*" quoted Abel, changing a word, and even, the entire original meaning of the

line. "I'm not, nor e'er shall be, enamoured enough o' his friendship t' gaze s' foolish-like inta th' eyes o' another male, me own
species 'r otherwise. Get a grip o' yerself, man. Get a grip."

"'Tis not ye, but yer skill, ensnared," replied the skippy, coming to his senses with a headshake, "Besides, anyone who'd hang
about with a girl of *her* fashion sense *can't* be all *that* significant."

"Hey!" protested Angelica, relieved he'd stopped spooking
Abel, "What's wrong with my fashion sense?!"

"Well," chortled the skippy, "it started in the toilet, then
flushed itself."

"It did *not!*" snapped Angelica, "I wear overalls all the time
just in case Abel shows up! Besides, who're you to talk?—you're
buck-naked and built like a squirt of toothpaste."

"'Tis a sin t' cover perfection," sniffed the skippy, "an' 'twas
rude of ye t' display yer ignorance of that fact. But, as I said once
long ago: *'What's past is prologue, what to come is yours and my dis-
charge.'*"

"Why are you all quoting *The Tempest*?" enquired Rawhide,
curious.

"'Tis simplicity itself," chuckled Abel, "It be a great play, a-
choke with wisdom, if I say so meself, havin' written it."

"*'Good wombs have born bad sons,'*" scowled the skippy at Abel,
all its previous, deranged enamourment gone. "*'As wicked dew as
e'er my mother brush'd with raven's feather from unwholsome fen drop
on ye both! A south-west blow on ye and blister ye all o'er!'*"

And with that, it submerged and wiggled off like a tadpole, to
everyone's amusement.

"Why did he get so mad?" chuckled Rawhide.

"He claims he penned *The Tempest*," replied Angelica. "Any
chance it's true?"

"None a'tall," countered Abel, eyes atwinkle, "As I told ye,
'twas I."

"You've got to help me, Rawhide," requested Angelica, "it's
starting to bug me. Let's find out who *really* wrote *The Tempest*. So

far it's Shakespeare, Marlowe, Bacon, Shamus, the mud skippy, and now Abel. Will you help?"

"No," laughed Rawhide, stepping into the stream for a cast of his hookless pearl, "I've no time for such nonsense."

Chapter Fifteen

THE BLUSH

By the time Winifred tracked down Shamus her irritation at his tykes had turned to chuckles and it was just as well, for she found the sorcerer both ludicrously garbed and introspective, even melancholic, squatting alone by a river.

"Ever notice when Celts sinks into depression it makes their face sag like an old horse?" she teased, "And by the way, what's with your apparel, is your robe in the laundry?"

"Why, 'tis th' garb o' a well-dressed Bermudan gent, o' course," replied Shamus, rising, "What think ye, do I pass fer a native?"

Bemused, Winifred stepped back and took in the full effect, as Shamus turned slowly about. At six-foot-five, three-hundred-odd pounds, and cheerily bald, he was breathtaking in his usual robes but costumed as he presently was he presented as preposterous a picture as any could wish to see. Sporting a blue blazer, a white shirt, a striped silk tie, pink Bermuda shorts, black shoes and, god help him, white knee socks held up with pink tasseled garters, one could only assume his sole purpose was to stand out in any company as blatantly as was humanly possible; the opposite of his intent.

"Diplomacy is pointless," laughed Winifred, "in the face of utter absurdity. Why on *Earth* would you want to go to Bermuda?"

"I have to," sighed Shamus, squatting again and tossing a pebble into the river, "Merlin just told me he's shiftin' his cave t' Prospero's Island an' Angelica an' Thunder an' a couple o' their old friends, Boris an' Winston, will be guardin' it, an' more—seein' as how Angelica's t' be charged with restorin' th' Islands' harmony by doin' battle with tastelessness."

"That's ridiculous," snorted Winifred, "there has to be more. Is dark Faerie on the move again?"

"Aye, 'tis partly that as well, th' two bein' related, but th' big danger be that damned dragon losin' patience with us all, demandin' its teeth back from th' loan t' Merlin; an' if it be so, if th' great fire-breather be insistin' on th' return o' its flyin' teeth, Bermudans be in danger, fer its liable t' up with a final snort o' disgust an' flap off in a pique, drownin' all an' sundry. No, 'tis me aid Angelica'll be needin'."

"Does Brenna know about you going to Bermuda?" asked Winifred. "Does she know what a burlesque spectacle you are all decked out like this?"

"Hey, now," grumbled Shamus, "Think ye I be entire incapable o' thought an' deed 'thout her directin' 'r opinion? Think ye I be s' hopeless domesticated I..."

"Yes," laughed Winifred, slapping him on the back, "Yes indeed, I'm pleased to say. And Shamus, darling, with the cave shifted and Angelica gone, who do you think will be needed to govern Elfindale when Abel's in Faerie or McGarnicle's valley, or Bermuda, now I think of it?"

"Me?!" gasped Shamus, delighted, "Me?! *I'll* be in charge?!"

"No, silly," chuckled Winifred, "Brenna, of course, and there's no way she'll let you go gallumping off to Bermuda to mess things up, when finesse is required."

"More babysittin'," sighed Shamus, "Me tykes *an'* me children; they'll suck me finer sensibilities t' th' marrow in no time flat, I warrant. How th' mighty have fallen."

"It seems to me," said Winifred, brightening, "that Merlin wouldn't send Angelica without *any* human companions. My guess is Cactus Jack and Charlie will be going along too. Jack needs a change and Charlie's been altogether too brave and kind about my inability to relieve his arthritis in this frequently-damp clime; no, I'd bet a day's baking they're off to Bermuda too and you'll be running the pub."

"Me?!" responded Shamus, shocked and elated, "Me?!—Well now, 'tis 'bout time. Just think, th' stories I'll hear an' tell. 'Tis an excellent idea. An *excellent* idea indeed." And with that, rubbing his hands together in anticipation, the rejuvenated Shamus rose, finger-danced while uttering a spell, and his absurd habiliments were no more. Then, surfacing from his delight long enough to notice he was naked in the presence of a somewhat shocked Winifred, he instantly covered his chest and privates in an abashed, undeliberate imitation of a shy, startled maid, and, blushing, tumbled modestly backwards into the river.

Chapter Sixteen

BURYING THE HATCHET

"'*T*is clear we got off t' a bad start," said the mud skippy to Angelica, plopping with a pleasing-to-him squishiness onto her startled shoulder from an overhead branch as she walked along, "So if ye apologize, I'll forgive ye."

"That's mighty big of you, squirt," retorted Angelica, faking nonchalance, "but, as always, you're outdistanced by my mercy; for I forgave your curse on me and Abel, with the comedy of your exit. Laughter's a great glue, don't you think? I'm even developing an affection for you. So, '*Thy thoughts I cleave to. What's thy pleasure?*'"

"It delights me t' hear ye're so well-versed in me *Tempest*, Angelica," smiled the skippy, "Sorry 'bout that crack a while back when I accused ye of borderline illiteracy. As for why I'm here: '*I come to answer thy best pleasure; be't to fly, to swim, to dive into the fire, to ride on the curl'd clouds.*'"

"Act Two, Scene One," laughed Angelica.

"'*She misses not much*,'" paraphrased the grinning skippy, combining two actor's lines, "'*No; she doth but mistake the truth totally.*'—it's Act One, Scene Two."

"Hmm," murmured Angelica aloud, "Hmm."

"'*Look, she's winding up the watch of her wit; by and by it will strike.'*" teased the skippy, paraphrasing again, "Act Two, Scene..."

"One, yes, I know," interrupted Angelica, "but: '*Prithee, do not turn me about; my stomach is not constant.'*"

"That's 'cause movin' time, for a woman, be very stressful, generally-speakin'. Don't waste the day-afore tryin' t' find out who wrote *The Tempest*, 'twas me an' that's all there be t' it."

"Please," requested Angelica, plunking herself down, as Shamus had done, by a river, dismissing even the possibility that the skippy was actually revealing the source of her slight abdominal upset, blaming, as she did, a surfeit of eggs at brunch with Winifred earlier, "Please, if I have to barf I'd just as soon no one was about—it's a female thing. So, '*By your patience, I needs must rest me.'*—kindly go."

"Act Three, Scene Three," replied the skippy, diving obligingly from her shoulder into the river. "An' 'twasn't the eggs, me darlin'; 'tisn't an up-chuck ye're facin', 'tis an up-stakes."

"He sounded so familiar, there," mused Angelica, watching the teeny fellow churn off upstream in the late afternoon sun, "What an odd little squirt he is."

Chapter Seventeen

PROLOGUE

"'Tis approachin' five, Thunder," said Merlin, shading his brow and looking off at the lowering sun, "Almost suppertime. Care for some honeycakes?"

"*'I will stand to, and feed, although my last; no matter, since I feel the best is'*—coming?" hinted Thunder, savouring in his nostrils one of Cactus Jack's beefsteak and kidney pies bubbling away on the hearth some two miles distant.

"Let him go, Merlin," encouraged Morgan, "He'll slide in an' out 'thout Angelica's knowledge. Don't worry; he won't spoil your entrance."

"Spoil me entrance?" huffed Merlin, "Why, I don't need this mutt t' make an entrance."

"*That* mutt," corrected Morgan, with a grin, for Thunder had already bounded cleanly out of sight.

Chapter Eighteen

THUNDER BLOWS IT

*T*hunder hadn't been kidding years ago when he told Merlin he preferred tangible reality to magic and Merlin hadn't been kidding when he said he agreed. Morgan, equally, hadn't been kidding when she said Thunder could easily avoid Angelica, but she was in present-happenstance error, misjudging as she did, his eagerness to beeline it to the pub and sink his teeth into his favourite-by-far all-time food, so, as chance or fate would have it, it was mere minutes later that he leapt out of the forest onto a riverbank and skidded to a halt, face to face with a seriously-startled and delighted Angelica; who pounced on him instantly.

"Thunder! Oh, Thunder, Thunder, Thunder!" she squealed, choking the life out of his powerful neck, "You've come for my birthday! Where's Merlin and Morgan?!" And with that, still hugging her beloved friend, she looked around expectantly.

"They're back in Merlin's glade, in the flesh," he admitted, "And it's supposed to be a surprise; as am I."

"I'll fake it," grinned Angelica confidently, "He'll never know the difference. Hey! My stomachache's gone! So it *was* the eggs."

"Eggs?" puzzled Thunder, "I'd have guessed moving-day jitters ... Oh, oh, there I go again, flapping my jaws. Oh well, at least you don't know about the crystal blade Merlin's fashioning you. *That* at least, will be a surprise."

"Crystal blade?" enquired Angelica, "What crystal blade? – and why?"

"Better get out of here," thought Thunder to himself, forgetting she could so easily read his mind, "If I don't I'll blow it; give away more of her birthday-party surprises, and all about her going to Bermuda with me." And with that, he bounded away, heading for beefsteak and kidney pie.

"Bermuda?" wondered Angelica aloud, "Going to Bermuda with Thunder? And a crystal blade? A crystal blade, for me?"

Chapter Nineteen

THE KICKOFF

*A*ngelica's parents, a half hour later to the minute, rolled up to Jack's pub on a great, horse-drawn wagon piled high with casks of cerveza from McGarnicle's fabled brewery in his far-off Mexican valley. Tanned, fit, and full of laughter, they stood with an arm each draped over Jack's shoulders, smiling at him affectionately.

"We took the slow route," laughed Evelyn, "Gave a dozen-odd pilots and hundreds of passengers and stews the chance to deny their eyes in court. It won't have the impact of Winifred and her saucer twelve years ago but it'll grind in many an ear till all who saw us, and a generation or two of their heirs, expire."

"It was her idea, not mine," chuckled Shawn, "My wife's become quite the prankster since she started visiting Ariel in Faerie."

"Yer a fine woman, I've got t' say," grinned Cactus Jack, squeezing her waist affectionately, "His admiration o' ye be warranted."

"'*Do not smile at me that I boast her off, for thou shalt find she will outstrip all praise, and make it halt behind her.*'" quoted Shawn.

"Decided t' help Angelica solve th' mystery o' who wrote *Th' Tempest*, have ye?" enquired Jack. "I've heard 'tis plaguin' her."

"No," laughed Shawn, "the passage was merely *à-propos*."

"She'll be sorry t' hear it," chuckled Jack, "Rawhide turned her down too. Well, at least yer not claimin' t' be its author."

"I'm not so sure," replied Angelica's father, "I've been getting strange whisperings I *was* Shakespeare."

"Well I'm certain she'll be pleased t' hear it!" guffawed Jack in delight, "Every girl wants t' be proud o' her daddy, an' Shakespeare be still her favourite quillster."

And with that, a leprechaun elder stepped forward and handed Jack a golden ceremonial mallet and spigot.

Holding them up, arms flung out wide, the old prospector then strode to the doorway and bellowed: "Let th' festivities begin!! A river o' cerveza awaits ye all!!", before jumping hastily aside as a host of thirsty leprechauns swarmed into the pub, up on its roof, and about its well-cropped perimeter.

Chapter Twenty

REMEMBRANCE AND LONGING

"It's coming on seven," mused Angelica, "and almost nobody's about. I bet they're all percolating down to the pub. Dollars to doughnuts my folks are there already, fresh from McGarnicle's valley; they look better every year. And I bet Shamus and Brenna are spelling their babies to sleep round about now, getting ready for big-time fun. Shamus is still the funniest person I know and nobody dances like Brenna—nobody; it's like watching joy and healthy lust embrace, coffee mingling with cream. Shamus' tykes will be there of course, popping off all over the roof, laughing at the inebriates in comic tumble. Rawhide will be sitting at his favorite table by the fire in the pub too, side by side with Shamus' "wee warbler", whose undoubtedly paralyzed the lot several times already with his haunting voice. Winifred will have organized the dessert in the pub's basement pantry and be outside now, sipping a raspberry cordial and talking to Charlie; they love each other so. Paddy and his wife will have brought mounds of pork chops and beefsteak and kidney pies too, along with her world-famous plum duff brûlé. Merlin and Morgan, of course, will threaten to upstage Ariel and McGarnicle's spectacular entrance by arriving second-to-last, leaving the final opportunity to those great leprechaun warriors; compelling them to ride the crest of Perfection itself, soul food for all who witness it, manna from heaven. Yes, they'd all be there," she thought, "or coming soon. All but Boris and Winston."

And with that, she lowered her head in remembrance and longing, loss blinding her heart and senses to the sudden arrival of both in the pub, beaming-in in a shower of sparks; sparks which reassembled themselves, as Abel had promised, before everyone's very eyes.

Chapter Twenty-One

SPARKY GETS A GIFT

"*B*limey!" gasped Winston, looking about at all the leprechauns, then up at Cactus Jack, "Blimey and bloody hell! I'll never do that again. Lost control of myself completely. Terribly un-British. Might I have a stout, to settle the nerves?"

"In a bowl 'r bottle?" enquired Jack teasingly, delighted to meet someone who'd been told something of his exploits, but determined to be polite and ask about the old bulldog's undoubted boring past before regaling him with personal escapades.

"Bowl," replied Winston, "A bottle, for me, sir, is undignified."

"Done!" said Jack, bending and pouring. "Now, tell me 'bout yerself."

"'*Tis a chronicle of day by day, not a relation for a birthday party, nor befitting this first meeting.*'" paraphrased Winston from *The Tempest*, surprising himself, though wise to Jack's intent and determined to remain in charge.

"'*O, rejoice beyond a common joy, and set it down with gold on lasting pillars:*'" quoted Jack in return, astonished he knew it, having never read the play.

"'These are not natural events, they strengthen from strange to stranger.'" quoted Winston back, entranced.

"'This is as strange a maze as e'er men trod;'" added Boris, bewildered, also having never read it. "Got any vodka? I could sure use a snort. I too, will never again permit Abel or anyone else to turn me into a sparkler. It was exhilarating, I confess, and all turned out well, but it *definitely* does *not* suit my temperament. When we return to Bermuda it will be on the QE2—first-class of course—lots of caviar."

"Agreed," promised Abel, hopping up on Cactus Jack's shoulder, prior to springing off in a shower of sparks right through the ceiling, bursting like a Roman candle above the delighted tykes on the roof, then reassembling quickly ten feet over them in cross-legged fashion, before sinking calmly towards their midst, the tykes emulating his position and descent as he came abreast of them, in unisoned eagerness.

"Will ye teach us how t' *really* 'splode inta fireworks an' reform like ye just did?!" begged Sparky, "'Twould put th' shame t' our silly out-o'-a-cake jump."

"'Tis why I sit 'mongst ye now," laughed Abel, "Lean forw'rd all, an' listen close."

Chapter Twenty-Two

TIMING

"*T*hat had to be Abel, going off so colorfully in the sky above the pub," thought Angelica. "It's just past seven, which means Shamus and Brenna are there by now too. Only the old folks are missing, and if McGarnicle and Ariel are showing up at eight like I suspect, Merlin and Morgan will be arriving at any moment. If I walk down slow I'll get there about ten minutes after they arrive and about a half hour before McGarnicle and Ariel. That should be just about right."

And with that, Angelica rose and headed, barefoot, in her new white cotton frock, towards the collective love awaiting her, bearing nobly the constant sweet ache dwelling in her heart for the absent Arthur, asleep in Faerie.

PART TWO

THE PARTY
(7:30 PM—3:00 AM)

Chapter Twenty-Three

A FINAL GOOD-BYE

The mud skippy, comfortable in a slick bowl Jack'd provided him on the mantle above the fire, looked about contentedly, seeking further opportunity to implant *Tempest* quotes in some innocent soul's psyche. He'd no reason for doing so other than it amused him and harmed no one; the two ingredients required, whenever possible, before almost any action. Thus, it could truly be said, he was nicely holding up his end of Angelica's party by following the prime directive—being entertained and entertaining. He still, however, had no idea who he *really* was, a thought which, at the moment, troubled him not a whit.

"'*We are such stuff as dreams are made on;*'" he sighed philosophically, "'*and our little life is rounded with a sleep.*'" And with that, he surrendered to slumber, drifting off after a double quote from *The Tempest*; the first for Angelica alone, revealing a personal sense of longing; and the second, gallantly, for Angelica and Arthur:

*"'Let grief and sorrow still embrace his heart
that doth not wish you joy.'*

'Look down, you gods, and on this couple drop a blessed crown.'"

Chapter Twenty-Four

WISDOM AND GRACE ARRIVE

$\mathcal{F}$or some mysterious reason, Rawhide and the singer rose from their table by the hearth at exactly the same moment, picked up their half-filled bottles of cerveza, and silently headed to the bar for an unnecessary replacement, only to wind up at the buffet table instead, guided by a purpose pleasantly unknown to them; and when they returned with half a melon each instead of the beer they thought they were fetching, Merlin and Morgan were seated there.

"Melons," said Morgan, "Yummy. I *love* melons."

And with that, Rawhide placed his lovingly before her on the table, and the singer placed his before Merlin, with tremulous, reverent hands.

"No spoon?" jibed Merlin, affably, "'Tis undignified gummin' fruit through a beard in public. I wouldn't recommend doin' it, much less watchin' it."

"O'- o' course," stammered the warbler, flustered.

"Sing us a song, ye ninny," laughed Merlin, snapping two melon spoons to life in the air, before sending one off to screw itself into Morgan's portion and the other into his hand, to tap ringingly on an ale glass, "Sing us a song, 'tis time t' calm the mob; they've obvious missed the subtlety of our elegant entrance, an' our presence itself, lest me aged peepers be rheumed."

And with that, the singer raised everyone's spirits while simultaneously bringing all to ground, with a personal-best-surpassing rendition of:

A LITTLE BIT OF HEAVEN

"'Have you ever heard the story of how Ireland got its name?
I'll tell you so you'll understand from whence old Ireland came;
No wonder that we're proud of this dear land upon the sea,
For here's the way me dear old mother told the tale to me:
Sure, a little bit of Heaven fell from out the sky one day,
And nestled on the ocean in a spot so far away;
And when the angels found it, sure it looked so sweet and fair,
They said, "Suppose we leave it, for it looks so peaceful there:"
So they sprinkled it with star dust just to make the shamrocks grow,
'Tis the only place you'll find them, no matter where you go;
Then they dotted it with silver, to make its lakes so grand,
And when they had it finished, sure they called it Ireland.

'Tis a dear old land of faeries and of wond'rous wishing wells,
And no where else on God's green earth have they such lakes and dells!

No wonder that the angels loved its Shamrock-
bordered shore,
'Tis a little bit of Heaven, and I love it more and more.

Sure, a little bit of Heaven fell from out the sky one day,
And nestled on the ocean in a spot so far away;
And when the angels found it, sure it looked so sweet
and fair,
They said, "Suppose we leave it, for it looks so peaceful
there:"
So they sprinkled it with star dust just to make the
shamrocks grow,
'Tis the only place you'll find them, no matter where
go;
Then they dotted it with silver, to make its lakes so
grand,
And when they had it finished, sure they called it
Ireland.'"

Chapter Twenty-Five

ANGELICA'S ARRIVAL

"'Tis a bland, innocent cloak ye've added t' your normal free-spirited blaze," opined Merlin, looking down at his dog's aura as Thunder entered and settled in next to him by the fire, "Run into Angelica this afternoon, did ye?"

"Literally," confessed Thunder, "I don't know how, some stuff just blurted out. I got away as fast as I could."

"Did ye tell her 'bout me gift?" continued Merlin.

"Not what it can do," assured Thunder, "That much is intact."

And with that, the heavens cleft outside as Sparky and his fellow tykes suddenly went off simultaneously in a dozen chrysanthemum bursts, followed by their youthful sense of the final touch: a ground-shaking, cataclysmic, Boris-and-Winston-leveling, "*BOOM!!!*"

Angelica, it seems, had arrived.

Chapter Twenty-Six

ANGELICA'S ENTRANCE

The ale casks having been opened some two hours before Angelica's appearance, leprechaun inhibition, a paltry thing at the best of times, vanished entire when they saw their beloved girl approach in her simple, elegant white shift; and a tumultuous, joyous roar went up from all and sundry.

"Good one, Sparky," applauded Angelica, "I never saw anyone blow up that good before. You guys are naturals. Where's Merlin?"

"He's inside with Thunder an' Morgan, sittin' by th' hearth," grinned Sparky hugely, "Mind if I 'nounce yer entrance by 'splodin' out th' fire at him like McGarnicle used t' do t' Uncle Shamus? Pleeeeeeze?"

"Go for it," laughed Angelica, "I'll give you thirty seconds."

But, like anyone else who deals with Merlin, he didn't get exactly what he expected. Oh, the explosion and shower of sparks went well enough but Merlin's recovery time from shock turned out to be somewhat instantaneous and Sparky found himself imprisoned a millisecond later in an inverted ale glass on the table, held firmly in place by Merlin's gentle hand, to the hilarity of everyone; especially Sparky, who revered speed and wit above all but love.

Then the doors swung smoothly open of their own happy volition, pleased to their very cells to serve the blessed maid, and the object of everyone's devotion entered in all her native splendour.

Chapter Twenty-Seven

THE HAPPIEST OF REUNIONS

*B*eing the centre of attention at a birthday party, especially one in your honour, is somewhat of an embarrassment and Angelica would have been no exception to that rule had she not immediately spotted the inconceivable—Boris and Winston holding court in a corner, amiably defending the virtues of Prospero's Island above all places on Earth. Her delight at encountering what she'd held impossible, the physical, and rejuvenated, presence of her 'long-deceased' childhood companions, caused her to burst into a richness of tears.

"Ooooooooooooh! The poor wee soul!" mourned Boris, touched as deeply as her and beyond, "My heart is breaking! Nothing will save it now!" And with that, the great Borzoi was at her side in a bound, revealing by his agile leap the size, speed, strength, and symmetry of the origin of his breed as the great wolf hunters to the czars.

Angelica, thrilled, would have thrown both arms around his long poetic neck and choked a stanza or two out of him in her great joy but she was willingly compelled to simultaneously share that hug with Winston, who, at half Boris' size and weight, attained the happiness of her other side a moment later, revealing in his forceful scurry the awesome bull baiting power of his ancestors.

"How I've missed you, Angelica," sniffed Winston, moist of eye and trembling with an uncharacteristic British emotion, "How I've missed you. Thank god you'll be coming to Bermuda to help Boris and I guard Merlin's cave. What times we'll have. We're both married now, did you know that? Married, with woolly youngsters tumbling all about. And wait till you see the *present* Merlin has for you. Why, with it you can..."

"*Hey*, now," grumbled Merlin, rising, "*Hey*, now. 'Tis me gift; an' timin', as well ye know, be all. How can ye guard me cave if ye cannot commit a secret t' silence? '*Loose lips sink ships,*' as they say."

"Quite right," agreed Winston, "Quite right. But I didn't tell her she was getting Thunder back, in the flesh, did I? I didn't tell her that."

"Whaaaaat?!" gasped Angelica, thrilled beyond measure, "I'm *really* getting Thunder back?! For how long?!"

"Till Arthur awakens, darlin'," offered Morgan, remaining seated. "'Tis the only way ye'll have the strength t' live separate from Elfindale an' Avalon; though I'm sorry t' say, even then ye'll be plagued by a constant, sweet melancholia: but with Thunder at least ye'll wear it becomin', rather than as a tragic, sorrowful burden. An' besides, 'twill make ye all the more charmin'; useful for socializin' an' politics."

"Politics?" puzzled Angelica. "Politics? I've got to become a politician? In Bermuda? Why, for heaven's sake?"

"I was hopin' t' tell ye all this later, in the wee hours after your party, Angelica darlin'," said Merlin, "Here's a birthday missive for ye from me friend, the great earth-dragon itself. 'Twill, unless I miss me guess, explain all." And with that, he handed her a sealed envelope and Angelica slit it open with an effortless, razor-like "ssssssst" of one of her pretty nails, then curiously removed a large postcard.

On its front was a map of Bermuda, without lettering; a map that fleshed out before her very eyes into a magnificent dragon, which suddenly shuddered and took to the skies, flying clean out of the picture, leaving only a vast expanse of twinkling blue sea for her to look at. Intrigued, and slightly disturbed, she quickly turned it over and read:

> *" 'While you there do snoring be,*
> *Open-eyed conspiracy*
> *His time doth take.*
>
> *If of life you keep a care,*
> *Shake off slumber, and beware.*
> *Awake! Awake! '"*

"So it's true you're moving your cave to Prospero's Island," marveled Angelica, looking at Merlin. "Some deviltry's afoot and you're going to stop it."

"Yes, dear; and no, dear," laughed Merlin, "as always. But seriously, me rest be more than a rest, Angelica, 'tis also a vigil, as ye learned twelve year ago. That bein' the case, me presence alone on the Islands will defer the ambition of dark Faerie, should it break through the current silly karma of that fortuned place. The immediate problem, howe'er, be far more significant. Me dragon friend has endured the cruel folly of mankind an' withstood the urge t' shake us off its patient back, but Mediocrity as well be beginnin' t' plague with constant itch, so its made it clear it'll not support us longer 'thout clear signs that curse be diminishin' rather than on the march. Fast-food, I fear, an' a surfeit of pollutin' conveyances an' tourism, be stretchin' its tolerance t' the limit. Ye've got t' sojourn there an' turn back the tide; then guard 'gainst its recurrence till Arthur be hale an' returnin'. Thunder, Boris, Winston, Cactus Jack, an' Charlie will be your companions an' allies; an' this will aid ye mightily."

And with that, he placed a prettily-wrapped present in her hands and all crowded round to see.

Chapter Twenty-Eight

THE GIFT

*E*veryone in Elfindale, to considerable degree, is unmaterialistic, but all who saw the crystal dagger spring to life in her hand, for a flash, lusted for it without knowing why. Its beauty, of course, having been fashioned by Merlin, was a given, but its real draw came from an intangible to most; its extraordinary, subtle, mesmerizing power.

"'Tis small enough, moderns will find it charmingly decorative, Angelica," explained Merlin, "but its real purpose be 'twill make ye, single-handed, a formidable force, for, drawn, it beguiles all about ye t' your will. Manifests your desires as theirs. Enables ye t' plant a seed of taste in the mind of those in need of such. A seed that, o'er time, will strangle, as a vine, the baser habits of those mortals, till their hearts too require beauty an' harmony t' breathe. Use it well, an' sparin'; for force alone ne'er outlasts the folly of our species."

"Know why dogs started hangin' out with people?" chuckled Thunder, to break the ice. "So they could get the parts they can't reach scritched."

And with that, he brushed up against Angelica's hip, then proffered her the spot on his back just above his tail, that, with all his skill, he'd never been *quite* able to reach.

Chapter Twenty-Nine

THE GENERAL

*T*o a casual observer, a stranger, Angelica's party would have looked like a host of identical little folk, salted with a few dogs and a handful of Anglo-Saxons but to Angelica each little face had a beloved name and personality, all of whom, simultaneously, sent her an explosive love-hug as she stepped outside, and almost on, her just-arrived, diminutive little buddy, Petie, the great Chihuahua general, fresh from McGarnicle's Mexican valley.

"Petie!" squeaked Angelica, sweeping him up, "Oh, Petie! I *hoped* you'd come!"

"Well," responded Petie with a chuckle, "As Shamus would say: *'Nothin' like a stream o' green-light coincidences,'* I was just passing by and..."

"*Right*," snorted Angelica happily, "Just 'passing by': everyone *knows* you can't be pried out of Mexico for love nor money."

"For money, you're right," confessed Petie, "But love, in your case, I'm afraid, overrode all; so here I am. Happy birthday, Angelica darling. Happy, happy birthday."

And with that, he gave her a kiss, pulled an eye patch he didn't need down from his forehead, hopped out of her arms, and headed for Boris and Winston, contented to relive his exploits, with the pals he'd not seen in over a decade.

Chapter Thirty

A ROYAL EXIT

"C'mon, hon," hurried McGarnicle, "'tis eight-thirty in Elfindale; Shamus'll have quaffed half th' brew by now, if I be not mistaken."

"Not since he wed Brenna an' fathered," laughed Ariel, pushing her husband's crown down firmly on his head, "He, I'm sure, as ye, has learned th' art o' moderation, thanks t' her patience n' will. Now, 'tis time t' awe all an' sundry."

And with that, she seized his wrist and they streamed off, up and out, making a mockery of their age.

Chapter Thirty-One

A ROYAL ENTRANCE

$\mathcal{A}$t the very moment McGarnicle and Ariel exited through the skies of Faerie, all in Jack's pub found themselves filing amiably outdoors to stare up at the stars, for no conscious purpose; and when the last did so, two brilliant comets came barreling in from opposite sides of the heavens, then spiraled down about each other in an ever-tightening double-helix, till, just before they smacked into Charlie's beautifully-cropped and crowded lawn, they pulled up in physics-mocking union and settled gently to earth, transforming themselves as they did so into the splendidly-garbed monarchs of leprechaun Faerie.

"'Tis parched, I be," chuckled McGarnicle, giving Angelica's legs an all-encompassing hug, "Parched, an' no mistake." And with that, he parabolaed up over Jack's roof and disappeared down the chimney, followed hastily, in like manner, by his old drinking buddy Shamus.

"I see ye've got yers as fine-tuned t' th' social graces as mine," laughed Brenna, embracing Ariel affectionately.

"Aye," replied Ariel, hugging Brenna back, "Let's supervise th' lads till they've eaten hearty; 'twouldn't do t' have 'em pass out afore they've lied their way through many a pleasin' hour."

And with that, accompanied by Merlin, Morgan, and Cactus Jack, they entered the pub and seated themselves about its cheery hearth; while Thunder and Petie and Boris and Winston took off for a moonlit run, awash in the joy of physical dogdom at its prime.

Chapter Thirty-Two

PARTY BABBLE

*I*t must not be assumed leprechauns, humans, Faerie denizens, or even animals, living in, or visiting, Elfindale, did not suffer, in varying degree, from all the virtues and faults of any reasonably-decent incarnate creature and Angelica well knew this, so the snatches of conversation she heard while outside, wandering amiably about her increasingly-inebriated party, proved, as in all parties everywhere, a mixed bag indeed. Wisely however, she took few possessing barbs to heart and laughed delightedly at the rest. Further, not being an imbiber herself, she failed to be cornered and embroiled in any prolonged and heated argument nor did she drown in an excess of maudlin treacle, as were so many about her. Consequently, she had little difficulty in picking up the following gems while passing smoothly through, and around, debate and emotionally-brimming hearts.

"I was worried fer a while ye'd be too good-lookin' but yer not."

"Every parent needs a safe."

"If ye fear decapitation, never approach an angry female, with logic."

"Keep yer distance. Yer cuddly but yer no teddy bear."

"'Tis true. I swear 'tis true, for at th' end: *'All but mariners, plunged in the foaming brine and quit the vessel.'"* ... *"'The strangeness of your story put heaviness in me.'*"—"Ha! *'Your tale, sir, would cure deafness.'"*

"'Highest queen of state, great Juno comes; I know her by her gait.'"

"Is it some kind of conspiracy?" wondered Angelica, "so many *Tempest* quotes? Is everyone poking fun at me?"

"'Thought is free.'"

"'Tweren't his last, I tell ye. 'Tweren't his last."—"Well, it shoulda' bin. What a long-winded, borin' piece o' drivel *Henry VIII* be. An old man's final, reluctant, obsequious gasp. 'Tis n' wonder th' Globe burned t' th' ground durin' its first p'formance."—"I warn ye now: *'One word further and, by this hand, I'll turn my mercy out o' doors.'"*—"Aye, aye: *'He that dies pays all debts.'"*

"This is ridiculous," puzzled Angelica aloud, "what gives?" Then, to her astonishment, her mouth joined in the absurdity. *"'Sometimes am I all wound with adders, who with cloven tongues do hiss me into madness.'*—Stop it," she told herself. "Just stop it,—*'Who be so firm, so constant that this coil would not affect his reason?'"* insisted her lips. "I'm starting to get annoyed—*'Hell is empty, and all the devils are here.'"* countered her tongue. And with that, Angelica hurried inside the pub, to be mercifully met with *Tempest*-free babble.

"Where's me blessed pipe?"

"Opinion be easy: Facts be difficult."

"Some souls' lives be s' clownish ye can't help but mock their misery."

"Never assume 'SUGAR' be sugar."

"Is that reprobate brother of yers still ensconced with the behemoth?"

"One o' th' things 'bout poverty an' wealth be ye can go all day barefoot."

"Ye've got t' be incompetent t' start with—how else does a body learn anythin'?"

"I can't tell when I'm lookin' at Italian movies if they be goofin' on each other or if they really be that nuts."

"Ever notice how a bad song seems t' last forever?"—"Aye, an' why 'tis it buildin's past a certain age be all *creepy*?"

"I don't like t' repeat meself. Heaven knows, I don't like t' repeat meself."

"Don't be fey, Adam, it's 'bout as annoyin' as coy."

"Personally, I prefer coke."

"Dinnertime!" shouted Cactus Jack, entering and clanging a triangle.

"Thank god," grinned Angelica, "It sounds to me like a lot of stomachs need food."

And with that, everyone crowded outside to feast under the stars.

Chapter Thirty-Three

"'TWAS I!!"

Vegetarians would find themselves feeling squeamish were I to describe in full measure the groaning boards the revelers settled about so I'll spare them the details of Jack's spread and skip to the old prospector's dessert specialty; tray after tray of blackberry cobbler mounded with diet-distressing Devonshire cream, washed down with his personal pride and joy, nail-dissolving, camp-brewed coffee.

"A toast," proffered Merlin, rising at just the right moment, "A toast to Angelica, a poem by Sparky, an' then her final gift."

"Long lives, patience, an' health t' ye!" chorused all, "Long lives, patience, an' health t' ye!" And with that, everyone, tykes included, quaffed little crystal cups of Winifred's secret, bliss-inducing cordial.

"Ye've got the floor, Sparky," encouraged Morgan, "Hop to it, lad; we're all ears."

And with that, Sparky, a stranger to shyness as always, leapt up on the roof and assumed the classic pose of ham actors everywhere.

"Ahem," he said, unnecessarily and dramatically, "Ahem," And then he set too:

"PRINCE O' HEAVEN

One day a snake
Who lived by a lake
Dinin' on splake
Had all he could take
An' decided t' make
A boat
But a goat
With a gloat
Said it wouldn't float
So th' snake at a run
Bit th' goat on th' bum
Then under th' sun
In a day
Built th' boat anyway
An' was gone
Like a song
With nary a bleat
From th' fresh tasty meat
Under th' seat."

"Well said," laughed Angelica, clapping delightedly, along with the rest, "Well said; and as profound as any can be."

"An' now, me darlin'," expanded McGarnicle, rising, "as M.C., 'tis me honour t' announce we've a gift fer ye in common. Th' request o' yer choice. Anythin'; anythin' a'tall."

"What I *want*," demanded Angelica, rising too, "is the truth, once and for all. Who wrote *The Tempest*, dammit?! Was it that little mud skippy who hung with me all blessed day? Was it him? Did *he* write it?"

"He did, right enough," assured Merlin, "I can vouch for it."

"But somebody told me *you* wrote it!"

"Your point?"

"Both of you *couldn't* have written it."

"We could, if we were one an' the same, an' we be," laughed Merlin, "So ye see, 'twasn't Shamus or Shakespeare or Bacon or eggs.

"*How?!*" guffawed Ariel, "could *anyone* who isn't Irish be *so* full o' th' blarney!? *I* be th' skippy, 'an *I* wrote *Th' Tempest*."

"No!!" shouted a host of grinning leprechauns, "'Twas I!! 'Twas I!! 'Twas I!!"

"Mock me all ye wish," chuckled Shamus, rising grandiosely, "Truth e'er limps in on th' shoulder o' Time. History will prove, 'twas I."

And with that, all, Angelica included, laughed uproariously.

PART THREE

POST-PARTY
(3:00 AM—7:00 AM)

Chapter Thirty-Four

FAREWELL

*T*he wee hours of the morning, after a most pleasant party, have a unique ambiance for those eschewing excess; no common thing for leprechauns or Celts. Thus it was, by 3:00 am, only Merlin, Morgan, Angelica, and Thunder remained standing of the happy hoard that, mere hours before, was leaping in the throes of dancing and merriment. The rest were slumbering contentedly, strewn about the pub, the lawn, in the trees, and blanketing Jack's roof. Amongst them could be found all the friends that inhabit Angelica's world, save the largest, Merlin's fearful ally, the great earth-dragon. Ariel and McGarnicle were there, glowing radiantly, resting in each others arms on Jack's bed; Emile, at nod in his hovering craft; Abel, curled up on Boris' comfortable, sleeping back; Angelica's parents, entwined contentedly under a bush, as were Paddy and his delightful wife; Winston and the singer, sawing wood noisily before the fading embers of Jack's hearth; Jack too, of course, outsnoring Charlie pillowing his head; Shamus and Brenna, side by side in a large, swaying hammock; the mud skippy, blissfully unaware he was an element of Arthur conjured by Morgan, snoozing contentedly in his bowl on the mantle, his corporeal presence gently fading with every breath; Winifred and

Rawhide, sleeping in large comfortable armchairs Jack'd placed outside for that purpose; Sparky and his pals, subdued at last by Hypnos, dozing all over the roof; and a few thousand-odd, passed-out leprechauns carpeting every square inch of Charlie's beautifully-cropped lawn. All, individually and collectively, awash in gentle slumber; each balmed by the presence of every-one else.

"'Twill be Shamus' task, governed by Brenna, t' execute the defense of Elfindale in Abel's absence, Angelica," informed Merlin quietly, tamping down a pipe she never knew he smoked, before putting fire to it and puffing luxuriously. "Petie, of course, curled up in your lap there, will govern McGarnicle's valley in Abel's absence as well. As for Prospero's Island, 'twill be ye an' ye alone, with Jack an' Charlie an' Thunder for company, who'll general the salvation of that fortuned place. 'Twill be no easy task but ye can handle it or I'd not be sendin' ye. As for Boris an' Winston, they an' their descendants will guard the now-vulnerable rest of Morgan an' I in our cave till Arthur's healin' be done. 'Twill be a long an' somewhat lonely task I've set ye but necessity commands. All, be assured, be as it must; an' all will be well."

"I love you Merlin. I love you and Morgan past telling," said Angelica, placing Petie gently on the lawn, "will I not see you again before that far-off day?"

"I doubt it," replied Merlin, "But predictin' the future be asinine, an' an insult t' God."

"It seems t' me," chuckled Morgan affectionately, "'tis your specialty; an' mine too, come t' think of it. That bein' the case, I'm sure, Angelica, we'll meet ye an' Thunder again a time or two afore that distant day. Till then, a hug will have t' do."

And with that, Merlin and Morgan, with a final embrace to each, vanished, leaving Angelica and Thunder seated alone under the stars.

"Will you miss them, Thunder?" asked Angelica, "Will I be enough for you?"

"No problem," promised Thunder, "I can do nine-hundred-odd year standing on my head, with you by my side."

And with that, they rose, and ambled off into the forest, content, in each other's company, to bid farewell to Elfindale.

—The End—

About the Author

*B*unking for over sixty years with diverse strata of societal pyramids (from penniless prisoners to mega-rich bluebloods), experiencing a gamut of habitats (from wilderness solitude to teeming megalopolis), Ian Lauder lives a literary life uniquely honed for chastising malfeasant man, while celebrating Divinity's gifts of life, laughter, and love. Elfindale, his first public proffering, is one of dozens of disparate volumes penned and polished over decades, all to be published in due course.

Painting shares equal billing with writing, in Ian's art-obsessed firmament, as does filmmaking, cartooning, sculpture, and photography—showcased on his Mud Valley Productions web site: *mudvalley.com*

ISBN 1425120033-4